Get Ready to Play Rough

Shay Beckham grew up idolizing her brother's best friend, star quarterback Joe Reilly. There was no one in their Texas town who had the moves to match Joe on or off the field. Years later, he's still a player who has what it takes to drive any hot-blooded woman wild. But Shay isn't a kid with a bad case of hero-worship anymore. She's grown-up and independent, with her feet on the ground and a serious head on her shoulders. If she could just say the same for Joe.

It's been fifteen years, but Joe Reilly hasn't forgotten the skinny little kid who used to follow him around like a shadow. What he can't get over is that the skinny shadow has grown into one hell of an incredible woman. One any man in his right mind would kill to get his hands on. And one who seems to be completely immune to him. He knows he and Shay could have something special together. If he could only convince her he's about more than just the game.

Visit us at www.kensingtonbooks.com

Books by Desiree Holt

Finding Julia

Game On Series
Forward Pass

Published by Kensington Publishing Corporation

Forward Pass

Game On Series

Desiree Holt

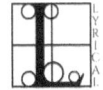

LYRICAL PRESS
Kensington Publishing Corp.
www.kensingtonbooks.com

Lyrical Press books are published by
Kensington Publishing Corp. 119 West 40th Street New York, NY 10018

All Kensington titles, imprints, and distributed lines are available at special
quantity discounts for bulk purchases for sales promotion, premiums, fundraising, and educational or institutional use.

Special book excerpts or customized printings can also be created to fit
specific needs. For details, write or phone the office of the Kensington
Special Sales Manager:
Kensington Publishing Corp.
119 West 40th Street
New York, NY 10018
Attn. Special Sales Department. Phone: 1-800-221-2647.

Kensington and the K logo Reg. U.S. Pat. & TM Off.
Lyrical Press and the L logo are trademarks of Kensington Publishing Corp.

First Electronic Edition: July 2015
eISBN-13: 978-1-61650-729-9
eISBN-10: 1-61650-729-2

First Print Edition: July 2015
ISBN-13: 978-1-61650-730-5
ISBN-10: 1-61650-730-6

Printed in the United States of America

First of all to my late husband, David, who said "I really want a wife who loves to watch football with me," then decided he should be careful what he asked for. All those games we watched, all the bets we made are stored in my memory banks.

Author's Foreword

A writer's life cannot move forward without the help and support of a lot of people. Many thanks to my son, Steven, who is willing to discuss sports with me for endless hours despite the fact he really does have a life of his own. When I wanted to go back to Michigan Stadium to see a game after so many years, he made it happen. Thanks for the memories and training to The Michigan Daily where I got my start as a sports reporter. Even sending me out on assignment riding a guy's bike or freezing my rear end off at hockey practice didn't deter me. I still love reading and writing about sports. A special shout-out to my sister, Sonya Langdon, the first person who taught me that watching football games could be fun. I'm so glad she roots for the New England Patriots because Tom Brady was a Wolverine. Special thanks to my friend and beta reader, Margie Hager, who labors through my typos and other mistakes and helps me whip every manuscript into shape. Then there's my daughter Suzanne and my granddaughter Brooke who are my assistants, virtual and otherwise, who run my street team and make so many things happen for me. And I have to give huge thanks to Paige Christian, who is just the best editor ever. You make me work for my stories but in the end they sing. Thank you so much. And last but hardly least, to Renee Rocco, who believed in me. This series is for you, baby.

Chapter 1

"Damn it, Hank. Why don't you answer?"

Shay Beckham pressed End on her cell phone yet again and sighed. She and her brother had been playing telephone tag for two days. When he called, she was in meetings. When she called, he was out of signal range. The only voices talking to each other were their voice mails. How godforsaken could it be in Wyoming, anyway? It was still in the United States, right?

And why was he trying so hard to reach her? They exchanged texts now and then, but they were both so busy they only called each other in case of emergency. The places he went, cell reception was spotty at best and talking to him was like playing leapfrog. Wait! Was he okay? Her heart stopped for a moment at the thought he might be hurt, but then she relaxed. If something had happened to him, his boss would have reached out to her. So what was on his mind that had generated this flurry of aborted phone calls? Obviously, he wanted something because he was the one who'd initiated this current game of phone tag.

She leaned back in the taxi as it turned from the airport access road onto the interstate. Less than half an hour and she'd be home, thank God, and she could get out of her sweatshirt and jeans that wore the remnants of her diet cola from the plane.

With the way her luck was running, maybe she shouldn't have accepted her complimentary beverage. On the flight out to New York a week before, a little turbulence had been responsible for her arriving with a huge coffee stain on her favorite yellow sweater. Maybe she should carry a bib with her. Or a large tarpaulin.

On today's flight, she had just set up her iPad and lifted her glass gingerly to take a sip when the plane hit an air pocket and everything bounced. Her iPad. The purse beneath the seat. Worst of all, her drink.

Her hand flew up, with it her diet soda and, most importantly, the ice cubes. Up in the air. Over the back of her seat. Into the seat behind her.

She could still hear the man behind her growling. "Shit!"

Then, "Damn it anyway."

She'd used the miniscule courtesy napkin to blot up what she could from her sweatshirt and jeans. Shay had cringed as the man behind her continued to mutter under his breath.

"Hey, you in front. Didn't you ever learn to pay attention on a plane? You got your damn drink all over me."

He hadn't seemed impressed with her mumbled apology so she'd just slid down even farther and buried her nose in her iPad again. And been damn glad to get to the end of the flight without further incident. When it was time to deplane, she'd avoided even looking back at the man, hustling up the Jetway into the terminal as fast as she could. Getting home was all she could think of.

Sighing, she brushed a few wisps of hair away from her cheeks and tugged on the brim of her red ball cap. A lean cougar prowled across the red background, a new graphic she'd created for Dazzling Designs. The company she worked for produced merchandise for college and professional sports teams. This prototype had been waiting for her when she flew in for four days at the main office and she'd decided to wear it on her trip home.

She was worn out from the long, intense days of discussions and brainstorming. This was her third round trip to New York since she'd made the move back to Texas. After five months, she was piling up plenty of frequent-flyer miles, which she hoped to use one of these days.

She realized with a start the taxi, which had slowed a moment ago, had come to a standstill. The driver's two-way radio crackled in the front seat, but she ignored its staticky sound as she checked her phone again. Still no answer from Hank. She leaned forward, seeing rows of vehicles stopped in every lane of the interstate as far ahead as she could see. Shit.

"Is there an accident ahead of us?"

"Yes, miss." The driver was nothing if not polite. "Dispatch radioed me a moment ago. Sorry, miss."

Well, crap. Just what she didn't need. She wanted a hot bath, a glass of wine, and pizza delivery.

She checked her watch again. Was it really only two minutes since she'd tried calling Hank? Maybe a text would reach him. Sometimes she had better success with that.

"In cab on way home from airport. What's up? Try a tin can for reception."

She hit Send and waited to see if he answered. In less than two minutes, her phone chimed.

"Good trip?"

"Yes. What's up with you? What's with all the phone calls?"

"Just wanted 2 let you know Laura had 2 vacate condo for repairs for 2 days. Told her she could stay at house. She knows where extra key is."

That was what was so important?

Shay snorted and wrote, *"I'll bet."*

"She'll be gone sometime 2day. Just a heads up." Shay ground her teeth. Damn it. Why couldn't the damn woman have gone to a hotel? And what was with giving out the location of the key? She loved her big brother and was grateful to him for sharing his house with her but she definitely needed to find a place of her own. She didn't need his females driving her crazy when he wasn't there.

"She'd better be out of there when I get home. Want peace and quiet."

"I'll text her now. Just wanted to get yr flight info."

"On my way home from airport now."

"Thx. I'll tell her. How was NY?"

"Same old same old. U home soon?"

"Maybe. Don't know. Take care."

"You, too."

Traffic was still not moving. Shay bit down on her frustration, sighed again, and unzipped the front pocket of her carry-on. She'd grabbed a sports magazine in the airport, planning to check the ads her company was running, but hadn't bothered to read it on the plane. Maybe she could use it to pass the time now.

Flipping it open, the first thing she saw was Joe Reilly's face smiling at her in full living color. Crap. Joe Reilly. Her childhood hero, her teenage crush, and the star of her adult erotic fantasies. The same Joe Reilly who'd called her squirt and pest when she tagged after him and Hank. The football idol who had been a babe magnet since his voice changed.

The man she'd been secretly in love with all these years, a love that stilted every other relationship she'd had. When was she ever going to admit that it was an impossibility? That she needed to stomp on it, bury it, and move forward?

In Texas, where football was the number one religion, high school stars wrote their own tickets. As the star quarterback for the Granite Falls High School Coyotes, Joe had had women hanging over him like so much drapery. During his outstanding career in college and then in the NFL, it seemed every time she turned on the television or checked sports online she saw his picture with one female or another. She was sure he had a black book that rivaled an encyclopedia in size. She might as well have been chopped liver for as much attention as he ever paid to her.

She'd wasted so much of her time studying football, until she could diagram games almost as well as Joe could. She could even point out the percentage of success for each play. Joe had always grinned and winked at her. Only in hindsight had she realized he'd tolerated her because she was Hank's baby sister, with the emphasis on baby, even as she stupidly wanted him to wait for her to grow up.

She needed to find a way to get Joe Reilly out of her head. For good. Certainly her obsession with him wasn't helping her love life. She needed to stop looking for Joe Reilly substitutes. The men she tried to build relationships with may not have been athletes, but they were ardent sports fans and that was what attracted her.

And look how far that had gotten her. One cheated on her with a coworker, one out and out lied about who and what he was, another wanted to move in with her and have her pay the rent. Thank God she'd never said *I love you* to any of them, probably because, in retrospect, she hadn't. All those experiences left her with a strong distrust of the male sex, Joe Reilly being no exception.

Yeah, she was the champion of stupid. What was with her, anyway? She was smart, savvy, successful at her work. She'd braved the Big Apple and found herself a dream job she loved, which paid her extremely well. People would be lining up to be her if she let them. Now she needed to find a way to get rid of this restless, unfulfilled feeling she hadn't been able to shake in years.

For weeks she'd been telling herself tomorrow she'd take the first step to build a new life here in San Antonio, back in Texas where her roots were. Reach out to old friends. Meet new people. Rebuild her life and shake the ghosts of the past. Stop burying herself in the house with her work and marathon sessions with old movies and popcorn. How pathetic was that?

What she needed was the right guy, one who understood emotion and who respected her. One who wasn't a Joe Reilly substitute. It wouldn't hurt if he was really hot and could make every one of her erotic fantasies come to life. And also didn't lie or cheat. Time to finally put the vestiges of her crush, her childish daydreams, where they belonged—in the mental Dumpster. She was through lusting after Joe Reilly.

Enough already.

If she was going to hero worship someone she should have stuck to Joe Montana. He'd be a lot safer. And better. Yes, way better.

She closed the magazine, putting Joe Reilly where he belonged. In her carryon.

Time to get on with life.

* * * *

Joe Reilly wheeled his rental car out of the parking lot toward San Antonio. Checking his cell phone for traffic alerts, he discovered an accident on Interstate 10 that had traffic at a standstill. He programmed the GPS for an alternate route and headed out.

He could still smell the traces of a soft drink on his slacks. He'd done his best to wipe away the stains but the rental clerk had given him the fisheye, probably thinking he was a real slob. It wasn't his fault some idiot who couldn't walk and chew gum, or manage to hold onto her drink on the plane, had dumped its contents over the back of her seat and onto him. Just another indication of how crummy his day was going.

He'd seen this trip as a chance to spend some quality time with Hank Beckham, who, despite geographical differences, was still his best friend. He didn't get to see as much of him as he'd like to these days. The last time had been three years ago.

Their schedules just hadn't allowed for any time together since then. Hank was an engineer who was always being sent to some assignment for his company while Joe ran around the country for Fox Sports One and for the Coaches Conference business he'd started. The latter was an important project for him, workshops for high school coaches on how to lead as well as coach. How to teach players personal values as well as diagrams and game plans. He'd seen too many kids come out of high school without understanding that playing was only half the deal. Personal responsibility was a big part of it. His programs were geared to help coaches pass that along.

Unfortunately Hank had texted that morning he was still in Wyoming working on plans to build a bridge, but Joe should make himself at home in the house.

"I'll try and catch a quick couple of days while you're there, buddy," Hank had assured him. "But if not, just make yourself at home."

He'd also hoped to spend some time with his parents, of course, who were happy in their new adults-only community, except they were away on a trip. Bad timing, but it couldn't be helped.

So he'd be alone in the house.

Joe shifted in his seat, trying to stretch out his left leg. The ache served as a constant reminder the glory days had come to an abrupt end.

His cell phone rang, interrupting his thoughts. He looked at the readout and swore. Lisa Margolin. No doubt calling for his help with Gina again. God. How had he gotten himself in this pickle anyway? Because his parents raised him to take care of people who couldn't take care of themselves. That was how. He let the call go to voice mail, not in a mood to deal with it right now.

He was aware the most recent company Gina worked for had gone out of business a few weeks ago. Employees had received a one-month severance package and Joe knew Gina was coming to the end of hers. She didn't deal well with uncertainty. Her dysfunctional family had set off her battle with the bottle to begin with and he knew the thread of sobriety was always very shaky.

Ten minutes later the ringtone chimed again and he knew without looking who it was. She was nothing if not persistent. Setting his jaw, he pressed Accept.

"What is it this time, Lisa?"

"You know I wouldn't call you unless it was important, Joe. Really." She always began the calls that way.

Except it was always important. "Yeah, okay. Just tell me what's up now."

"I hope you aren't mad."

She was as good at sounding tearful as Gina always had been.

"Lisa, I'm kind of busy. What's the deal?"

"Well, um…" She paused.

"Look." He chuffed with impatience. "Just spit it out. How much?" It was always money. Of course.

"She's got a few job interviews coming up and she could use a couple new outfits."

Joe squeezed the phone so hard he was amazed he didn't crush it. "What happened to the money I just sent her?"

Pause. "She got sick." Lisa's voice was very quiet. "I mean, really sick. She needed medicine."

He could only imagine. Medicine that came in bottles of cheap booze.

"She really wants to make a good impression at these interviews," Lisa added.

A headache began to burrow its way into his temples.

"Fine. Give me an hour and I'll transfer some money into your account."

"Can't you just meet me with a check?" she whined.

"No. I'm busy. It's the transfer or nothing."

"Whatever." Her heavy sigh was clear across the connection. "Sorry. I just want this to happen for her."

"We're coming to the end of the road here, Lisa. It's time Gina took responsibility for her own life."

"But you're all she has," Lisa protested, a familiar refrain. "You can't let go of her now. I-I'll make sure she stays clean. Gets a job. Goes to work."

"Do that. I'll check back with you to see what's going on." He disconnected the call in the middle of her thanks, grinding his teeth.

Gina Rivera. High school bombshell. Wild child who'd captured his virtue. He hadn't seen her, had even forgotten about her, until his third year in the NFL. She'd shown up at a game, waiting for him at the player's gate, all masses of blond hair and tight clothes. He'd been high enough on the excitement of the win to succumb to her sexiness and spend the night with her.

He hadn't thought much of it, not even when she showed up twice more. Then he'd discovered her secret, answered her one plea for help and after that he was trapped, just because he was basically a good guy. Occasional contact turned into regular contact. And when he'd stopped taking her calls, she'd had Lisa contact him with a sob story that plucked at his conscience.

How long was he expected to offer aid to a raging alcoholic who didn't help herself? He should have told Scott Manchin, his agent, about it from the beginning. By now so much time had passed if word got out, the media wouldn't look at him as doing something kind for a friend. They'd want to know why he'd kept her hidden all this time. Did they have a child together? All that shit. He'd seen it happen to others and hadn't been smart enough to protect himself. It would be gossip fodder for weeks and kill all the work he'd done to clean up his act. He really had to cut the cord here.

Okay, enough of that.

Following the GPS directions, he pulled off the interstate and into an attractive neighborhood of larger homes and mature trees. A little farther on and the GPS directed him to turn left into the long driveway of a two-story colonial. *Nice digs, Hank,* he thought. But the guy was making big bucks. He deserved a good place to come home to.

He parked in front of the garage door. Maybe when he got inside he could grab the opener from Hank's car and use it while he was here. The key was right where Hank had said it would be. He opened the front door, pulled his suitcase inside, and headed toward the room Hank had said was his to use. On the way he passed a room that looked far too feminine to be Hank's. He wondered briefly whose room it was. Hank hadn't mentioned anything about sharing the house with someone.

Too much for him to think about right now. He wanted a shower, and then he'd see about ordering some dinner. Less than five minutes later he was under hot, steaming water, washing away the grime of the day.

* * * *

The taxi moved forward with a jerk and Shay's eyes popped open. She leaned forward and tapped the driver on the shoulder.

"Did they clear away the wreck? We're finally moving, right?"

"Yes, miss." He shrugged. "But slowly."

She rotated her neck, trying to work out some of the kinks. She'd been sitting in uncomfortable seats since she got in the shuttle to the airport and every muscle in her body ached. The hot shower was looking better and better. Or maybe she'd fire up the hot tub Hank had installed on the rear deck.

Hopefully, with all this delay caused by the wreck, by the time she got to the house Laura would be packed and gone. They pulled off the interstate and she mentally crossed her fingers and silently chanted, *Let her be gone.* But bad luck was still with her. When they turned onto her street and she spotted the car parked in the driveway, she swore under her breath. Laura Whoever was still here. Well, she'd better be getting ready to leave. Shay was in no mood to put up with bullshit. Sighing, she hauled her suitcase into the house, closed the door, and headed through the living room to her bedroom.

And stopped.

A hissing sound came from the shower in the bathroom connected to her bedroom and the guest room. Damn it! The least Hank could do was tell his little friends to use the master bath and leave hers alone. He had, after all, promised her that she'd have complete privacy.

"I travel a lot," he'd told her. Then grinned. "And I'll keep the sleepovers to those times you're in New York."

Yeah, yeah, yeah.

So how come this female hadn't gotten the message she was supposed to be gone?

Crap! The door wasn't even closed. Clouds of steam billowed in the bathroom and obscured the figure in the frosted-glass shower enclosure. Okay, enough was enough.

Shay stepped into the bathroom and banged her hand on the glass.

"This is my bathroom," she ground out. "I've had a tough day and you don't want to mess with me. Next time use Hank's bathroom. This one is off-limits. Get your ass out of here in five seconds, or I won't be responsible for my actions."

She turned away, not the least bit interested in a glimpse of Laura Whoever's nudity. She just wanted her out of the house.

The water stopped and the door slid open.

"Okay. I don't want to cause you any more stress. But Hank said I should use this one."

The deep voice shocked her and she turned around before she even thought about it. And nearly swallowed her tongue. A very wet, very naked Joe Reilly stood in her shower stall, grinning at her.

Just when she'd finally made up her mind to stop thinking about him and obsessing over him.

At that exact moment her cell phone chimed. A message from Hank.

"BTW, Joe's in town. Take good care of him."

Chapter 2

Shay couldn't stop looking at Joe, at his broad shoulders and hard chest with its scattering of dark curls. Water ran in rivulets over his flat stomach and his lean hips, his long legs and his—*Ohmigod!*—erection that exceeded even the most outrageous expectations. Whatever she'd imagined in her dreams, the reality was way beyond it.

All these years she'd nursed her secret feelings for him, all the time she'd lusted after him as a teenager, all her erotic fantasies he'd starred in—nothing ever came close to this incredible reality. She wanted to run her hands over those six-pack abs and feel the hard muscle beneath the skin. Let her fingers drift through the dark hair on his chest. Maybe let her fingertips glide over his flat male nipples. Lick the few drops of water still glistening on his shoulders.

Breathe, Shay. Slow, deep breaths.

She was enchanted by the sight of him, aching for him in every hot place in her body.

He's not the first naked man you've ever seen.

But this was Joe Reilly! In all his glorious nudity. And glorious it was indeed. Her breath caught in her throat and her nipples hardened of their own free will. She felt the thrumming of the pulse in her cunt and moisture pooled in her panties. In fact, her entire body was doing a happy dance.

Oh. My. God.

Joe's low laugh plucked at her nerve endings and vibrated through her body, shaking her out of her erotic reverie.

"Seen enough? Think I could get a towel now?"

The heat of embarrassment suffused Shay's face and she backed away, turning so fast she almost bumped into the wall.

"Get some clothes on. Please." She dragged in a breath. "I'll be in the living room. And do it now," she snapped.

Pacing, hands shoved into the pockets of her jeans, she scrabbled for the edges of her control. Her mind whirled, totally unsettled, as the implications of this situation peppered her. Joe Reilly. Here. In this house. Just the two of them. Alone. Was Hank crazy?

Maybe. He'd probably given less than two seconds of thought to it, off there in the wilds of Wyoming as he was. Had it even occurred to him she might not want to play housemates with a man who'd treated her all her life as if she were *his* kid sister?

This was ridiculous. She was an adult. No big deal.

Yeah, it was a big deal. Because this was Joe, the secret hero of every one of her dreams since she was eight years old.

Obviously, the car in the driveway belonged to him. Good thing he'd parked by the half of the garage that held Hank's car. Like her, Hank always cabbed to the airport and back.

"Usually women are telling me to take my clothes off." The deep voice behind her had a teasing edge to it. "This is a novelty."

She whirled around to find him inches away from her. It was obvious he'd given drying off a quick pass. His dark hair curled from the dampness of the shower and tiny drops of water still snaked down his chest, drawing a path toward the waistband of his jeans. Her gaze dropped automatically to his crotch, and she forced herself to jerk it away.

Not. Good.

"There's nothing funny about this. At all." She fisted her hands on her hips. "Just what in the hell are you doing here, anyway?"

He grinned and she noted he still had the tiny dimple at the left corner of his mouth. A very *sexy* dimple. It just wasn't fair. No man should be this downright appealing, especially when she wanted desperately to be angry with him.

"Simmer down, squirt." He chuckled. "There's a simple explanation."

"Don't call me squirt." She spat the words out through clenched teeth. "I'm not a kid any more, in case you hadn't noticed."

His midnight-black eyes took a slow tour of her from the red ball cap on her head to her sneaker-clad feet. Heat surged through her as if he was undressing her with his eyes and she wanted to cross her arms over her chest.

"Oh, I noticed. Believe me. I'd say you've grown up a whole lot." He actually had the audacity to wink. "So what are you doing here?"

Her jaw dropped. "What am *I* doing here? That's a lot of nerve coming from you. I live here. What are *you* doing here?"

"You live here?" His eyes widened. "I thought you lived in New York."

"I moved back about four months ago. Hank's giving me house room while I take my time looking for a place of my own."

"Well, damn." He scratched his head. "Old Hank didn't mention that when he said I could crash here for a few days."

"Are you kidding me?" She was going to kill her brother the minute she laid eyes on him. "I can't believe he did this. What's wrong with a hotel?"

Joe frowned. "That's not very hospitable of you. Hank told me to make myself at home. Much better than a hotel."

Yes, killing was definitely on the agenda. Except she was torn between wanting to throw Joe out of the house or throw herself at him bodily. After all these years, at the very moment she'd decided to pack him into the memory closet and move forward, here he was. *Control,* she told herself. She had to stay in control and not get any wild ideas. The time for that was long past.

Anyway, why would he be interested in her? He had a gazillion women rotating in and out of his bed. He still saw her as a kid, so she'd better not get any wild ideas.

"Look." Shay took a step backward. Joe had moved way too close into her personal space and his clean male scent was making her crazy. "Hank should have checked with me first. I'm sorry, this is just not going to work."

"I don't know why not." He moved closer again. "You've got plenty of room here. Anyway, I have things to take care of so we'll probably hardly see each other."

"What kind of things?"

He shrugged. "Just business."

"Fine. Whatever. It's not as if I care." Shay threw up her hands. "I'm going to my room to unpack. Do us both a favor and find a hotel room." She turned to look at him. "And get your stuff out of my bathroom."

One corner of his mouth turned up in a half grin. Shay did her best to ignore the dimple winking next to it.

"But isn't this the bathroom for these two bedrooms to share?"

"Yes, but—"

"Then I'm sure this is what Hank meant for me to do. I promise I won't get into your cosmetics. They probably aren't my skin tone, anyway."

"You're trying to drive me crazy, right?"

His rich, low laugh made the pulse between her thighs throb like a drum. "Would I do that?"

She started to roll her suitcase out of the room as if everything was settled when strong male fingers closed over her arm.

"Hold on just a minute. That cap. I've seen that cap before."

"My cap?" She frowned. "I doubt it. I'll bet there's a million red caps out there and this one is one of a kind."

She tried to pull away but Joe's grip on her was firm.

"But that's a distinctive red." He frowned. "Let's see. You're just getting home from out of town. You flew in from New York. Not too many flights from there to here landing at this time. I don't have to be too bright to think you might be the idiot who tossed her drink all over me on the plane."

Her stomach plummeted. "You must have me confused with someone else."

He moved to block her path. "I don't think so." He reached behind her head and tugged on her ponytail. "I definitely think you're the culprit. I should make you pay for my dry cleaning."

"Fine. Whatever." She had to get away from him. His nearness was driving her nuts and his touch sent threads of heat to various parts of her body. "Send me the bill."

He tipped her chin up with one finger. When his eyes looked directly into hers, everything in her body went liquid. All her damn danger signs were flashing. He was just playing with her, nothing more. Just being Joe. She needed to remember that.

"I'd say it entitles me to guest privileges here, too. Don't you agree?"

He wasn't going to leave. That much was obvious.

"I said I'd pay for the damn dry cleaning. Just leave the stuff on the counter in the utility room."

"I think that's worth a lot more than just paying a bill," he repeated. "Even more than house privileges. I should get special privileges. Like maybe having you cook my dinner, too." Laughter lurked in his eyes.

"In your dreams," she snapped. She knew he was yanking her chain, and he was doing a good job of it. Somehow she would find a way to get him out of the house while she still had her wits about her. Good thing she was more than over Joe Reilly. If only every one of her nerve endings didn't sizzle when he was within two feet of her.

He chuckled, obviously enjoying himself. "Maybe I can think of a few more things to add to the list."

"Forget it. Not happening." She pushed past him, tugging her suitcase. "You clean up after yourself and don't leave a mess in the kitchen." At the door to her bedroom she looked back at him.

"Just be sure to stay out of my way. And if you insist on sharing the bathroom you'd damn well better keep it clean. House rules. I don't even want to see a razor lying on the sink."

"Wow. Stiff rules." He laughed again. "I'll do my best not to break any of them."

Shay slammed the door to her bedroom and threw herself on her bed. Great. Just freaking great. She didn't have enough stress in her life. Now she was forced to deal with Joe Reilly as a temporary housemate. Lying there with her arm over her eyes, something else occurred to her. She jumped up, yanked open the door, and stormed into the living room. Joe, unfortunately, was not there. She found him in the room he was using, pulling a shirt out of a suitcase.

Shay stopped, momentarily mesmerized by the sight of his solid chest with its dusting of dark hair. Again her pulse thrummed and the blood heated in her veins. She scrubbed at her cheeks that suddenly felt too hot.

Please don't let him notice.

"Come right in," he teased, slipping the soft, collared shirt over his head. "Make yourself comfortable."

"How long?" she demanded.

He cocked an eyebrow. "That's an ambiguous question. How long what?"

"Will you be here, damn it. How long?"

That sexy laugh rumbled out again. "Ready to toss me out so soon?"

She fisted her hands. "I just want to know when you plan to leave."

He shrugged. "When I finish my business. Hank said no rush."

"Argh!" She stamped her foot, then immediately regretted it. He'd never see her as a woman if she kept acting like a child. Oh, wait. He'd never see her that way at all. She let out a calming breath. "So? When?"

The grin disappeared from his face.

"Shay, is there some reason you don't want me here? I thought we were friends."

"Friends?" she squeaked. "What makes you say that? You never treated me as anything but Hank's pain-in-the-ass little sister. We were never friends. And it's too late to start now. Trust me."

The look he gave her ignited every space in her body. The air around them crackled with sudden, unexpected sexual energy and the heat that flared in his eyes shocked her. Holy hell. She swallowed hard and sent a silent message to her body to behave. Now, after so long, was not the time to respond to Joe's masculine sexuality. Actually, for her sanity, the time would be—never.

"So what's the answer?" she persisted, ignoring the hungry look Joe suddenly gave her.

"The answer," he drawled, "is I don't know. Preseason's not for a couple more months. That gives me time before I have to be back to get ready for the show. I have some things to take care of here." His gaze seemed to bore into her. "Maybe as long as I'm around we can try to be… friends."

"Friends."

His gaze took a leisurely tour of her body again, as if mentally cataloging each of her assets. It took every bit of self-control to tear her eyes away, but the new Shay wasn't going to be tempted.

"I don't think so." She frowned. "Let's just try to stay out of each other's way. Oh. And one more thing. I'd appreciate it if you didn't bring any of your women here."

He lifted his eyebrows. "My women?"

"Yeah. You know. Your usual harem. By the way, if your phone still has Bad Company's *Feel Like Makin' Love* as a ringtone, put it on mute."

A smile threatened again. "You don't like the song?"

"Well, it's certainly appropriate for your lifestyle, I'll say that."

His face sobered. "Shay—"

"I'm sure your salary's plenty big," she interrupted. "You can spring for a hotel room when the need arises." Under her breath she muttered, "Which will probably be about every night."

"What did you say?" he demanded.

"I said you probably won't be sleeping here much."

"That's a low blow." She heard the edge of anger in his voice. "Is that how you think of me? Really?"

"It's the truth, isn't it?"

Before he could say anything else, she headed back to her room and slammed the door again. She knew she was being childish. Juvenile. But holy hell. Joe Reilly in her space for a whole week. Maybe more. How was she supposed to handle that?

* * * *

Joe stared at himself in the bathroom mirror, now clear of the earlier steam from his shower. Not bad-looking, he told himself. A few more lines in his face and just a hint of gray in the hair. The thing bothering him, however, was the lust flaring in his eyes, lust put there by the little go-round with Shay Beckham.

The image he'd carried with him from the last time he'd seen her, however brief the contact, was spot-on. Something he'd wanted to chalk up to an aberration on his part. An overactive imagination.

Hank had been in New York, staying with his sister for a couple of days, and Joe drove into the city to have dinner with him. When Shay opened the door and he'd looked at her, his system had gone into full-blown shock. Gone was the skinny kid and the developing teenager. In their place was a ripe, mature woman who made the spit dry up in his mouth and his cock try to urge him to do things strictly off-limits.

Then he saw her today and bam! The vision slammed into him again. Even tired and cranky, with no makeup and dressed down in jeans and a sweatshirt, she made his body sit up and take notice. His cock was already sending him a message and his balls ached like crazy.

This was Shay. Hank's baby sister. The skinny little kid who used to stick to them like gum to a shoe. She wore a big Keep Away sign.

As a teenager, having a little kid hero-worship him stroked his ego. It tickled him to have his best friend's sister hang out with him and Hank and talk football, unless of course there were females around. Then he'd made sure to let her know she was a pain in the ass.

He cringed now as thoughts from the past bounced around in his brain, memories of the dismissive way he'd always treated her. There was no dismissing her now. This Shay was a luscious, desirable woman and the way his body responded to her froze every nerve with shock. If she were anyone else, he'd already be figuring out a way to get her out of her clothes and horizontal.

"I said you probably won't be sleeping here much."

Her barbed words cut deeply. To think Shay still saw him the same way.

He'd always thought of himself as a man who loved women. Who was lucky women loved him. He enjoyed the hell out of them. For a lot of years he'd been jazzed by the dating game. It was heady stuff to be envied by others for a steady string of gorgeous women and certainly fed his ego. All those years he'd never given a thought to how people saw him. He rocked it on the field and reaped the benefits of his success with the female population.

Still, it had stunned him to suddenly realize he was tired of the eternal conga line of women in and out of his life. What was once his juice had suddenly became old hat.

Things had changed so much in the past five years. He was in a much different place. As his life continued to evolve, so did the things he wanted from it. Like settling down. Getting married.

What he really needed was a woman like Shay.

Joe blinked and looked around, as if someone had actually spoken the words out loud. Where in hell did that thought come from? Again he reminded himself that she was off-limits to him. Right, right, right. Maybe he could tattoo it on his brain. Even thinking of her that way was off-limits. He needed to keep telling himself that.

Okay, time to get dressed and find someplace to eat. Maybe he'd pick up a pizza and bring it back. Or Chinese food. Then early to bed. And sleep, if he could do it with Shay only a few feet away from him.

He wondered what she'd say if she knew about the work he did with kids? With teenagers? Obviously her entire image of him was crafted from those wild years and the accompanying tabloid coverage. But so much had changed. He had changed. Did she ever watch his television show? If so, what did she think of it?

Fuck, Reilly. Enough. Get your head out of your ass. Once more, idiot. She's Hank's baby sister. It would be nice if she liked him but it wouldn't kill him if she didn't.

He hoped.

Heading toward the front door, he bumped into the woman in question coming out of the kitchen. In place of her travel outfit, she now wore a T-shirt and skimpy shorts and was carrying a glass of water. When they bumped, her hand jiggled, spilling drops from the glass on both of them.

"Crap." She shook her hand to rid it of the moisture.

"I already showered," he teased. "Remember? You saw me?"

"Okay, okay, I'll say it." She bit her lower lip. "I'm sorry. And I'm clumsy. Shoot me."

She hurried into the kitchen for a paper towel, bright red staining her cheeks. Joe swallowed a smile when she busied herself blotting his shirt, frowning as she did so.

"There." She stepped back and studied his chest. "I think you're good to go." She crumpled up the paper towel. "Wherever you're going."

"Shay." He cupped her elbows and kept his voice low and even. Steady. Why did he get the impression he spooked her? He'd have to think about that. "It's okay. It's just a shirt. And it's washable. Got it?"

"Yes." She still wouldn't look at him. "I, um, think I'll just go back into my room."

Damn!

"Wait." He didn't want her to retreat, even though he knew he should just leave it alone. Especially since—shock!—just touching her made him so horny he was afraid his cock would strangle itself.

"I'm going to my room, Joe." Why did she refuse to look at him?.

"Wait. I, um, was going to head out for some dinner. Want to join me?"

She looked down at her outfit and then raised her eyes to him, a tiny smile teasing her mouth. Finally. "Where are we dining? Goodwill?"

"You know what? I don't think I'm in the mood for a restaurant. How about if I order a pizza delivered? You can choose the toppings," he coaxed.

What the hell was he doing? He needed to put space between them until he figured out what was happening here. Preferably several city blocks.

"Why do you want to eat with me?"

Of course he didn't have a sensible answer for her. He just knew it was important to get her to say yes.

"Um, because I'm hungry and you're hungry so, food together?"

She narrowed her eyes at him. "There's a special on tonight about Joe Montana and I plan to watch it." She waved her hand at the living room. "In there, on the big-screen television."

He chuckled. "Really? Your big hero? The man you raved about incessantly when you were younger? Okay, I think I can handle that." He winked. "Although we both know I've got him beat in all categories."

"In ego, maybe." She tilted her head and looked up at him again. "You sure you want to do this? Buy a pizza and share it with me?"

"Sure, kid. It will be like old times. Only without Hank. We'll just eat his share."

"Oh. Okay."

Was that disappointment on her face, or was he just imagining it? What did it mean? Did she regret accepting his invite, or did she read something more into it? Well, regret just wouldn't work. This pizza thing was just damn stupid if he wanted to put space between them. Where was his brain when he needed it to work?

"I'll call it in," she told him. "I have the number on speed dial."

"You and Hank don't do much cooking?"

"Hardly." She fetched her smart phone from her room and punched in the number, snapping out her order. "Lots of pepperoni and mushrooms," she warned Joe when she hung up.

"Yeah?" He crossed his arms over his chest and leaned against the kitchen counter. "I would have thought with all those years in New York you'd want pineapple chunks and chicken."

"Please," she mocked. "Do I look like I'd eat designer pizza?"

He watched her refill the water glass and take a long drink from it. The play of muscles in her throat as she swallowed fascinated him, as did the shift of fabric over her breasts when she lifted her arm. He noted the outline of her nipples beneath the flimsy T-shirt, a sure sign whatever was scratching at him was doing the same to her. His palms itched to cup those mounds and he curled his fingers to keep from reaching out to her.

Again the devil in his head, the really horny one, reminded him this was Shay. Hank's baby sister. He needed to keep repeating it to himself. What the fuck was wrong with him? Now here she was. In this house. With him. Alone. And his brain and his dick seemed to be getting different messages.

Shit!

"Hello?" A hand waved in front of his face. "Anyone in there?"

"What? Oh, sorry." Damn. He'd just spaced out. He hoped drool wasn't running down his face. "Late hours catching up with me."

"Maybe you should cut back on that list of women."

Again with the women.

"Shay, look at me. Put down your empty glass and turn around to me."

"You don't tell me what to do," she snapped.

"*Please* turn around and look at me. Okay?"

She set the glass in the sink and turned slowly, leaning back against the counter. Unfortunately when she did it stretched the T-shirt even more against her nicely rounded breasts and her nipples that reminded him of the gumdrops he loved. He forcibly restrained himself from smacking his lips.

"What?" The word was filled with belligerence.

"We haven't seen each other much in a lot of years. Many, many, many years."

"Yeah? So?"

"Did it ever occur to you I might have changed? Maybe I might not be the guy with the overload of testosterone anymore?"

She barked a laugh. "Right."

"Maybe I'm a lot more like Joe Montana than you think, him who you so revere."

"Hardly." Was it possible for someone shorter than him to look down her nose at him? "He was never Mr. Playboy with a gaggle of females hanging off his arm. He was always business. Nothing more."

In two strides, he was in front of her, his fingers wrapped gently around her upper arms. She tensed immediately and her lips thinned. He eased his hold, but he didn't back away.

"I may not be Montana but I'm *not* the person you think I am, either. And somehow I'm going to make you see the truth of it while we're here together."

He was close enough to her now he could feel the outline of her body. The way her eyes widened, he knew she could also feel his, including his raging hard-on. Faint pink crept up her cheeks and he moved an inch or two backward. The air between them, though, still crackled with shockingly unexpected sexual energy.

"So." Her eyes were still glued to his. "Exactly how were you planning to do that?"

Fuzz was wrapped around his brain, the effect of being this close to her. "What? Do what?"

She gave a breathy little laugh. "Make me see how different you are now."

As he was digging in his woolly brain for an answer, the doorbell rang. Shay pressed her hands against his chest and pushed.

"I think the pizza's here. You need to get your wallet out."

Pizza. Wallet. Yeah.

He took another step back and headed for the door. Pizza. What he needed more than food, though, was another shower. A cold one.

"Bring the food in here," Shay hollered from the living room.

When he put the box down on the coffee table he saw plates and glasses already set out, and—hallelujah!—two ice cold bottles of beer.

"Can't watch Joe without beer," she joked.

"Which Joe?"

"Ha!" She busied herself dishing out the pizza. "The real one, of course."

* * * *

Why did he have to sit this close to her? His very nearness panicked her, eroded her self-control. She'd grasped at the Joe Montana thing like a lifeline, hoping to create a barrier between them. Change the feel of whatever it was buzzing in the air between them.

Needing distance, Shay had deliberately taken a seat at the far end of the couch, leaving the rest of it for Joe to stretch out. Instead he plunked himself down right next to her, sending her body temperature spiking. This was a bad idea. Very, very, very bad. She should have turned down Joe's invitation and sent him out to eat. Someplace. Anyplace. And worn a caftan that covered her from neck to toes to disguise her body's automatic reaction. It seemed not even Joe Montana could do anything about her reaction. How pathetic was that?

Where were all her good intentions, the resolutions she'd made in the cab ride from the airport? Here she was sharing a house with Joe Reilly, with temptation rapping on the door. It just wasn't fair. If Hank were here, she'd kick his ass for putting her in this position. She wasn't a saint, for God's sake.

Damn him, anyway.

"So what made you move back from New York?" Joe asked, startling her out of her reverie. "I thought you really liked it there."

She realized she was staring at him and gave herself a mental shake, shrugged and swallowed a bite of pizza. "It got old after a while." And the men sucked.

Joe cocked an eyebrow. "Hank mentioned you were doing gangbusters in your design job. Told me you were excited about it."

She nodded. "I was. I still am. I enjoy creating the designs, making someone's idea come to life."

"But?"

She took a sip of beer. "But I decided I liked San Antonio better. And my boss made me a great offer. I work from here and head into the city about every six weeks for meetings. Thus the plane ride today."

The look he gave her was filled with curiosity. "I can't believe you're happier here away from the glitz and glamour of the Big Apple."

"Yeah?" She sniffed. "Maybe you never noticed, I'm not exactly a glitz-and-glamour kind of woman. I love San Antonio. This way I get the best of both worlds."

His gaze poured over her like warm melted chocolate. "There wouldn't be some man in the mix, would there? I'd be very upset if someone messed with my girl."

"Your girl?" She chuffed. "One, I'm not yours. I'm not anyone's. Two, I'm not a girl any more. And three, my private life is none of your business."

"No?" He picked up another slice of pizza, bit off a piece, and chewed thoughtfully. "Maybe it should be. Hank not being here and all, I should probably make sure you're doing okay. You know, kind of be your guardian."

"My guardian? Are you for real?" Shay barked a laugh. "Hank doesn't meddle in my business. You don't need to, either. Remember, I'm not a kid who needs her nose wiped."

He reached out and cupped her chin with one of his large warm hands—quarterback's hands—and looked straight into her eyes. The look in his eyes stunned her. He was actually looking at her as a female. Desirable, even. His touch sent delicious shivers racing over her skin and the look in his eyes made her body want things that were impossible with this man. She needed to pull away for her own salvation but she couldn't seem to make herself do it.

"No." His voice was hot and slow, plucking at her nerve endings. "You are definitely not a kid. Not anymore."

Shay wanted to tell him not to touch her but those fingers were like electric wands sending jolts through her system. She couldn't tear her gaze away from him. When he reached for a napkin and dabbed at her lower lip, she wanted to bite him instead of the food.

"A little sauce." His mouth turned up in a lazy smile. "Wouldn't want Montana to see it, right?"

Montana.

The program.

Right.

When she turned her head, he was forced to move his hand. She picked up the remote and clicked on the television. "It's about time for the special on Joe, so, no talking, please."

For the first time she had to work to concentrate on a program about her hero. Video of him played out on the screen, shots of him tossing his unbelievably accurate passes to his favorite receiver, Jerry Rice. Of the celebrations following each of his four Super Bowl victories. Of his cool head under fire as the ultimate field general.

To her dismay she found her mind wandering to the Joe sitting next to her, all six foot four of his powerful masculinity. She was more acutely aware of him than she could remember. She couldn't help stealing glances at his very male body next to her, long legs stretched out to the coffee table, muscles flexing in his thighs every time he shifted. Whatever he'd splashed on his body after his shower was driving her nuts, too. The clean woodsy male scent she always associated with him drifted across her nose and seemed to surround her. Tantalizing her.

No, no, no. This was all wrong. *Control,* she reminded herself. Control, control, control. She could do it.

"—don't you think?"

"Huh? What?" Embarrassed, Shay realized she'd zoned out and Joe was saying something to her.

His sexy laugh rumbled through her. "I guess old Joe really does have you hypnotized. You haven't heard a word I said, have you?"

"Um, sorry." She picked up her bottle of beer. "You know how I block everything out when my hero is on the screen. What did you say?"

"Not important." He recrossed his legs at the ankle. "So, still got the love affair going on with Joe, huh?"

"Hard not to. He's the ultimate."

Joe was silent for a long moment, holding a paper plate with another slice of pizza on it.

"Question," he said at last. "Did you ever, you know, see any of my games? Look at my stats?"

"Why, Joe Reilly." She couldn't help laughing. "Are you jealous of Joe Montana?"

"Of course not. Just curious." He nodded at the screen. "But I measured up pretty good against him. Just sayin'."

Surely her ravings about Montana never bothered him. He was an icon in his own right. No, wait. Only his ego was affected, right? Because she was sure Joe Reilly didn't give a rat's ass if she idolized him or not. All those women more than did it for him.

The program ended and the silence between them was suddenly thick enough to touch.

Shay cleared her throat. "I'm going to clean this up and then do some reading."

"Here. I'll give you a hand." He sat up and reached for the empty pizza box at the same moment she did, and their heads collided.

"Ouch!" Shay rubbed her forehead.

"Oh. Sorry. Here, let me look at it."

Joe cupped her face and turned her head so he could see where they'd bumped. Suddenly the air around them changed. Her heartbeat ratcheted up at the hunger that flared in his eyes and her breath stalled in her throat.

For a very long moment neither of them moved. Maybe it was curiosity to finally find out what it would be like to kiss him. Maybe it was the simmering heat of the moment. Whatever it was, she didn't pull away. So slow the movement was barely detectible, Joe leaned closer and touched his mouth to hers. His lips were cool yet their contact scorched her, heat sizzling through her body clear to her toes. His lean fingers cradled her cheeks with a touch light enough that a whisper of wind would have brushed them away yet Shay was unable to move, afraid to breathe. Every brain cell froze and her heart was beating hard enough she could hear it pounding in her ears.

When Joe's tongue came out to trace the seam of her mouth, everything in her body went liquid. Her pussy throbbed, her nipples sprang to life, and a desperate hunger gripped her. The soft glide of his tongue was like the touch of velvet, coaxing her to open for him, to accept him. When he slid it between her lips she welcomed it, opening wider for him and letting her own tongue begin a dance with his.

All her life she'd wondered what kissing Joe Reilly would be like. The reality was so much better than anything she'd imagined.

They stayed that way for what seemed forever, exploring each other's mouths, tasting, licking. The scent of his cologne still tantalized her nostrils and invaded her senses. Everything faded away for Shay except this incredibly sensuous contact. This was not a voracious kiss but a testing. A sexy little dance where neither partner was sure who would lead. As his tongue swept in slow glides, touching sensitive nerves, she hummed with pleasure and explored his taste the same way. Back and forth, an erotic dance that needed no music.

When Joe finally lifted his head enough to break the contact, he stared at her, shock written on his face. Shay locked her gaze with his. Who should speak first? What should she say? What *could* she say? She'd just exchanged a totally erotic kiss with Joe Reilly.

Joe Reilly!

He still cradled her cheeks in his warm palms, as if unable to let her go. Still neither of them moved or spoke.

Shay was trying to unscramble her brains when Joe dipped his head again and this time there was nothing light or gentle about the kiss. It was a predator's kiss, ravenous and claiming. His tongue was a slither of flame burning the inside of her mouth everywhere it touched. He didn't wait for her to offer her own tongue as she'd done before. Instead, he tugged it with his teeth and closed his lips around it, sucking it hard.

He continued to cradle her face, using strong hands to tilt her head this way and that to give himself a better angle. His body, hard and muscular, pressed against hers until she was lying back against the cushions. One lean, jeans-clad thigh insinuated itself between hers, nudging against her quivering pussy through her skimpy shorts.

Her responses were primal, an explosion of the need that had been building for years.

One of his hands slipped down to her arm, then eased beneath her T-shirt. His warm palm cupped one breast, his thumb rasping over the hardened tip. The heat of his body permeated hers, surrounded it. A moan floated in the air and she wasn't sure whose it was, exactly.

He trailed his lips across her cheek and down the length of her neck. She ran her hands along the hard muscles of his back down to his hips, pulling him more tightly against her. When she arched to him, he took little nips, then soothed the skin with his tongue. Every one of her nerves was firing, her body so hot she was sure she would instantly combust.

He licked the hollow of her throat where her pulse fluttered wildly.

More. I want more.

She dragged his shirt free of his jeans, yanking it over his head, and touched his naked skin with her fingers. His chest was just as hard as she'd imagined, and the curls of hair covering it just as soft and silky. Touching him was like sticking her finger in an electric socket.

She felt his hands grasp her own shirt, pulling it loose.

"Lift up," he whispered and tugged the shirt over her head.

Next to go was her bra and then his mouth was on her, his lips closing tightly over a beaded nipple. Streaks of high voltage raced to her core as he fed on her like a man with an insatiable appetite. A man in the grip of unquenchable desire. She tried to touch him everywhere, suddenly frantic with need. He sucked and nibbled, the tug of his mouth reaching way down to her pussy.

Her brain melted. With his hot mouth back on hers, feeding impatiently, she was only vaguely aware of the movement of his hands everywhere on her body. Sliding into her shorts and cupping her ass, then easing around to find her very, very wet slit. When he slid two fingers inside her, she clamped down on him and rocked her hips, focused only on satisfying the need raging through her.

"That's it," he whispered, his lips at her ear. "God, Shay, you are so hot you're burning my fingers."

He moved against her, the heat of his body surrounding her. The hair on his chest brushed erotically against her naked skin as he shifted position slightly. He licked the shell of her ear and traced the line with his tongue. Her responses were primal, raw, uncontrollable. Shivers raced along her spine. She lost all sense of time and place, her entire being focused on the unexpected climax swirling up through her body. It had been such a long time, and her body was so eager, and this man seemed to unlock every one of her secret places.

"Let go." His voice was raw and urgent. "Let go for me."

He pressed his thumb to her clit and as if a button opened a magic door, she exploded. Wrapping her legs around his waist, she pulled herself as tight to his touch as she could and rode his hand like a wild horse. When the last spasm subsided, when the last tremor had rippled through her body, she lay there gasping, her heart galloping and her breathing ragged. When she opened her eyes at last, Joe's face was barely a millimeter away from hers, his eyes still burning with lust.

And then…

Reality slammed into her. Ice water dumped all over her couldn't have shocked her more. What the hell had she done here? Allowed to happen?

No, no, no, no, no. Big mistake. Huge mistake.

She pushed at him, trying to move him away from her body. She could tell when his brain snapped into focus again and the look of desire was replaced by shock.

Abruptly he sat up, shaking his head. "Jesus. Shay, I—"

"Don't say a word. Not one word." If he tried to apologize, she might have to kill him.

"Listen, I don't know what—"

"Shut up, Joe. I mean it. Just shut up."

She was hot and cold by turns, mortified and embarrassed by what happened. By what she'd *allowed* to happen.

No more hiding your feelings now, Shay, the ones you were so sure you'd buried.

She scrabbled around for her T-shirt and bra, clutched them to her, and pushed herself off the couch. If she could have somehow melted into the floor she would have. She could tell he was already regretting what happened and she just didn't want to listen to it. Ignoring the debris from their dinner, she raced to her bedroom and slammed the door.

She'd never be able to face him again. What in God's name must he be thinking?

* * * *

Joe was actually doing his best not to think. His big brain seemed to have vaporized and his little brain was screaming orders at him. Speaking of his little brain, he was rock hard to the point if he bumped into anything he was afraid his dick would break off and fall to the floor. Maybe it would be best since it seemed intent on dragging him into such trouble.

What the hell was wrong with him? This was Hank's baby sister. The squirt. The tagalong.

Not any more, hotshot.

That was damn sure. Tonight he'd been seized with the unexpected desire to lick her all over. Because this Shay was a very sexy woman who turned him on full blast. And tempted him. Hell, temptation didn't even begin to describe her. He only wanted one tiny taste of her. A little something to satisfy him after he'd carried the image of a mature Shay in his mind for so long. Well, he damn sure got his taste. What was the matter with him? Hank would kill him when he found out.

Maybe Shay wouldn't tell him.

As he carried the empty pizza box, the plates, and bottles into the kitchen, he tried telling himself it would be okay. He'd find a way to make it so. He'd apologize to her.

No, not an apology. No matter how he worded it she'd take it wrong. What was he apologizing for, anyway? The fact he was hot as a pistol for her or the fact he'd acted on it? Would she be insulted? Angry?

Shit. He was supposed to be the expert on women. Now he realized just how little he really knew. Life had always been easy for him in that department. The Bad Company song she'd teased him about, *Feel Like Makin' Love,* could have been his theme song.

So he'd cleaned up his act. So what? After tonight he was sure nothing he said would do any good. He'd certainly lived up to her image of him, pawing at her the way he had.

What the hell had come over him, anyway? If he could, he'd kick himself in the ass.

He sure as hell hadn't the first idea what to say to her now. Her snarky, get-in-your-face attitude certainly wasn't going to make it easy. Combine that with her image of him as the ultimate playboy and he had a big wall to climb here.

Heading down the hallway, he saw Shay's door was still closed. As hard as she'd slammed it he wondered it hadn't fallen off its hinges. He raised his hand to knock, then dropped it. What would he say to her? *Sorry I'm an ass? I thought you were someone else?* Oh, yeah. That would go over like a lead balloon.

He should go out somewhere. Anywhere. Out of the danger zone.

Perversity made him head for his bedroom, instead. Anyway, where could he go with such a raging hard-on he could barely walk? Yeah, he definitely should have taken himself elsewhere tonight. Lying on his bed, however, with his arm over his eyes, a thought struck him with alarming awareness.

She'd liked it!

Not only liked it, but came apart right there on the couch in his arms with nothing more than his mouth and his fingers touching her. Lifting his right hand, he sniffed the perfume of her liquid, then tortured himself by lapping the traces of it from his fingers.

Pathetic. Completely pathetic.

Yet here he was, obsessing over a woman he had no business even touching and hard as a spike because he never had a chance to get past first base. First base? What was he, in high school?

He still couldn't wrap his mind around the fact he wanted to plunge himself inside her, let her wet heat surround him, and ride her until they both exploded. He had to get over this. Especially if they were going to share this house for more than five minutes.

Chapter 3

At eight in the morning, after a mostly sleepless night, Shay reluctantly dragged herself out of bed. Her dreams had been filled with images of Joe Reilly and the feel of his hands as he moved them over her curves. She could still feel the scratch of his stubble as she touched her palms to his cheeks. Still feel the abrasion of the curling hair on his chest against her breasts, teasing her nipples to agonizingly hard points. The heated look in his eyes after he stroked her to orgasm still scorched her body. She ached with rising need even as her brain tried to shut everything down.

She felt stupid. Humiliated. Completely embarrassed as the tendrils of the erotic dream still wound themselves around her. So much for her good intentions and new resolutions.

But oh holy God. The touch of his mouth, his kisses hot, wet, teasing. The way his hands caressed her. The heat he created in her body. Her teenage dreams had barely scratched the surface of the reality. What was it Hank always said? Oh, yeah. Expect the unexpected. No kidding!

Never mind. She could handle this. She just needed to keep reminding herself Joe was still—well, Joe. Hot sports figure who never took anything serious except the game of football itself. Ladies' man. What happened last night was an aberration, in his life as well as hers.

What prompted him, anyway? She'd give a week's pay to know what had been going through his mind and what he thought now. For her part she'd just chalk it up to a surge of hormones. That's all. Her hormones had to be way out of whack. Maybe she could take a pill, or something. Anything to get this out of her system before she made a bigger fool of herself.

She had no idea how she'd face him today. She wanted to jump back into bed, pull the covers over her head, and stay there until Joe left town. Or found someone to shack up with. Of course, that was totally unrealistic.

Her cell phone chimed, and she picked it up from her nightstand.

"Laura out of there okay?"

Shay ground her teeth at Hank's text. Laura would have been a lot easier to handle. For a moment, she was tempted just to ignore the message. He'd just text her again until she answered him, though. Crap.

"She was gone." She paused a moment, then typed, *"Different houseguest. He needs to leave."*

A long moment passed before Hank texted back.

"Oh, yeah. Forgot. Told Joe he could bunk there. All good."

No, it was not all good. Not even a little.

"He needs 2 go 2 hotel."

"B nice, Shay. He's good friend."

"Call him. Tell him 2 leave."

"Told you to take good care of him, right? Do that for me."

"I can B nicer if he's in hotel. CALL HIM!!!!!"

She waited and waited. Kept watching the screen. Nope, no more texts came through.

"Damn you, Hank."

Shay tossed the phone onto the bed. Now what? She'd have to come out of the room sooner or later. She strained her ears to catch any sound of movement in the house but heard nothing. Maybe he was already gone for the day, doing whatever it was he was here in town to handle.

She cracked the bedroom door an inch and listened intently. Still no sound. Okay. If he wasn't gone maybe he was still sleeping. In which case the tank top and boy shorts she'd slept in would do fine for a quick trip to the kitchen to fix a cup of coffee. Just in case, she walked on tiptoe and held her breath as she moved down the short hall and through the living room. The kitchen was empty. Good so far. She let out a sigh of relief and set about brewing her coffee in the single-cup machine.

"Think you can fix one of those for me?"

"Jesus, Mary, and Joseph!" Shay jumped at the sound of the deep voice, banging her knee against a cupboard door and nearly cracking her elbow on the counter. She turned slowly, praying her face showed no emotion. Holy Mother, it was a sin to look that good in the morning. The Fox Sports T-shirt and running shorts did little to disguise the hard, masculine lines of his body. Despite the fact Joe Reilly hadn't played one down in five years, he obviously worked hard to keep himself in shape. She couldn't keep her eyes from taking in every inch of his still-athletic body. The scruff on his cheeks and slightly mussed hair only enhanced the sexual hum in the air around him.

Shay closed her eyes for a moment and prayed she was still in her bedroom. That she was just imagining this. Then reality set in, she blinked and realized Joe was taking in every detail of her body as she'd done to him. The tank top and boy shorts seemed suddenly insubstantial, and she wished for a shroud to appear and wrap itself around her. No such luck, so she tried for an attitude of nonchalance.

"Um, yes. Coffee. Sure." She busied herself taking down mugs and putting the little prepared cups in the machine.

"I need a slug of caffeine before I head out for my run." His voice was rough with a gravelly, early morning rumble.

Sexy. Way too sexy. A pulse with a mind of its own set up throbbing between her thighs and her nipples hardened and tingled. Damn body! Traitorous body.

"You run every day?" She tried to make distracting conversation.

"Sometimes work prevents me, but I try to get a run in as often as I can. Keeps the leg limber."

Shay turned to hand him his coffee and her gaze fell automatically to his knee where a white scar bisected the flesh. The knee he'd wrecked in the last game he played. The one the doctors had replaced. She was sure for him it was a constant reminder of the end of his dreams. Shay knew how vital knee flexion is to a quarterback. He needed the ability to keep his legs slightly bent as he stepped in to make the throw and to rotate over the leg on the release. When that was gone, the ability to play disappeared with it.

He saw the direction of her gaze. "I'm good with it. God's truth. Football gave me a lot of good years and now I have a new career I love. I'm luckier than a lot of guys."

"Yes, you are," she agreed.

For a very brief moment, sorrow for everything he'd lost swept over her. Then their fingers touched as she handed him the mug and high-voltage electricity shot through her. Joe's gaze dropped to her tank top where she was sure her traitorous nipples poked back at him. At least if the flare of heat in his eyes was any indication.

So much for wiping last night out of her mind. She wanted him, plain and simple. All these years she'd wondered what an erotic touch from him would feel like. Now she knew and she wanted more. He was like addictive chocolate—one bite and you wanted it all. Maybe she should look at this differently. What would it hurt if she indulged herself? Gave in to temptation? She could get him out of her system once and for all.

But not until she was sure she had her act together.

And had her heart well protected.

Maybe.

Shay took a step back, picked up her own mug, and started toward her bedroom.

"Shay."

She stopped, still facing away from him. "What?"

"About last night." Uncertainty tinged his voice, as if he wasn't quite sure whether to bring it up or not.

"Forget it." No, she wasn't ready to talk about it now. Not until she was sure she had full control of herself. "You got carried away. I understand. No explanations necessary." She paused. "You probably thought I was someone else, anyway." She took a step forward again.

"Shay!" This time the word was almost a shout. "Damn it, take a minute and listen to me."

"I can't imagine what you'd have to say to me. We'll just forget it ever happened." If she didn't get out of the room soon, she might say something she'd regret. Like let's do it again. And she wasn't quite ready for that yet. "That's what you were going to tell me, right?"

"That's not what I was going to say."

Was that desperation in his voice? Maybe he thought she had expectations now. She could certainly disabuse him of that in a hurry.

"It's okay, Joe. Listen, enjoy your coffee and have a good run."

Speaking of running, she almost ran to her bedroom, holding her mug so no liquid sloshed over the rim. She closed her door and leaned against it, hoping he didn't follow her. Her pulse was racing, and she had trouble catching her breath.

Think, think, think.

What if she did this, gave in to all her urges? If he wanted to have sex with her again she'd go for it, making it very clear he was under no emotional obligation. She was a big girl. The thought of finally being completely naked with Joe and having wild, uninhibited sex was way too tempting.

She could do this, especially if she could manage to control the situation.

She waited, listening for any sounds in the hallway. The soft *tap* on the door sounded as loud as a thunderclap.

"Shay? Come out here and talk to me. I owe you a huge apology."

Oh, great, an apology. The kiss of death. He was going to apologize for forgetting who she was and thinking she was one of his hot numbers, just when she'd made up her mind to go for it.

"It's okay. Please just go for your run. And don't knock again. I'm heading for the shower."

Which she did, closing the door loudly enough that he could hear it in the hallway. She turned on the shower full force, then sat on the closed lid of the toilet and took a swallow of her coffee. She didn't need his apology or his pity, if that's what he was offering. She took another swallow of coffee, easing the lump in her throat. Finally, convinced he'd left the house, she stripped off her shorts, and top and stepped under the hot water. Maybe, if she stood there long enough, she could wash away the memory of his touch.

* * * *

Joe enjoyed running whenever he got the chance. People always focused on a quarterback's arm, not realizing strengthening his legs was just as important. A big part of the precision and timing of a throw depended on leg action. After the surgery, he'd forced himself to start again as soon as he got the all clear. Even though his playing days were over, he maintained the routine. He'd discovered when he ran for pleasure it felt very, very good.

There was a small park about three blocks from Hank's house, which he headed toward. He set off at an easy lope, enjoying the freshness of the morning air. Stopping when he reached the start of the jogging trail, he took a minute as he was doing his stretches to check on Gina. He'd transferred the money as he promised Lisa, but he wanted to make sure she used it for the right purpose.

She answered right away.

"Hi, Joe. I got the money. Thanks so much." Her voice sounded a little strained, or was that his imagination?

"Everything okay?"

"Sure, sure, sure. Why wouldn't it be?"

He leaned against a thick oak tree. "You took her shopping, right?"

"I did. And to a salon to get her hair styled and a manicure."

"When's the interview?"

"Tomorrow. In the afternoon."

Did Lisa sound a little hesitant or reserved?

"Fine. I want you to text me afterward and let me know the results. And Lisa?"

"Yes?"

He closed his eyes and let out a breath. "This is going to have to be the end. You hear me?"

"But—"

"No buts." He shook his head, even though she couldn't see him. "Seven years is a long time to carry her. Now she's got to carry herself. Make it happen."

He disconnected before she could say anything else and zipped the phone into his pocket. It was past time to be done with this. With the impression of him Shay had built up over the years, God only knew what wild things she'd imagine if she found out he'd been giving Gina money all this time. It was suddenly important to him what Shay thought of him. How she saw him. What her opinion was.

By the time he hit the jogging path, his muscles were warmed up and he could set a steady clip. This morning, in addition to sticking to his routine, he wanted to work the restless energy out of his system. And his unsatisfied sexual urges.

What the fuck had he been thinking last night, anyway? One minute they'd been sitting there watching a program about fucking Joe Montana. The next he'd had his mouth on hers and his hands everywhere on her body. This was Shay, for crap's sake. Little Shay. Only she wasn't so little anymore. She was a warm, desirable woman. One touch of her mouth, one taste of her, and she completely blew his mind. Where did this hot, sexy female come from, anyway?

Hank was going to kill him.

Yeah? Then he should have been smart enough not to leave the two of them alone in that house. He'd studied biology. He knew all about how sex worked.

Now what the fuck did he do? He not only didn't regret what happened, he also wanted to do it again. And more. Lots more. He wanted to strip them both naked and watch his cock slide into her sweet, delectable pussy. Feel her clamp those hot muscles around him, the ones that singed his fingers last night. The problem was figuring out what she wanted and what last night meant to her.

Shit, shit, shit.

He pounded along the path, his body on automatic pilot, as every single moment of the previous evening replayed itself in his mind. By the time he slowed and began his cool-down, his cock was hard enough to use for a tree trunk and his balls ached like a sonofabitch. When at last he dropped onto a park bench and leaned his head back, he was thoroughly confused and thoroughly aroused.

Two things stuck out like the trip wires they were—Shay Beckham had grown up to be a very hot, very enticing, very sensuous female despite her girl-next-door appearance, and he wanted her more than he'd ever wanted anyone in his life. Wanted? Wait, that wasn't even half of it. The little seed of something planted inside him last night when he laid eyes on her now burst into full bloom through his body.

He was fucking in love with Shay Beckham! Holy shit! In love? Where the hell had that come from? People didn't fall in love this fast, did they? Did you fall in love with someone in less than the blink of an eye?

But Shay was no stranger to him. Truth be told, she'd been on his mind for a very long time. Had this been growing inside him since that brief episode in New York or maybe even before that, even while he'd been so busy living the high life?

Jesus! In love with Shay, a woman who pushed all his buttons the right way?

His entire body felt as if a thunderbolt had speared through it, delivering the shocking realization that he was in love with Shay Beckham.

Yes, you ass. All this time you've just been too stupid to realize it.

Until now. Until they'd been thrown together in a situation where the attraction had exploded and consumed him. He'd had just a taste of her and now he wanted all of it. Everything. And not just for the here and now.

God. He could hardly wrap his mind around it.

He certainly had a lot to overcome with her. All those years he'd dissed her as Hank's pesky kid sister. The overload of women he'd drowned himself in. The reputation the tabloids had hung on him. He needed to change her image of him and at the same time make her realize things were different now.

Oh, yeah, sure, jerkoff. Because she doesn't have her defenses up, right? Taking on a Super Bowl championship team with a broken arm would be a lot easier. First he had to get past whatever she was feeling about last night.

For him it had been an awakening. Had it hit her the same way? That's what he'd wanted to tell her, ask her, this morning before she shut him down, avoided the subject completely. Did she regret what happened? Was she ashamed of it? Somehow he had to get her mind turned around about it because he wanted more. With her.

He needed to breach her defenses because his desire for the grown-up Shay had exploded into a living, breathing thing. This was a whole lot more than sex. He wanted all of her, the whole package. Forever.

If he was going to move forward here, he needed a plan. This was no different than quarterbacking a game. Register the pitfalls presented by the other team, set the objectives and put the field plan together. He could do that, right?

Then he would get her to change the way she looked at him. The person she thought he was. He hoped. Show her she wasn't just another addition to a long list she seemed to think he kept. He just needed to get her to listen to him.

Slow, he told himself. *Just take everything real slow.*

Okay. Now he knew what he had to do, but business first.

He mentally ran over his agenda for this trip. He'd be speaking to a couple of the coaches groups Scott had set up as part of his Coaches Conference. He was also meeting with the committee planning a big fundraiser for scholarships for athletes. He'd agreed to make an appearance at the event and use his connections to solicit sponsors and merchandise. Because it was close to his hometown and because football had been very good to him financially, he agreed to match all the funds raised from other sources. Keeping this out of the media until the last minute was the only promise he'd extracted from them.

That was the one thing he and Scott continued to disagree on—using his Coaches Conference program, his speeches, and his fundraising for publicity purposes. He didn't mind personally soliciting people for contributions for worthy causes, or speaking to coaching staffs of varied sizes. As he changed the flow of his life, however, it occurred to him discussing his charity work would seem too much like puffing himself up. Telling people how wonderful he was for doing these things.

"We've been over this a bunch of times, Scott." The agent's words had irritated him. "You're the one who told me I was too much of a publicity hound, remember?"

"I do. But that was more your life-of-the-party image. This is good stuff, Joe. People need to know about it. To see who you've become. Which is a damn fine person."

"I'm the same person I always was," he'd snapped. "Just older and wiser. And I don't want to look like I'm buying a new image with money and good deeds. Doing this for a less than stellar purpose."

"Joe," the agent had begun.

"Isn't it enough the gossip hounds aren't after me anymore? That I'm off the gossip pages," he'd pointed out. "That alone should make you happy. And I think it's time to keep my private life just that. Very private. If I can tap into my connections to help people, I'm more than happy to do it. But I won't use any of them to, as you say, polish up my image. I'd feel cheap doing it."

"That's very noble of you," Scott had told him, "but hiding your good works won't get people to take you seriously. You cut a pretty wide path through the female population for a long time, sport. Your bosses at Fox Sports One would love to see you settled down."

"How about if I just promise to keep my social life out of the media? If people want to quietly discuss my other activities, okay, fine. No big publicity campaign, though. I mean it."

"Wow!" Scott had grinned. "A conscience. My baby boy is growing up."

This afternoon he would be meeting with the people putting on the fundraiser for athletic scholarships. The past few weeks he'd wrangled major commitments from former teammates and some of the Fox Sports One guys. He had Scott working his current sponsors and he even got commitments from a couple of his former backers. He felt good about not just reaching but surpassing the goal, especially with what he planned to contribute himself.

He gave a brief thought to telling Shay where he was going today but changed his mind immediately. Better to wait for the right moment, when things with the two of them were on a different footing. Between her firmly etched opinion of him and last night's grope-a-thon, she'd just think he was blowing smoke to make himself look better. If he told her about his meeting today, just dumped all of it on her like that, she probably would. Cleaning up his image with her would take some work.

Instead he'd casually ask her if she was going to be home tonight. Tell her he had some game videos to review for his show—no lie, he actually did—and would she like to watch with him. Yeah, low-key it like that and hope she didn't have plans.

If she was home when he stopped to change, he'd put on his friendliest face, not mention last night and see if he could at least get them on friendly footing. Yeah, okay. Good plan. Friends first. Then they could ease into the rest of it when she began to trust him. Which she obviously didn't at the moment. He wanted to tell her how much he'd changed, how different his life was now, but he knew it would take a lot to convince her. He'd just have to set the stage.

On his way home after his meetings, he'd pick up Chinese food for dinner. Then he'd find the place that made those cookies she liked so much. They used to get them from a bakery in Granite Falls, a branch of the one in San Antonio. That should buy him some brownie points. He pulled his cell phone from his pocket and looked up the San Antonio address. Right on his way home. Perfect.

Cookies. And maybe ice cream. They could watch the videos together. He hoped.

He also hoped when Hank found out he didn't cut off his balls.

As if conjured up by magic, his phone chimed and he saw a text from Hank.

"Settled in? Everything okay?"

Joe blew out a breath.

"Fine. Thx. All good."

Yeah, right. Everything was just peachy keen.

* * * *

Normally, the day after she returned from one of her New York trips Shay hung around the house in slop clothes, read, and watched sports to decompress before going back to her current project, or starting a new one. A minimalist where makeup was concerned to begin with, on those days she never even swiped a lipstick over her mouth. She'd put her hair, usually still damp from the shower, up in a messy ponytail and pull on a very old Granite Falls Coyotes T-shirt with a faded pair of jeans shorts. Until she got a good read on where this thing with Joe was going, she didn't want him to think she dressed in any way for him, so she stuck to her routine.

And what exactly was this thing? Maybe it was just once and done for him. Maybe he'd decided to satisfy her craving for him. God, she couldn't stand it if that's all it was. Then she really would have to kick him out of the house.

But what if he wanted more? What if he wanted…everything. Full-blown, all-out sex?

She told herself to quit overthinking it. So she'd had almost sex with her childhood hero. They were both adults now. Things were different. Hadn't she decided she'd just take it for what it was, enjoy the ride while it lasted, and walk away with her pride intact? Anyway, he probably wouldn't be around all the time. Not Joe the ladies' man.

Passing the mirror in her bedroom, she got a glimpse of herself. Yeah, she looked like a first-class slob all right. Certainly a far cry from the glamorous females Joe was used to. Besides, he'd probably get back from his run, shower, and head out to hook up with whatever women were waiting for him.

Images from last night kept playing over and over in her mind and she couldn't quell the little thrill of expectation wriggling through her when she heard his car pull up in the driveway. She did her best to focus instead on the glass of orange juice she'd poured. Maybe its icy coldness would smother the heat building inside her.

"Hey, Shay."

The gravelly voice made her lady parts stand up and take notice, especially the inner walls of her pussy that contracted at the memory of his touch.

"Um, hey, Joe." She didn't need the sound of his footsteps to tell her he'd come into the kitchen. Her body had an uncanny ability to sense his presence. "Have a good run?"

"Yeah. I like the little park near here. Not too crowded. Nice and pleasant. So, uh, listen."

"Yeah?" Okay, here it came. The excuses. The apology. She wanted to tell him just to keep his thoughts to himself and then run into her room.

"I have a couple of meetings this afternoon...."

Was that a euphemism for hooking up? Okay, she could handle that.

"Have a nice time." She sipped at the orange juice.

"Anyway, I thought if you didn't have any plans for tonight, I've got some DVDs of games I need to watch before my show starts up again. I know you like football. It isn't Montana, but I'd like it if you'd watch them with me. Get your opinion on some things. If you want to, that is."

Did she want to? Hell, yes. She also wanted to get completely naked with him. Too bad what he offered didn't sound close to an invitation to seduction. She'd shut him down that morning when he wanted to bring up last night, but maybe that was a mistake.

"Um, yeah. Sounds okay." Right. Couldn't let him know her hormones were jumping up and down. She could wait and read whatever signals he sent out.

"So how about if I pick up some Chinese on the way home and maybe some dessert?"

Now she turned to look at him. She had to see the expression on his face, but it was carefully blank. But the blatant heat in his eyes nearly ate her alive. Allrighty, then! The muscles in her pussy gave a hopeful flutter and her mouth suddenly went dry. She cleared her throat.

"That would be very nice. Thank you." Orange juice in hand, she eased out of the kitchen.

"See you around six," he called after her.

Her nasty voice, the one she'd been listening to for so many years, wanted to ask him if the afternoon would give him enough time. But he was being so nice she pressed her lips tightly together to keep from saying anything. At least until she knew what his game was. Because this Joe

Reilly was nothing like the one she'd always known. She wondered just how much of it was an act.

* * * *

"Shay?" He called out her name as he carried his packages into the kitchen. "I brought goodies."

Silence greeted him and his stomach dropped as he realized she might have gone out. Maybe she'd had second thoughts, regretted last night, and planned to just avoid him until he left town. Then the sound of a door opening broke into his consciousness. Yes! She was here. In a minute the delicious scent of whatever soap she used tickled his nostrils and he sensed her behind him in the kitchen.

"Goodies? Besides the Chinese food?" She pounced on the bakery box on the counter. "Ohmigod! Is this what I think it is? Snickerdoodles?" She started to untie the ribbon.

"Uh-uh-uh." Joe playfully slapped at her hand. "No dessert until you eat your dinner."

"Then let's get to it." She pulled the big brown paper sack toward her and began removing the cartons of takeout. "What did you get?"

Joe was relieved to hear the casual, almost playful tone in her voice. She'd either decided to pretend last night never happened—bad—or was hopeful it would happen again. That was good, right? Right? He voted for option two.

When he turned to look at her he almost swallowed his tongue. Her hair, the color of corn silk, fell softly to her shoulders, framing her face. He wanted to fist his hands in it, let it sift through his fingers. White shorts cupped her sweet ass and she'd paired them with a T-shirt, the soft fabric the same deep blue as her eyes and draped gently over her breasts. Oh, God, were her nipples actually visible through the material? No makeup except some pink gloss slicked over her lips, but as far as Joe was concerned, she didn't need anything else. Didn't those lips just beg to be kissed? He had to stop himself from licking his own.

Shit. Kill me now.

He was in such big fucking trouble here. How the hell was he supposed to take things slow? How could he make time to establish a new relationship with this woman—and she most definitely was a woman, not a little girl—when just looking at her made him hot as a pistol and harder than steel?

Suck it up, he told himself and grabbed two of the cartons from her. He was anxious to have something to do with his hands before he put them all over her.

"Here, I'll do that. Why don't you get the plates and silverware?"

"What's in this other bag?" She unrolled the flap on a white paper sack. "Ice cream?" She squealed like the little kid he remembered. "Cookies and cream. Yum, yum, yum."

He took the sack away from her and shoved it in the freezer. "Like I said, dinner first. This is to ease the pain while I bore you with a bunch of football crap later."

She cocked her eyebrow, giving him a quizzical look. "Boring? Football? You must have me confused with someone else."

"Okay." He chuckled. "It's just not Joe Montana football."

"I'll suffer through it." She turned away from him and busied herself with plates and silverware. "Come on, let's eat. I'm starved."

Joe made sure to sit across from Shay at the table, not next to her. He needed to avoid touching her as much as possible. Put distance between them until he could figure this thing out. As it was, it took every bit of the discipline he'd learned playing football to look away from the way her T-shirt fabric caressed her breasts, the outline of her nipples visible beneath the soft material. His blood pulsed heavily through his veins, pressure building in his cock. He hoped if Shay noticed him drooling she'd think it was for the Chinese food. He gave thanks the table hid his ranging hard-on, which apparently appeared now whenever he was in her presence.

Conversation. They needed conversation. Anything to distract his body and his little head, which seemed to think it was in charge.

"Sorry New York turned out to be a bust for you."

Shay speared a piece of orange chicken, popped it into her mouth, and chewed thoughtfully. When she licked a drop of sauce from her lower lip Joe was afraid he'd combust right there at the table. The look she gave him reminded him they'd had this discussion before but he was desperate for a safe conversational topic. Anything that dropped a virtual ice cube in his pants and cooled him off.

"It was okay for a while. I had the big-city adventure and scored a fabulous job." She shrugged. "The bloom just wore off quickly. Besides, I'm a Texas girl through and through." Her voice was flat and uninflected.

Joe would give a lot to know what was really behind her decision to move back.

"So, no hot guys?" he teased. "No broken hearts left behind when you came home?" He made his voice as casual as possible.

Another bite of chicken. More chewing. Joe tried not to focus on the smooth play of muscles in her neck as she swallowed.

"None that you'd find interesting. They were all too sharp-edged. Too high energy, I guess. Too—" She waved her fingers in the air. "Too New York."

Joe sensed an intense story behind her casual comments, but she sure wasn't going to open up to him tonight over takeout.

"Besides," she went on, "I get my fix of sidewalk hot-dog vendors and pizza by the slice when I go back for a few days of meetings."

He frowned. "And that's what New York is to you, hot dogs and pizza?"

She laughed, the now familiar musical sound that cut right into him. "I guess. Apparently I'm just not a city-slicker girl at heart. What about you? You like it? You're living in Los Angeles now, right?"

"Actually I don't live there anymore." He scooped more fried rice onto his plate. "Too metrosexual for me. I guess I don't like the city any better than you do."

"So where are you living now?"

Hadn't Hank told her? Exactly what information had her brother given her about him? More than that, did she even ask or show interest?

"Houston. Fox Sports has facilities there as well. And I like it much better than the West Coast."

"But you flew in yesterday from New York," she reminded him.

"Meetings on one of my endorsement contracts with a company rep and my agent."

She studied his face, her eyes serious. "Forgive me if I'm stepping into forbidden territory, but does it bother you? Not being able to play again?"

Joe thought he'd gotten past those feelings pretty well until the little taste of bitterness surged in his throat. "I think I'll always miss playing, but I'm lucky. My agent hooked me up with a terrific television contract and my bosses seem to be happy with me. We're going into our fifth year and there doesn't seem to be an end in sight."

"Unique name, *Inside the Helmet.* Good show, too."

He quirked an eyebrow. "You watch it?"

She flipped a hand casually. "When I get a chance."

Alright! She watched his program. He gave a mental fist pump.

"Well, let's clear this stuff away and you can help me watch some video for the earliest fall shows."

"Me? Help you?" She laughed. "I don't think anyone knows more about what's in a quarterback's head than you do, Mr. Hotshot Quarterback Joe Reilly." The smile left her face. "I'm sorry. I didn't mean to tease—"

"It's okay. I'm past it." Mostly. "Let's do this."

"What about dessert? I want my ice cream and cookies."

"After the first video. A reward for your help."

In the living room, Joe pulled a disk from his briefcase and slipped it into the DVD player. He picked up the remote, careful to take the recliner and leave the couch to Shay.

"So what's up first?" she asked.

"The young quarterback for the San Antonio Mustangs, as a matter of fact. I'll be doing a piece on him before the first preseason game. Maybe even analyzing their entire quarterback situation. We'll see. I have some background work to do, but first I want to watch the kid in action."

"Is he any good?"

He shrugged. "You tell me. Let's give him a look."

He was so conscious of her his skin felt as if he'd sandpapered it. He wondered if she felt the sexual tension as much as he did. He wanted her with an intensity that stunned him. He couldn't just sweep the remnants of dinner aside, though, and jump her bones, much as he might want to. He had to move slowly. He could not afford to give her the idea this was some casual hookup, like the ones she seemed to think he enjoyed on a regular basis. Somehow he had to dredge up every bit of discipline he'd spent a lifetime learning and keep a lid on things until the right moment. The next time it would be a lot more than a grope session.

Managing to do it was going to be easier said than done.

* * * *

Shay studied the man standing in front of the television. It was hard to wipe away the image of him naked from the shower, the one from yesterday that was etched in her mind with acid. He still had the toned athlete's body only now it belonged to a mature man. She wanted to see it again, without any of those clothes concealing it. Run her hands over his muscles and squeeze his very fine butt.

After last night, just being in the same room with Joe made her pussy throb and her blood heat. She didn't know about him but for her it had occupied nearly every waking moment during the day. He sure didn't seem like he was going to make another move on her. If she had half a brain, she'd take her dessert and hide in the bedroom. Wait! Wasn't that what she'd been doing this morning before she finally snuck out to the kitchen?

Okay, no more hiding, not if she really wanted sex with Joe Reilly. Real sex. She wished she knew if he was being so nice to her because she was Hank's sister, because he was afraid he'd pissed her off last night or because he wanted more with her. He'd brought her ice cream and her favorite cookies and asked her to watch the videos with him. Exactly what did that mean?

She tried not to look at him stretched out in the big chair, his masculine sexiness like an aura clinging to him. He still wore the clothes from the afternoon, the khakis outlining the lean length of his legs, the dark green of the soft-collared shirt stretched across wide shoulders and a muscular chest. Her palms itched to touch him again, feel that soft chest hair scattered over hard chest muscle. God, she wanted him more than a snickerdoodle.

She was so lost in her imagination the sound of his voice startled her.

"Shay? You with me?"

"What?" She blinked. "Sure. Sorry." She tried hard to focus. The last thing she needed was for Joe to catch her salivating over him.

"I'd like to hear more about your take on this kid. You've got a sharp eye."

"Um, okay." Damn straight she had a good eye for players' strengths and weaknesses. She'd studied them all these years. She took in a breath. "Sure. Be happy to."

Joe pressed Play on the remote. "He declared for the draft in his sophomore year and pretty much rode the bench as a rookie. I saw him in training camp last year when he was still a raw recruit. The coach says he's come a long way since then. Watch his two-step dropback when he gets ready to throw."

Shay curled her legs beneath her and forced herself to concentrate on the screen. The young quarterback actually had good moves, a good rhythm. In some ways, he reminded her of Joe in his college days. The lithe athleticism on the verge of maturity. She watched Joe making notes in his iPad as the video unfolded, then eject the disk when it came to the end.

"I wanted to be able to study him before I meet with him," he told Shay. "Like I said, the Mustangs have great hopes for him and my producer wants to lead off the show this season with his interview. What did you think?"

"Good footwork," she told him. "Good timing. He shows a lot of promise." She grinned. "Like a young Joe Montana."

"Yeah? Well, maybe Montana can show up and get you some ice cream."

"No, hey." She jumped up from the couch. "You can't get out of this. I want my treats."

"Do you now." He winked at her. "Ask nicely."

She wrinkled her forehead in a mock scowl. "Give me my ice cream and cookies, or I'll have to hurt you."

Joe threw back his head and laughed. "If that's nicely, I don't want to be around when you're ticked off. Come on. We'll dish it up. I have more video to watch."

Shay followed him into the kitchen, her body heated just from their close proximity. How on Earth had she allowed herself to agree to this "friendly" evening? She was torn between wanting a repeat of last night—no, *more* than last night—and wanting to hide until Joe finally left the house and the city.

Sighing, she plated the cookies while Joe dished up the ice cream and they carried their food back into the living room. She set the cookies on the coffee table and picked one up. Biting into it, she hummed with pleasure as the sugary flavor exploded in her mouth.

"Shay?" Joe's voice broke into her thoughts. "You okay?"

She drew in a breath. "Just enjoying my treat. Mmm. This is yummy good."

"They always were your favorite."

"I can't believe you remembered."

"It's hard to forget," he told her. "I don't think there was ever a time I was at your house you weren't eating those cookies or begging for them."

He remembered? The thought gave her a warm feeling. Of course, then she'd just been Hank Beckham's little sister. But now? Had last night changed how he looked at her?

Drive yourself nuts, why don't you, Shay?

"Well." She licked her fingers. "Thank you for remembering. And for getting them today, although it wasn't necessary."

He looked at her as if about to say something then shook his head. After sliding in a new disk, he hit Play again.

It took every bit of Shay's willpower to sit there quietly watching game video and discussing the details with Joe. What was going on here? Were they just going to keep pretending last night hadn't happened? She was ready if he ever made another move, but she was pretty sure she couldn't make the first one herself. Staying in the house with him under these circumstances was going to be a strain on her self-discipline. Maybe she could bunk with a girlfriend until Joe left. Her problem was her few friends from the past years were in New York, people she'd chosen now to disconnect herself from.

She hadn't exactly made time since she moved back to reconnect with anyone. In fact, it depressed her to realize how much time had passed since she saw or spoke to any of the people she used to hang out with from Granite Falls. She'd left home for college and apparently left them behind, too. Why? Was she just so focused on herself, on getting away from Granite Falls, she wanted nothing to do with them?

No help there. If anyone was going to leave, it would have to be Joe, and that didn't look like it was going to happen.

Argh! She wanted to pull her hair.

Damn Hank, anyway.

"Shay?" Joe's deep voice cut into her thoughts. "Are you with me? I just asked you a question."

"What?" Oh, great. Her mind had been wandering again. He probably thought she was bored to death. She set her ice cream dish on the table. "Oh, yes. Sorry. I thought the guy was terrific. Great hands."

Joe's deep laugh rumbled in the air again. "Nice try. That was ten minutes ago. Here. Let me have your ice cream before it turns into soup."

"No, no, no." She gripped the bowl. "I was paying attention. Truly. And I want my ice cream."

"Then let me get you some that isn't melted."

He stood up and reached to take the bowl from her. When his fingers touched hers, she nearly dropped the bowl. The color of his eyes darkened now to polished onyx, the savage heat so incendiary it could have singed off a complete layer of her skin. They stood there, frozen, staring at each other. A muscle twitched in his jaw and electricity jolted through her to her breasts and her pussy. Her hands shook.

Lordy!

Joe opened his mouth as if to say something, closed it, then practically grabbed the bowl from her.

"I'll get us some fresh ice cream." He looked over at the plate, a corner of his mouth turning up in a crooked grin. "I see you did a number on the cookies. I guess we need to put out the rest of them. Then I'll pop in another video."

Ice cream. Cookies. Video.

Okay. She made herself move, one foot in front of the other as she walked toward the kitchen. Was he playing some kind of game? One minute he looked like he wanted to lick every inch of her naked body. The next he was treating her as if nothing had happened between them. And damn it! Something had happened. Now that she'd decided she wanted it to happen again she was having trouble waiting for him to make the next move.

She certainly wasn't about to throw herself at him. She'd watched women do that for years. No, whatever happened she was going to wait for him to take the lead. But she'd certainly be a willing participant.

She just had to keep her emotions under control. No way could she let Joe be aware of her real feelings for him. Ever. She'd never let him know she'd been in love with him all these years.

Love. Crap.

Yes, Shay. You're in love with him. It's your little secret, and it's going to stay that way.

Because she knew it was pointless. He'd never see her as a woman, never have those feelings for her. It was easier just to be at odds with him. Then she'd never get hurt. Everything she'd ruthlessly suppressed over the years, that she buried behind a snarky attitude whenever she was with him, had just boiled over last night and now here she was.

God. Make up your mind, Shay. Bring it up, don't bring it up, but quit driving yourself crazy.

For one fleeting moment she'd thought, from the look in his eyes, he might feel the same way. Yeah, right. Joe might be in lust with her, but that's all it would ever be. Of course, she could always tell him she thought he'd turned into Joe Montana.

Yeah, right.

Dumb, dumb, dumb.

Why did life have to be so friggin' complicated?

"Cookies?"

Joe's voice nudged her into awareness. "Oh, yeah. Cookies. Coming right up."

At least, she thought, it seemed like they were going to be friends instead of adversaries. Maybe she could get through his stay without letting her real feelings show, as long as he wasn't here for too long. She was strong. She could handle it. As she plated the rest of the cookies, she swallowed a sigh. Maybe she should have stayed in New York after all.

Chapter 4

Joe turned off the shower, slid the door open, and reached for the towel he'd left on the vanity counter. The hot water relaxed his muscles and the tendons around his knee, but he was sure what he really needed was ice-cold spray. Since the first night here, when he'd given in to temptation with Shay, bringing her to climax with just his hands, he'd sported a perpetual boner. Just looking at her made his balls ache and the blood rush to his cock. He didn't seem to be getting very far in his campaign to woo her. With each passing day—hour—he found himself wanting her more and more. What an unexpected switch. He hadn't felt this strongly about a woman since—ever. Go figure it would be Shay Beckham who tied him in knots.

At night, his dreams were filled with erotic images of the two of them. Naked, on the king-size bed in his room. Her blond hair like a curtain of hot sunlight dusting her shoulders, her breasts lifted to him, her rosy nipples swollen and wet from his mouth. In his dreams, he felt the silken smoothness of her skin beneath his hands, the wetness of her hot pussy as he slid his cock into it. Her inner walls gripping him like a heated fist as he pumped into her. Yet when he woke up, he was still harder than a spike and had to resort to his hand for relief.

Jesus H. Christ! Where did all this come from? Her effect on him totally blindsided him, leaving him scrambling for a way to deal with it. She was the first woman ever who made him feel uncertain. Joe Reilly uncertain? His friends would kill themselves laughing if he told them that.

He didn't know how long he could go on this way, keeping his feelings for her in check while he tried to convince her he was now a nice guy. Not that he hadn't been nice before. At a distance now, he knew his overindulgence in female company could have created a negative image. But holy crap! He was a healthy guy with a healthy appetite. It wasn't as if he'd fucked them naked on Main Street.

This was not going to be as easy as he'd hoped. He wanted her with a desire so fierce it shocked him. He'd just have to keep working hard to maintain his famous self-discipline if he wanted to keep a leash on himself as he worked on making her comfortable with him and convincing her he was someone she could trust. Especially making her believe his sudden craving for her went beyond just sex.

His brain was still trying to sort things out when his phone signaled an incoming text. Hank's contact picture stared at him from the screen.

Shit!

"U and Shay doing ok?"

Yeah. Just dandy.

"All good. When will I C U?"

A long pause.

"Sorry. Client needs me. L8tr."

Well, this message was highly unsatisfactory. Of course, it was probably better for Hank not to show up right now. He'd take one look at Joe, read his thoughts, and punch his lights out. He needed more time for Project Shay. Slow and steady, he kept reminding himself. Slow and steady.

For the past three days, he'd brought her stuff like the special cookies and a bottle of the wine she'd mentioned she liked. Taken her out for hamburgers, just something casual. Nothing to frighten her off. She seemed to be bewildered by his behavior. Confused, even. Not that he could blame her. He'd spent more than two decades looking at her as a pest and treating her like one. Now he'd experienced an unexpected awakening, a jolt of awareness that drew him to her. Convincing her of how he felt was going to be a difficult task.

Sometimes he wondered if he should just address the situation head-on. Tell her how he felt. Make a real pitch. Because this friendship thing and dropping little hints wasn't doing a damn bit of good. He wasn't very good at this because he just wasn't used to it. He saw a woman, he liked her, he asked her out, and they went from there. Even in the past few years, when he'd been a lot more discriminating with his dating habits, he'd had a confidence that came easily to him. In fact he hadn't been this uncertain since high school when he asked a girl out for the first time.

He'd already been for his run this morning. Now he had work to do on his laptop. He pulled on a pair of jeans and a Fox Sports T-shirt and fastened his watch around his wrist. Glancing at it, he realized it was almost ten o'clock. He could hear computer keys clacking in the den and knew Shay would be hard at work. He wondered if she'd eaten anything.

The last two mornings he'd only seen her with coffee, so today he'd taken a detour to a bakery and picked up fresh chocolate chip muffins. The way to a man's heart was through his stomach. Maybe it worked for women, too.

In the kitchen, he filled a mug with fresh coffee, plated two of the muffins, and carried them to the den. Any other woman would have hugged and kissed him and slobbered over him for his thoughtfulness. Shay just looked up from her computer and frowned.

"What are you doing?"

"Bringing you some breakfast. I heard you in here when I got up. I took a chance you hadn't eaten anything yet." He grinned, setting the mug and plate on the desk. "Gotta feed the brain cells."

She stared at the muffin as if it might bite her.

"It's not poisoned," he joked. "Go ahead and taste it."

"Thank you." But she left it sitting on the plate, staring at it as if it might attack her. "Shouldn't you be meeting some hot chick for breakfast? Or getting ready for a nooner?"

Shit! Were they back to that?

Joe ground his teeth and reached for his patience. He supposed this was no more than he deserved. As far as she knew, it was the same old, same old. Who was it who said our sins always come back to haunt us? He nudged the plate closer to her.

"Take a bite. Chocolate chip. Gives you energy."

"Chocolate chip? Honest to Pete?"

"Yeah, honest to Pete. Or anyone else. Go on. Take a bite."

A smiled teased at her mouth. She broke off a bit of the muffin and popped it into her mouth, then closed her eyes and hummed with satisfaction. "Mmm. Yum. Love the chocolate."

Joe glanced at the computer screen. "Nice design, Shay. Can you tell me who it's for?"

She shook her head and swallowed the piece of muffin. "I wish. In-process designs are sort of under wraps until the big unveil."

"Even for close friends?" he teased.

She stared up at him. "Is that what we are? Close friends?"

"I hope so. At least to start with." He stroked his fingers along her cheekbone, her skin silky soft beneath his touch. "Maybe I'd like us to be more, but not until I have a chance to show you who I am now. How I've changed."

For a moment she sat absolutely still, studying him. A thick stew of emotions flashed in her eyes—distrust, anxiety, pleasure, uncertainty, even—yes—desire. When the snarky mask dropped in place again, he wondered if he'd misjudged his plan. Was he moving too slowly here? Damn, she was just so hard to read.

"Changed? Uh-huh." Skepticism outlined her words even as he saw the barest flash of hope in her eyes. "We'll see."

"Come on, Slick, give me a break, okay?"

Her eyes widened. "Slick?"

"Yeah, I think that's a good nickname for you. I reach out for you and you slide away from me. Slippery. Will I ever be able to catch you?"

The pulse at the hollow of her throat fluttered. She swallowed, and then slid her tongue along her lower lip, his dick hardening at the sight. He wanted to press his lips to hers and run his tongue over her full lower one. Was he going too slow here? Had he lost whatever edge the other night had given him?

"If I let you, will it be okay?"

"Try it and see. I think it will." His eyes fell on an item on her desk, a signed Joe Montana in a silver frame. "He's a lot of competition for me to overcome."

"You know Montana will always come first," she teased.

He lifted an eyebrow. "Always?"

"Live with it. But thanks for the muffin and coffee."

"You're very welcome."

Joe was a Montana fan, too, only right then he wanted to toss the picture out the window. Stupid idiot. At least she'd given him a very tiny indication she'd be open to "friendship." That was a good starting place. Who knew he'd want something like this—whatever *this* was—with Shay Beckham. His instincts told him he'd better proceed with caution. One wrong step and they'd be back where they were before the other night. Maybe even worse. And Hank would definitely cut off his balls and roast them over an open fire.

This would require a lot more thought on his part.

Meanwhile he had a phone call to make. An edgy sensation at the back of his neck reminded him he hadn't heard from Lisa about Gina's job interview. The other day he hadn't been too happy with their conversation. He reminded himself again how uneasy he'd been with her tone of voice. Lisa sounded as if she was holding something back. He decided to take it out to the screened-in deck. For a lot of reasons, he didn't want Shay to accidentally overhear any of it. He wandered to a corner of the outside deck to make his call and punched the numbers for Lisa's cell. If Gina had screwed it up like she'd done a few other times…

"Hi, Joe." Today Lisa's voice sounded friendlier, more relaxed. Maybe he'd been reading something into it when he didn't need to.

"Hey, Lisa. Just wanted to make sure Gina was still doing okay."

She chuckled. "Just as good as she was when we spoke the other day. I'm keeping an eye on her."

"Job hunting going okay for her? The interviews go well?"

"Yes, they did," Lisa assured him. "Callbacks on three of them. She seems very positive about the whole thing."

"You can wait until she gets one of the jobs for sure before letting her know the bank is closed, okay? But make no mistake. I mean what I say."

He didn't think he could repeat it too many times.

"You've done a lot for her," Lisa assured him. "You always have. I'll do my best to handle it from here on out."

"Just keep me in the loop."

"I will. I promise."

Still, the feeling of apprehension persisted after he disconnected the call. He didn't need the situation with Gina to explode in the middle of everything going on—developing his relationship with Shay, meeting with coaches, and working on the fundraiser. He had too many balls in the air and he was juggling as fast as he could. Everything he was working for—*had* worked for—could be destroyed in a heartbeat.

* * * *

Shay saved the work on her screen, took a last sip of coffee, and picked up her cell. Earlier when Joe came into her office she'd more than half expected him to finally—*finally!*—bring up the other night. Was he playing some kind of game with her? The looks he gave her melted her panties, so what was with this ignoring the whole episode?

It wasn't that she didn't know how to act with men. She was hardly a shy virgin, for God's sake. She'd had her fair share of dates and three somewhat serious relationships. But as secure and confident as she was in every other area of her life, she couldn't seem to kill the tiny bit of insecurity that swept through her when she compared herself to the other women she'd seen with Joe. He seemed to go for the tall, willowy females with an air of sophistication who knew what the game was, not short women with too many curves. She was so totally the opposite.

Had she disappointed him in some way the other night? Was that it?

Could she drive herself any crazier?

What would Hank think about what was happening here? She could sure use him as a sounding board.

Hank! Was her rat-fink brother ever coming home? She typed in a text.

"When r u coming home?"

She pushed Send and waited for Hank to answer her text. Five minutes passed before her phone chimed at her.

"When I'm finished here."

Oh, great. Swell answer.

"U have a houseguest."

The next answer came back almost at once. *"I know u can be a good hostess. It's just Joe."*

Shay wanted to slam the phone on the desk. Good hostess. Right.

"Get ur ass home."

She waited long minutes for an answer this time, ready to send him another angrier one when her phone chimed.

"Have fun."

Fun? Have fun? Who the hell was he kidding? She was wound up tighter than a drum, hoping Joe would get on the stick and make his next move. More coffee, that's what she needed. She carried her plate and mug into the kitchen and popped a fresh cup into the Keurig machine. As she was waiting for it to brew, she glanced to her left through the sliding glass doors. Joe was outside on the big deck Hank had built onto the back of the house, cell phone to his ear, one foot propped on the cover of the hot tub and his hips leaning against the picnic table as he talked.

Shay snorted. Probably one of his "babes." She figured he was making the call outside so she didn't hear him making arrangements for a hookup. Not that she gave a tinker's damn...or a damn of any kind. If he was still going to be the old Joe Reilly, he could go poke his penis in any woman he wanted to.

And yet she knew, felt in her melting bones, that he'd been just as involved in it as she was the other night. Give it another shot, the devil in her head whispered. Put it out there a little more. She'd already made up her mind whatever happened she'd walk away with whatever memories she had and her pride intact.

Damn, damn, damn. Why was she making this so difficult?

The coffee finished brewing and she grabbed the mug, lifting it to take a sip. And burning her lips because of course it was scalding hot.

"Damn!" This time she said the word aloud, jerking the mug away from her mouth and sloshing some of the hot liquid over her hand.

"Hey!" The glass door slid open as Joe came back inside. "Careful there. Hot-coffee warning."

Before she realized what he was doing and could protest, he'd removed the mug, set it on the counter, and was holding her hand under cold water.

When she tried to jerk it away, he simply tightened his fingers around her wrist.

"Just another few seconds," he told her. "To make sure you haven't done any serious damage to your delicate hand."

"Don't make fun of my hand," she snapped, automatically on the defensive.

His gaze locked with hers, so penetrating she could feel it deep inside her core. "I'd never make fun of you. Don't you know that?"

"Yeah?" She quirked an eyebrow. "Seems to me you spent a lot of years doing just that." Ohmigod, couldn't she just shut her mouth? This was no way to get him out of his clothes and into her bed.

But his eyes darkened, and there was no mistaking the lust flaring in those pools of polished ebony. An answering warmth surged through her, sending moisture to her panties and igniting spasms in her cunt. Holy fucking damn! Apparently her body had its own control mechanism where he was concerned. Or lack of one.

He turned off the water but held her hand for a long last moment, his thumb brushing the pulse point on her wrist. It reminded her of his touch on her body the other night.

Shay stood there, his fingers holding her, and for a moment time stood still and they were back in the mood of the other night. Joe had a stunned look on his face and she was sure hers wore a matching one. The kitchen suddenly seemed much smaller, the air in the room much heavier. She tried to draw in another breath but her lungs constricted. She looked back up at Joe's eyes, and from what she saw, he was having the same difficulties. She wanted to wrap herself around him and press her lips to his firm, cool ones. From the look in his eyes, she guessed he wouldn't stop her.

Then she recalled the sight of him on the deck with his cell phone and it shook her out of her trance. Joe reached for some paper towels, dried her hand, and released it. Shay turned away, pulling up the edges of her sarcastic self.

"You didn't have to go outside to call your latest hot date." She emptied a packet of sweetener in her coffee and lifted the mug. "It means nothing to me if you want to schedule hookups every night. Every hour, even."

He chuckled. "You give me a lot of credit for stamina."

"Are you saying you're not up to it?"

He moved to stand in front of her, blocking her path. "You'd be surprised what I'm up for." He blew out a breath. "Let's start over here. I wasn't making a hot date, Shay. Or any kind of date. In fact, I was hoping you'd let me take you out to dinner tonight."

"Dinner?" Shay stared at him. Wow! Okay maybe things were back on track here. "Did you just ask me out? On a date?"

"Would that be so bad?" His voice rolled over her like warm molasses. "Dinner? You and me? Just two people having a meal and good conversation and getting to know each other better?"

Oh, yes. She could get on board with that. She definitely wanted to know Joe as intimately as possible. No wading in shallow waters for her, she was going to take the plunge into the deep end of the pool.

Images tumbled in her mind like a kaleidoscope of the two of them at an intimate dinner for two. Him touching her. Giving her that melt-your-panties smile. The thought made her smile. He cocked his head.

"You think my taking you out is funny?" He wrapped his hand around her free one, his thumb doing that stroking thing again. "You afraid to have dinner with me? Is that it?" His voice was low and sensuous and vibrated through her.

"No. Of course not." She smiled. "Why would I be?"

"Then let's do it. Tonight."

Tonight? Really? Her hormones did a happy dance. Then she remembered her deadline. She was already late with this project. Well, damn.

"Tomorrow night. I'm finishing a design that's due tonight."

He looked at her with that penetrating gaze she was fast becoming familiar with, one where he seemed to see right into the center of her. "All right. Tomorrow night. And Shay?"

"Yeah?"

"I want to take you someplace nice. Really nice.

"Fine," she said at last. "Someplace nice. Now I need to get back to work."

His wicked mouth curved in a smile. "Tomorrow night at seven. Okay?"

She blew out a breath. "O-okay."

Only now that she'd made what she thought of as the big decision, how would she last until then?

Joe finally released her hand and she escaped to the den, closed the door, and set her mug down on a coaster before she dumped it all over everything. Then she leaned back in her chair and touched her wrist where Joe's thumb had caressed it so softly. She could still feel the sensuous brush of his thumb across her pulse point. Feel the heat of him surrounding her, the essence of his male scent invading her nostrils. And the memories of the other night? What happened had been incredible. Indescribable. The stuff of erotic dreams. Which certainly kept replaying in her mind in living color.

Would they have a repeat tomorrow night? Would he take her to bed? Take off all her clothes and make slow delicious love to her body? She wanted to do the same to him, indulge in every erotic act she'd ever known about, read about, dreamed about. She harbored no illusions about where this was going. She fully expected it to end when he left town, but she wanted as much as she could get before he took off. Memories that would keep her warm on a lot of cold nights.

Maybe, if she got enough of him, she could quit obsessing about him and get on with finding the right man for her. She might always be *in love* with Joe but surely she could find another man she could love.

She pressed her fingertips to her temples, trying to chase away the headache determined to wiggle its way up. She had to stop driving herself nuts. She had work to do and work came first. She'd just have to tuck tomorrow night in the back of her mind for the moment before she drove herself completely nuts.

But like a bumblebee buzzing just at the edge of her vision, she couldn't help wondering who he'd been talking to on the phone that made him take it outside for privacy.

* * * *

Joe took a swallow of his coffee and leaned back in the patio chair, his cell phone to his ear.

"So the fundraiser is still on track?" Scott asked.

Joe nodded, even though the man couldn't see him. "Coming along nicely. A lot of my old high school teammates have signed on, either with cash or items for the silent auction. Rafe Ortiz has been out of town on a job, but I'm meeting up with him for lunch today."

"We had drinks with him once, right? He'd just retired after only eight years with the San Antonio Mustangs?"

"Uh-huh. Said he wanted out while his brain still functioned."

"He was sure a great running back. So good defensive tackles were always all over him. Retiring was probably a smart move for him. What did you say he's doing now?"

"He's got a great position. Heads a team of security specialists."

"Didn't you tell me one time he wanted to be a cop?"

"Yeah." Joe shifted in his chair. "He got lucky. This is probably even better. He's with Lone Star Security, the agency that provides protection at the Mustangs stadium. I'm sure he makes more money than if he was a cop."

Scott laughed. "Like he needs the bucks after what he made in the NFL. Well, tell him hello for me. And text or e-mail me about the agenda for the Coaches Conference you've got set up. I wish to hell you'd let me give it a lot more publicity."

"We've been over this enough times. Give it a rest already."

He could almost see his agent heave a sigh. "I hear you. And yeah, you've been a good little boy with your social life since you got the job with Fox Sports. I guess I'll have to settle for that."

"Good. Let's leave it there. By the way, you still planning to fly in for the fundraiser?"

"I am. This has turned into a major event. You might be trying to keep your participation low-key. But, I'm sure you can understand if I want to do a little glad-handing and promote you quietly to the movers and shakers."

Joe laughed. "As if I could stop you. All right. I'll see you a week from Saturday."

He disconnected the call and scrolled through for Rafe's number.

"Hey, buddy," Rafe greeted him. "You're not calling to cancel lunch, are you?"

"Not at all. Just checking to make sure we're still on."

"One o'clock at Andover's. It will be good to see you again, Joe."

"Thanks. Same goes."

He hung up, thinking about that long ago team and the heady excitement of the trophy years. They'd all thought they were such hotshots, every one of them. Big stars, with the girls—especially the cheerleaders—falling all over them. College hadn't been much different, even though they'd all ended up in different places. Ditto for those who went into the NFL.

Sometimes it bothered him they hadn't all stayed in contact with each other. For those in the pros it was a little easier when their teams played against each other. Some of the players either chose not to enter the NFL draft at all or else weren't selected and so they moved on with their lives. He wondered if he and Hank would still be as connected if they hadn't been friends since they were twelve years old and on the same pony-league team. He was just grateful their friendship continued to grow stronger over the years.

The fundraisers gave him the opportunity to reconnect with some of them and he made a mental note to see where everyone was these days. Even if they no longer were connected with sports, they'd still been friends. This weekend he'd make it a point to sit down with his laptop and do some research.

* * * *

Shay leaned back in her desk chair, stretched out her arms, and flexed her fingers. She'd been at this for three hours straight and her muscles were protesting. But the design was coming along nicely. A few more hours at it and she should have it about ready for a first pass by her boss. He was accommodating her with her telecommuting. In return, she always pushed herself to meet or exceed her deadlines.

Looking at the clock on her computer, she realized it was past noon. If the time hadn't reminded her to break for lunch, her stomach suddenly did by growling at her. Good thing Joe wasn't around to hear it.

Joe! Was he even still in the house? Had he gone somewhere without her even realizing it? When she focused on a project, everything else disappeared from her consciousness. She rose from her desk chair, opened the door partway, and listened, trying to pick up any sounds of activity. Only silence greeted her. Almost on tiptoe, she made her way down the little hall into the kitchen. No Joe there. And no signs of him she could see either in the living room or out on the deck.

Okay, then. He'd obviously taken himself off somewhere. So what? Why should she feel slighted he hadn't checked in with her?

Damn it, Shay, you're doing it again.

No reason in the world why he shouldn't come and go as he pleased. He was here on some kind of business, whatever it was—and he certainly hadn't chosen to share it with her—so maybe he was off tending to that.

Or maybe he really *was* making a hot date on the phone earlier and just didn't want to tell her.

Stop!

She wanted to give herself a smack. Letting her mind wander in that direction could mean nothing good. She'd do her best to believe Joe, until she discovered he was lying. If he was.

And his new nickname for her. Slick. Smooth and slippery, he'd said. She kind of liked it. Meant she could slither from his grasp any time she got scared and needed to run. Wait. Scared? Of what?

Of your feelings for him, stupid.

Okay, enough introspection. Meanwhile she was hungry. The refrigerator yielded very little that appealed to her. She hadn't grocery shopped nor apparently had Joe. She needed to take a break now, anyway, so she could kill two birds with one stone. When she grabbed her purse from her bedroom, she took a quick look at herself in the mirror and made a face. No makeup, hair in a messy ponytail, outfit consisting of an oversize tee and an old pair of yoga pants, comfy clothes she threw on to work at home. Ugh! Well, what the hell. She wasn't liable to run into anyone she knew, right? Besides, if she hadn't scared Joe off this morning she could at least consider herself presentable.

That lasted until, in the produce department, she heard someone call her name.

"Shay? Shay Beckham? Is that you?"

The voice was only vaguely familiar. For a moment she was tempted to ignore it and just hurry to the next section. Years of good manners being drilled into her took over, though, and she turned slowly to see who had called her name. And came face-to-face with a woman who had been a girlhood friend. One she'd lost contact with as with so many others. Even though they hadn't seen each other in more than ten years, memories washed over her like a summer rain. The pretty teenager had grown into a very attractive woman, one who still had the same embracing smile she'd been known for.

"J-Jilly?" She clutched the handle of her cart and wished the fashion fairy would wave a magic wand over her. "Jilly Knight?

The woman smiling at her was perfectly put together, curly red hair pulled back in a gold clip, light blue T-shirt and capris without a wrinkle, and of course full makeup.

Oh, shit. Where was a bag for her head when she needed one?

"Jilly Mackenzie now." Her smile widened. "I married Jason Mackenzie. Remember him? He was on the Coyotes team with your brother."

Who could forget the awesome starting left guard?

"Of course I do. Are you guys living in San Antonio now?"

Jill nodded. "Uh-huh. Jason's with a big law firm here in San Antonio. He bypassed the NFL for law school. You know we discovered a couple other members of the old team have settled here, too. I'm not sure anyone stayed in Granite Falls."

"You have to want the slow-paced, small-time life. I loved growing up there, but I think most of us wanted something beyond that."

"I think you're right." Jilly frowned at Shay. "I thought I'd heard you were in New York."

Shay nodded. "I was. For a long time. Now I telecommute." Her lips quirked in a deprecating smile. "I work from home. Thus the fashionable outfit."

"We need to spend some time catching up." Jilly looked at her watch. "Do you have a few minutes now? We can get a table in the little coffee shop the grocery has in the front." Her smile faltered for a moment. "If you want to, that is. Jason says I tend to steamroller people."

"No, no," Shay protested. "It would be great to catch up with you. I was just thinking the other day it was time to see if people still remembered me. I've been bad about staying in touch."

"Let's do it, then. Right now."

Shay had forgotten how much she enjoyed girl time until she and Jilly were sitting across from each other with foaming lattes, splitting a gooey cinnamon roll. The conversation was stiff at first, at least on her part, but Jilly was as bubbly as she'd always been. By the time they were gathering their trash, Shay felt she had someone she could call if she needed to. Of course, Jilly was married—with three kids!—so it wasn't as if they'd be two single females hanging together. But it was a start.

"So where are you living now?" Jilly asked as they pushed their carts back toward produce.

"Actually I'm staying temporarily with Hank. My brother. You remember him, right?"

"Sure do." The other woman chuckled. "He and his tight buddy Joe Reilly broke a lot of hearts before they graduated. And from what Jason has let drop now and then, I understand Joe kept on breaking them."

"Hank's an engineer now," Shay told her, hoping to steer the conversation away from Joe.

"No kidding? He always was a smarty. Are he and Joe still as close? Do you ever see him?"

Shay cleared her throat. "As a matter of fact, he's in town on some kind of business for a couple of weeks and staying at Hank's house."

"Oh, yeah?" Jilly grinned. "You always had such a crush on him. Good thing you have Hank there to act as a buffer, right?"

"Well, um, to tell you the truth, Hank's in Wyoming."

Jilly stopped dead in the aisle. "You're staying in a house alone with skirt chaser Joe Reilly? Shut the front door! You finally got him to yourself."

Heat crept up Shay's cheeks. "It's not like that," she protested. "We hardly see each other." Except for a brief sexual encounter that still scorched her body when she thought about it.

"Uh-huh. Is that why your face is so red?"

Shay wanted to hide behind the end cap of cereal boxes. "Nothing's going on," she insisted.

Yet.

Jilly gave her a hard look. "Really? You're alone in that house with the man you always idolized and nothing is happening? Pardon me for saying so, but don't ever play poker. Your face gives you away, not to mention the look in your eyes."

Without realizing she was doing it, Shay lifted her hand to her face and brushed it across her cheeks.

Jilly chuckled. "I thought so. And you don't have to tell me any of the juicy details. I get it." Then her face sobered. "But let me just say one thing, something I hope you'll keep in mind. Joe can be dangerous to your emotional health, and I knew how you always felt about him. If you need a listening ear, just call me any time."

Impulsively Shay reached out and gave Jilly a hug. "Thanks. That means a lot to me."

"Just…tread softly with the big man, okay? I know how badly you always wanted this, and I hope it doesn't blow up in your face."

"It won't." She hoped.

"Well, I'm here if you need a friendly shoulder." She grinned. "Or a lot of ice cream to soothe the pain. And I'm calling you next week for lunch. Maybe I can pull a couple of our old friends along, too."

"Sounds great. I look forward to hearing from you."

"When Hank gets home, have him call Jason. I'm sure he'd like to get together with him."

"I will. Odd, isn't it, how many of the guys ended up in San Antonio?"

Jilly laughed. "You know what they say. You can take the boy out of Texas, but you can't take the Texas out of the boy."

"That's so true."

Jilly gave her another little hug, then took off across the parking lot.

For the first time in ages, Shay felt less disconnected from everyone. Now if she could just figure out how to handle Joe and the electrical charge that crackled in the air whenever they were in the same room together.

Chapter 5

Shay's phone chimed with a text just as she was slipping her feet into her shoes.

Hank, the rat.

"Howzit going?"

How was it going? She'd tell him how it was going. Despite her decision to do *this* thing with Joe, she thought she was about to make a huge mistake. What if she ended up in one of her typical disasters? That's how it was going.

Of course she couldn't tell him that.

"OK. U evr cming home?"

The seconds ticked by as she waited for his answer.

"Cple of glitches with prject. Wrkng on them."

Yeah, she'd just bet he was working on them. When she didn't send another message her phone chimed again.

"U & Joe doing OK?"

Oh, yes. Just dandy.

"Gotta run."

Let him make of her cryptic message what he would.

She checked herself in the bathroom mirror yet again. As much time as she'd spent getting ready she could have outfitted and made up ten people. Her hair was pinned up with a clip, stray curls drifting across her cheeks and down her neck. The dress was a simple black sheath she'd had forever with a classic style that definitely made the most of what she thought of as her body's best assets. Silver hoops dangled from her ears and killer heels completed the outfit. Okay. Yeah. She was as ready as she was ever going to be.

If only Joe had dropped more of a hint about where they were going.

"Some place nice." He'd grinned. "With good food."

Yeah, that had been a huge help. Even living in New York, her choice of wardrobe always leaned toward casual. That's just who she was. *Well, shit*, she'd finally told herself. *Just give yourself the full treatment and knock his socks off.* Maybe the rest of his clothes, too. She might not come from the same mold as his usual playmates, but if Joe Reilly didn't see her for the smart, sexy woman she was then it was his problem. Tonight she'd leave him drooling and walk away with her heart and her pride intact.

If only she could do something about the bad case of nerves jittering through her system.

It was just a damn dinner. A meal. In a public place. No expectations. Just enjoy the meal and she'd be fine. Whatever happened after, she'd deal with it then. If it turned out to be just one very great night, well, at least she'd have that. And if something else happened, then she'd have great memories to replay in her mind when it was all over.

Joe was waiting in the living room, lounging on the couch, the evening sports report on the television. She took a moment to admire his muscular build in its well-tailored slacks and sports jacket, the crisp dress shirt, and the discreet tie. Shoes that probably cost more than her computer. An expensive razor cut tamed his thick hair.

Wow. She drank him in while he wasn't watching, branding the sight of him on her brain for future reference when this all blew away.

Letting out a slow breath, she cleared her throat. "I'm ready."

"Great." He turned off the television and unfolded himself from the couch.

When he turned to her his grin faded, his eyes widened and Shay swore his jaw dropped. For a moment, she thought he'd swallow his tongue. He just stared at her, heat smoldering in the inky blackness of his eyes, a muscle twitching in his jaw.

"Is something wrong?" she finally asked, slightly teasing. "Do I have something out of place?"

He swallowed. "No, everything's just—fine. Jesus, Shay. Where did you get that dress?"

She was tempted to say *Oh, this old thing?* But she hated women who reacted that way to compliments.

"It's just your basic black dress," she finally answered. "You didn't tell me where we were going so I wasn't sure what was appropriate."

He took two steps forward until he was directly in front of her and tilted up her face with the tip of one finger.

"It should probably be outlawed. I'm not sure taking you out in public dressed like that is in my best interests. I'll have to beat off the crowd with a big stick."

She laughed giddily. "Thanks for the compliment, but I think you're exaggerating."

"You do? Well, how about this. We need to get out of here before I forget we've got dinner reservations and see how fast I can get you out of your sinful outfit." He took her hand and tugged her toward the door. "Let's go. I think I need a drink. Badly."

Shay forcibly tamped down the little thrill wiggling its way through her at his words, sending messages to every one of her erogenous zones. A drink. Yes, she could use one, too.

Joe turned on the radio and soft music played as they negotiated evening traffic on the drive to the restaurant. Nothing, however, could dissipate the unexpected sexual tension crackling between them. His compliment bounced around in her head, scraping her nerves and threatening her self-control. Shay was so nervous she was tongue-tied, well aware she was about to get in over her head. Why, oh why, had she agreed to this? No way could she and Joe Reilly be just friends. When the fairy-tale evening was over, when his business was finished in San Antonio, she'd be lucky if she ever got a Christmas card from him. It was just the way he rolled, and she knew it.

She wasn't surprised when they pulled up to the door of Andover's, a very pricey upscale restaurant on the city's northwest side. Hank liked to take his dates there and twice they'd celebrated her birthday there when she'd been in town. A valet who didn't look old enough to have a driver's license opened the car door for her and held out his hand to help her out.

"Welcome to Andover's."

Joe nodded at him. "Thanks."

With his hand pressed against her back, Joe guided her inside. The restaurant was designed and decorated for intimate meals. The tables in the center weren't too close together and booths with curved backs creating a sense of privacy lined the walls. Thick carpeting on the floor and upholstered walls muted the sounds in the room. Crystal chandeliers cast a soft light over everything, matched by the amber glow of the candles in each table. Joe gave his name to the hostess and urged Shay through the room as they were led to their booth.

"May I take your drink orders?" A waiter materialized next to them.

Joe looked at her. "Would you like to split a bottle of wine?"

She lifted an eyebrow. "I didn't peg you as a wine drinker."

One corner of his mouth quirked up. "There's a lot about me you don't know."

"We don't know if we're having beef or fish, though," she pointed out.

"Well, see, I've always been of the mind you should drink what you want with the meal, regardless." He grinned, the dimple at the corner of his mouth flashing. "How about you? Ready to be adventurous?"

She exhaled slowly. "Sure. Why not? A white, semidry."

Joe made the selection, the waiter reappeared with the wine and a cooler, they did the tasting thing, and at Joe's nod the man filled their glasses. Then Joe lifted his glass and touched it to hers.

"To a very special evening."

At the unexpected heat that flared in his eyes for a moment, Shay forgot to breathe. She had a feeling the night was going to end with both of them naked. Now that she was on the verge of having her dreams fulfilled, she didn't know if the realization tempted her or scared the hell out of her. Then he lifted his glass to his lips, and she did the same. The smooth wine with a tiny bite to it slid down her throat and eased the jangling of her nerves. Shay set her glass down carefully, determined to keep her anticipation under control. She'd made the decision to go for it and now it seemed her body was trying to speed up the process. She wanted to savor every bit of this evening, from start to finish. If she had one worry, it was that Joe might not find her as hot in bed as the other women he'd been with. No sense worrying about it now. It was what it was.

"Shay?" Joe sounded amused. "Special evening? That work for you?"

Yes. Okay. She'd make it a nice evening and enjoy the hell out of it, knowing it meant absolutely nothing. They could go back to irritating each other and she'd at least have one nice memory.

"Sorry." She smiled. "Yes. To a special evening. And thank you very much for inviting me."

"Is it an outrageous idea for you to think I actually am enjoying myself?" He grinned. "Or I would if you weren't quite so uptight. This is just a nice dinner between friends. Relax, okay?"

She exhaled slowly. "Okay. Friends." Hopefully with benefits.

"Joe Montana couldn't make it tonight," he joked. "He asked me to take his place. I hope I'm an acceptable substitute."

"More than acceptable." His teasing eased her tension. "I guess he's home with his wife and four kids." She took a sip of water. "So tell me more about your show on Fox Sports." There. His job was safe ground. "Like I said, I do watch it." She paused and then teased, "Now and then."

He laughed, the sound a low, sexy rumble. "I'm flattered. Okay, what would you like to know?"

From then, the conversation flowed smoothly, the atmosphere between them easing. The food was excellent and they ate slowly. But Shay was still on the alert, her tummy tightening when Joe's hand brushed against her, her breath hitching when he gave her one of those devouring looks. She was proud of herself for keeping it together despite her reaction. The wine helped a lot, she had to admit. As the evening wore on one thing became abundantly clear to her. Full-out sex with Joe Reilly would give her a permanent addiction, but she wanted it with a craving that had built steadily over the years. If he walked away, she'd find the strength to deal with it. She wasn't going to miss out on the one thing she'd wanted all her life because she had no guarantees. She'd settled for poor substitutes for too long. Now she wanted the real thing.

* * * *

Joe had no idea how he managed to keep it together during dinner. As he stared at the woman across from him, a million wicked possibilities chased through his mind. She was so mouthwatering, so tempting, he was glad the tablecloth covered his dick. She didn't need to see it standing at painful attention. At least a dozen times during the meal he wanted to say to hell with it, get the check, pull her out of there, and take her home to ravish her. He forced himself to drag his gaze away from the upper swell of her breasts above the low neckline of the dress and the way they moved with each breath she took. Just watching her chew her food so daintily, seeing the flex of muscles in her throat as she swallowed her wine, was enough to drive him nuts.

But the worst was the chocolate cake. They'd decided to share the Decadent Delight, a moist cake with creamy frosting. Every time she ran her tongue over her bottom lip to lick away the crumbs or a dollop of frosting, he wanted to pull her across the table and thrust his tongue into her mouth. He wanted her to taste *him*. To share her flavor with *him*. To bury himself in this woman who could tempt Satan.

And smart. He always thought she had a smart mouth but her brain and her wit were just as much a turn-on as her physical traits. The other night, when he'd tasted lips as sweet as sin and had his hand inside a pussy that could make grown men weep, his mind and his body sent him a huge message: this woman was the real deal and he wanted her.

It embarrassed him to admit how many women he'd fucked in his life, a sexual history that no longer made him proud. But he didn't remember a single one of them who was as warm and hot and responsive as Shay Beckham. He hadn't had nearly enough of her. Not even close.

He wanted to bang his head on the table. He was making this too complicated. Just test the waters, he told himself. See what she liked or didn't like. He had to do this very carefully, though.

No missteps with this one, Joseph. First you have to get her into bed, stupid. Then you can take it from there.

"You're staring again."

Shay's voice broke into his steamy thoughts.

"What?" He blinked. "Oh, just making sure you don't get more than your share of the dessert." As if to emphasize, he scooped up the last large bite and stuffed it in his mouth, then made a show of licking his lips.

Shay burst out laughing, a musical sound like bells tinkling in the wind. "Of course you got more than your share. Don't you always?"

Her words were like ice cubes bouncing on him. "Okay, I might have at one time. It embarrasses me to admit it. Please believe me when I tell you I'm not that person anymore and haven't been for a long time. Somehow I'm going to make you believe it."

She stared at him for a long moment, then picked up her wineglass and drained the last of the liquid. "If you so say." Then she smiled again. "But if we ever do this again, I get the last piece of dessert."

"Agreed." He definitely planned to do this again, even if she didn't know it yet.

Again he used his hand at the small of her back to guide her through the restaurant to the front door. He could feel the heat of her body through the soft fabric of her dress. The tips of his fingers just grazed the curve of her ass, a part of her body he wanted to explore in great detail. He'd fastened one button on his sports jacket before sliding out of their booth, using it to camouflage the erection that only seemed to swell more as the evening progressed.

He tipped the valet who brought his car around and took another opportunity to touch Shay as he helped her into the passenger seat. He had to drag his eyes away from her legs as she swung them gracefully into the well beneath the dashboard. He just hoped his tongue wasn't dragging on the ground.

"Thank you for dinner." Shay finally broke the silence in the car. "I enjoyed it. A lot."

"It was my pleasure. I'd like to do it again." And a whole lot more.

When she didn't say anything more he turned on the radio to fill the silence. Hoping he wasn't pushing his luck, he reached over and closed his hand over one of hers. At first, she tensed beneath his touch. Then, as if at some point she'd made some decision, she relaxed, turned her hand over, and laced her fingers with his. Joe's heart rate stuttered like it had when he was a teenager out with a hot cheerleader. He'd better get himself under control pretty soon.

At the house, he took the keys from her hand, unlocked the front door, and moved with her into the small foyer. Shay had left a lamp on in the living room and it cast a fuzzy halo of light into the darkness, just enough for him to see her face when he turned her and pulled her into his arms. He should probably ask her if this was okay, only he was afraid if he did she'd say no and that would be that.

Instead he cupped a cheek with his hand, bent his head, and touched his lips gently against her. Her entire body tensed, rigid as a cement column, and he waited to see if she objected. Pushed at him. Moved away. He hardly dared to breathe, wondering what her decision would be. Then, as if someone pulled a ripcord, the tension eased. She just stood there, soft against him, the touch of their mouths barely a kiss. Emboldened, he slid the end of his tongue across the seam of her lips, tracing the line and swirling the corners. Pleasure shot through him when she opened her mouth, tentatively at first, as if making up her mind. Then the hesitation disappeared and she met his tongue with her own, dueling and dancing with it. Her arms slid beneath his sport jacket, slipped along his spine to his shoulder blade and pressed into him as he deepened the kiss.

He banded his other arm around her, the tiny space between their bodies disappearing, her breasts soft against the wall of his chest, her nipples like hard tips digging into him. With their lips still fused together, he licked every inch of the inside of her mouth with his tongue as if he'd never get enough of her taste. He could feel the soft roundness of her mound where his cock branded itself against her. He wanted her every way he could take her—in his bed, on the couch, bent over a chair with her sweet ass tempting him. He wanted nothing more than to tear off their clothes, thrust inside her, and fuck both of them blind.

Slow. Take it slow. Don't screw it up.

When neither of them could breathe, he lifted his mouth from hers and slid his lips across the satiny skin of her cheek, down the slender column of her neck, and back up to the soft spot behind her ear. He nibbled at the delicious lobe of her ear, his balls tightening at the sigh that escaped her lips. As slowly as he could manage, he eased one hand up her rib cage until one warm breast was nestled in his palm. Unable to stop himself, he squeezed the nipple between thumb and forefinger and waited to see if she'd object.

She surprised him when she licked the tender spot beneath his jaw and tugged at his jacket with both hands.

"I think I need to point something out to you." The words came out on a soft whisper of breath. "If we're taking this any further, you have too many clothes on."

"You, too." He dipped his head toward her.

He should have waited to turn on the music. Create a mood. Maybe see if there was any wine in the house. No, no more wine. He didn't want either of them drunk for this. Been there, done that too many times in the past. Instead, he shrugged out of his jacket, draped it over one arm, and guided her out of the little foyer and down the hall toward the room he was using. He wouldn't presume to take this to her bedroom, her space. Maybe next time, and God, he sure hoped there was a next time.

When she stopped at the threshold of the bedroom, he was sure she was about to turn and run. Instead, she curled one of her hands into his and let him lead her inside. He tossed his jacket onto a chair and turned her to face him.

"Let me undress you. I've been dreaming about this body every night."

"O-okay."

He caught the hesitancy in her voice. Was she inexperienced or just nervous about him?

"I promise it will be good." He brushed a kiss over her mouth. "Better than good. Just leave everything to me." He kissed the corner of her mouth. "And I promise you won't hate yourself in the morning. Or ever. Trust me."

When she didn't say anything else, he pressed his mouth to hers, deepening the kiss and at the same time gliding the zipper down the back of the dress. Still with his mouth fused to hers, he slipped the dress off her shoulders and down her body, letting it pool at her feet. Now he took a moment to look at her and nearly choked on his tongue at the sight of her in a black lace bra and matching tiny panties, tied with bows at the hip. She was petite, just as she'd always been, but now with nicely rounded breasts and a graceful curve of hip. He wanted to lay her down and lick every inch of her, and maybe he'd do just that.

He reached for the clasp on her bra but she gave him a tiny smile, batted his hand away, and took care of it herself. With her breasts free, he couldn't help himself. He had to reach out and palm them, testing their weight and brushing his thumbs over the dusky-rose nipples. She shivered at his touch.

"Cold?" he asked.

"No." She ran her tongue over her lower lip in the way guaranteed to drive him nuts.

"Don't worry if you are. I'll warm you up."

More with the tongue. Jesus!

"I hope so." Then she pulled the ribbons holding the panties in place, freeing them, and she widened her stance, letting them fall to the floor.

Now she was completely naked except for those fuck-me high heels. The hair covering her mound was a shade darker blond than on her head but looked just as soft and silky. He reached out a finger to touch it and discovered it felt even better than it looked. Before he could stop himself, he ran the tip of his finger into her slit, touching her clit and feeling the moisture waiting there for him.

"Aren't you going to take off your clothes, too?" she asked. Heat danced in her eyes.

"If I do, I'm liable to embarrass myself."

Her laugh was a soft musical sound. "I think I should get a look, too, don't you?"

His gaze still glued to her naked body, he unbuttoned his shirt, yanked it off, and tossed it on top of his jacket. Slacks next, the zipper on his fly sounding abnormally loud in the room. He slid them down carefully with his boxer briefs, taking care not to injure his very swollen cock as it sprang free and pointed toward Shay's pussy like a homing device. Her eyes widened and a small grin curved her lips.

"You certainly got your share and then some." She ran her tongue slowly over her bottom lip, making him even harder.

"The better to fill you with." He chuckled.

Shoes and socks were next for him, the high heels for her. They stood, naked, staring at each other, and their breathing in the room sounded like the rasp of leather on steel. Then he couldn't stand it a moment longer. He swept her up in his arms, carried her to the bed, where he drew the covers back and settled her on the crisp cotton sheets he'd taken the time to change earlier in the day.

He came down beside her, pulling her against him, feeling her naked body against his. He skimmed his hand down the line of her back and over the curve of her ass, squeezing each globe gently. When he ventured just the tips of his fingers in the hot crease between them, she gave an erotic little moan and pressed herself against him.

Jesus!

He wanted to fuck her there so badly his balls actually hurt. He had to remind himself again to go slow. Test the waters. He settled for just sliding his fingers up and down in the heated crevasse, dreaming of what it would feel like when his cock pressed for entrance to her tight opening.

He started with her mouth, taking it in a devouring kiss and she welcomed his tongue, offering her own in a sensual dance of thrust and retreat. When he broke the kiss, he moved back to her neck again, pausing at the hollow of her throat to suck at the pulse pounding beneath the delicate skin.

She squirmed against him, doing her own exploring with her warm hands and nimble fingers. She wriggled them between their bodies, tracing the line of his shoulders down over his chest, skimming her palms over the mat of chest hair. When she raked her nails over his nipples, he shuddered and his cock flexed.

"Mmm," she hummed against his shoulder.

He was humming himself as he trailed his tongue down the valley between her breasts before swirling it around first one nipple, then the other. Was it possible they hardened even more at his touch? He nipped each one lightly, and pleased with the little erotic sounds she made, bit each one a little harder.

Reminding himself to take things slow, he wrapped his fingers around her wrists and tugged her hands over her head, holding them there while he ravished her breasts. His cock tightened against the softness of her tummy, a tummy he took his time kissing and licking his way over, tasting every inch of skin. He drew a line with his tongue through the crease where hip and thigh joined. She shifted beneath his grip, arching herself up to him.

God, she tasted so sweet. He couldn't wait to get to the heart of her. To fill his mouth with her juices. It was torture to move slowly, but he wanted to build her desire slowly, ramp up her need to where she craved him as much as he did her.

He urged her onto her back and positioned himself between her thighs, spreading them with his shoulders. He could smell her musk, the scent teasing at his nostrils. Inching himself down a little more, he pressed her labia open with his thumbs and sucked in his breath at the sight of her deliciously tempting pussy, all pink and wet.

"Just like I said." His voice was so gravelly with need he didn't recognize it. "Slick. In a lot of ways."

With the tip of his tongue, he traced a line down one side and up the other, pausing briefly to rim the opening of her channel.

"Ohh." The soft whimper came out on a whisper of breath.

Joe's cock was hard and pulsing, demanding he pay attention to it. Not now. He wanted a lot more of delectable Shay Beckham before he was actually inside her.

Closing his lips around her engorged clit, he sucked hard as he slid two fingers inside her. She clamped her legs around his neck, pulling him in tighter, making little sounds of pleasure. The harder he sucked, the more he slid his fingers in and out, the tighter her legs gripped him. She grabbed his hair with her slender fingers, pulling tightly on it as if she could just hold him in place that way.

She tasted far better than the wine they'd shared at dinner, better than any drink he'd ever had, a delectable combination of sweet and tart he could feast on forever. The harder he sucked her little bundle of nerves, the more she arched into him. He added a third finger to the other two, her wet walls clasping him. Adjusting his fingers, he curved them slightly to hit the sweet spot tucked inside her channel. As he did, he bit down on her swollen nub of flesh and she rocketed into her climax.

He sucked and thrust, fucking her with his mouth and his hand, and rode her through the spasms, not letting up until she lay limp and quivering. "Watch me," he told her.

Her eyes opened slowly, as if the lids were weighted down. He slipped his hand from her wet flesh and carefully licked every finger. Then he captured the remaining drops on his lips.

"Best I ever tasted," he told her, his voice low and rough with need.

Before changing position, he coated his fingers with her cream again and slid them down into the crease between her buttocks.

"Keep this in mind, darlin'. One of these days I'm going to take you here and make you mine in more ways than you ever thought possible."

He reached into the nightstand to grab one of the condoms he'd stashed there ahead of time. He really wanted to slide his cock into her mouth, see those kiss-swollen lips wrapped around it. Come with her sucking him as hard as she could. Just the thought of it pushed him close to the edge. That was why he'd have to wait. Because if he didn't get inside Shay right now, he'd be in big trouble.

His hands shook as he rolled the latex on, the action made more difficult by how engorged his dick was. Then he was ready. He braced himself over her and put his face close to hers.

"I can't hold out any longer, Shay. I'm at the end of my tether here. I have to be inside you right now. Okay?"

She nodded, excitement dancing in her eyes. "Yes. I want you. Now."

He lifted her legs and positioned them over his shoulders to give him better access to her slick cunt and nudged the head of his shaft at her opening, his eyes on her all the time. Even with her recent climax she was tight, so he took his time. Inch by inch he worked his way inside her hot sheath, pausing now and then to give her time to adjust. The pulse at her throat beat harder and her breath came in uneven gasps.

Then he was in. Oh, sweet Jesus. He closed his eyes, determined to hold onto his control as long as he could, but the feel of her hot flesh around him nearly sent him right over the edge. Despite all the sex he'd enjoyed these past years, he'd never felt like this before. It was almost a religious experience. He didn't want it to end, yet he wanted to fall off the cliff with her into an erotic whirlpool.

Slowly he began an in and out glide, her tight inner grip on him making the friction almost unbearable.

"Touch yourself," he rasped. "Please. I'm so close. Help me get us both there together."

Her gaze locked with his, she slid her hand between their bodies until she found her clit and moved her hand in rhythm with his plunges.

"Yeah, that's it. Oh, God, you feel so fucking good. Yeah, yeah, like that."

He watched her carefully and when he saw the signs she was almost at her peak, he drove into her once, twice, three more times and they exploded together. His entire body shuddered with the force of his orgasm and his cock emptied in thick spurts into the latex sheath. The walls of her pussy milked him until he had nothing left and collapsed forward, catching himself on his forearms to keep from crushing her with his weight.

He didn't know if it was her heart pounding or his he felt, her seesaw breathing or his own. He only knew he'd never experienced a climax this intense and all consuming in his entire life. He rolled to the side, still firmly inside her, and pulled her to him with his arms wrapped around her. Sweat slicked their skin as they struggled to come down from the erotic high.

Finally he inched himself from her body, padded to the bathroom to dispose of the condom, and made his way back to bed, lying down next to her.

"I know we should shower," he murmured as he pulled her back against his body. "I just don't have the strength tonight. Okay?"

"'S okay," she mumbled. "Can't move anyway."

"Sleep, darlin'. More good stuff in the morning."

She hummed her satisfaction as she spooned herself to him.

Joe just hoped to ever-loving Jesus Christ when she woke up she didn't have a sudden change of heart, because he had no intention of letting her go. Now if he could just convince her this was real and she could trust him.

For that he needed sleep and the energy it would give him.

Chapter 6

Shay came awake slowly, aware at first of a pleasant ache throughout her body, of soreness in interesting places. Maybe it was from the dream. She'd dreamt about hot, stupefying, incredible sex with Joe Reilly. She smiled as she shifted position. That's when she realized there was a man in bed with her. She reached behind her and touched a muscular thigh. Yes, a man. No doubt about it. Curled next to her, a hand resting on her hip. Joe Reilly's hand!

And there it was, exploding back to her. The previous night. The dinner. The sexual tension she'd felt building throughout the evening. The hot sex. Yes! She'd had mind-blowing sex with Joe Reilly. And not just once. As her brain began to function, she remembered he'd woken her during the night to take her twice more, each time unbelievably more intense and impossibly more amazing than the others.

Oh. My. God. She'd actually done it.

She knew about first morning-afters. They could go any way, and she had no idea what Joe's reaction was going to be. Would he regret it? Be embarrassed? Worse yet, be flippant about it? The trick was to manage expectations. For a brief moment, panic surged through her, sudden and fierce, gripping her in its ugly fist.

Stop this!

She'd gone into this knowing exactly what might happen, and she didn't regret one minute of it. If she never had anything else with Joe, last night would keep her dreams fed for a very long time. If she wondered how he'd polished all those skills, well, maybe she should be grateful to all those women who helped make him such an incredible lover.

The question was, now what? How was she supposed to act with him? If he wanted cool and sophisticated, no clinging or endearments, she could definitely do that. She'd made up her mind, right?

Holy shit, Shay. Time to get her freaking act together and stop behaving like a teenager. Last night had been great. Joe was great. *She* was great and she needed to enjoy the residual afterglow.

She did her deep breathing thing and sent her brain a message to quit running around like a maniac. Even to herself she sounded like an idiot. She was an adult, in an adult situation. Joe had basically asked for a chance to show her he'd changed. How he felt. And she'd agreed to it, like the adult she was supposed to be. Which was exactly what she should do because this was *Joe Reilly*. If she had a real chance with him, she didn't want to do something stupid and blow it. Fine. She'd shower, wash the cobwebs out of her mind as she soaped her body, and see where they went from here.

Moving very carefully, she folded back the edge of the rumpled covers so she could ease out of bed. Suddenly the hand on her hip moved and Joe wrapped his strong arm around her to band her against the rest of his gorgeous naked male body. Naked! And obviously aroused.

"I hope you don't think you can sneak out of here and pretend like nothing happened between us, Slick." Joe's voice was gravelly with the edges of sleep. "Because that's not happening."

Shay wondered if he intended to have sex again this morning before they got out of bed. Before they even had coffee? She wanted to kick-start her brain but his morning woody was poking into the crease of her ass and his thumb and forefinger were lightly pinching her nipple. She could feel her own body responding already.

"Um, listen, Joe."

He slipped his hand up to cup a breast, sending prickles of sensation skittering through her.

He shifted and put his mouth close to her ear. "Uh-uh. I think *you* need to listen."

"But—"

"No buts, darlin'. I have some things to say, and I guess I have to get to them before we get out of bed. Not even a civilized cup of coffee. So you're going to lie here and listen. You with me?"

Slowly she nodded her head. What else could she do short of breaking his arm to get away from him? What if he decided last night was no big deal? Okay, she'd treat it the same. Protect herself. She'd enjoyed a night of stupendous sex, but it was time to get her shields ready.

"Answer me." His breath was a warm breeze on her ear. How was she supposed to think straight?

"I'm with you," she said at last.

"Whatever is going on in that sharp brain of yours I can assure you is probably a long way from the truth of what happened."

"Okay, what *did* happen? Tell me, so I don't make a mistake." She closed her eyes, ready for whatever speech he intended to make.

"Damn it, Shay." He rolled her resisting body to face him and wrapped an arm around her to keep her in place. "Look at me. Open those gorgeous eyes and look at me. I have things to say to you." Their faces were close enough their noses nearly touched and something dark and emotional swirled in his gorgeous eyes.

She could hardly breathe this close to him, all their body parts touching, his cock now rigid against her mound, the soft hair on his chest tickling her breasts.

"Okay, go ahead." She watched his face carefully, trying to read his expression. Whatever he said, she'd never regret last night. Ever.

His mouth curved in a slow, sexy grin and suddenly her pussy was slick with need and the pulse in her womb set up a jungle tempo.

Hunger flared suddenly in his eyes and she saw the effort he made to bank it. "This thing between us is something special. Very special. I hope you think so, too." He stroked his fingers down the sheet. "I don't want to jinx anything by giving it a name yet but I know you feel it, too. I want to pursue it. And," he continued, when she opened her mouth to say something, "I want the chance to show you I'm not the same shallow horn dog you always thought I was."

"With damn good reason." She couldn't resist pointing that out, despite her good intentions.

"Maybe. Sort of." His face sobered. "I've changed, though. A lot. And I'm going to prove it to you, if you'll give me a chance." He brushed a few strands of hair back from her cheek. "I know we can have something solid. I feel it. I believe it. Let's give it a real shot, okay?"

I love you.

What would he say if she just blurted it out? But of course she'd never do that. She still had too many reservations. But it played in her mind like the refrain of a song. She'd never know if they had it if she wasn't all-in.

"Okay, here are the ground rules," she told him. "Don't say things you don't mean. Don't lie to me or make promises you have no intention of keeping. That's the only thing I'm asking of you. Either of those would be a deal breaker."

"All I want is a chance with you." He brushed her hair away from her face. "No lies. No pretense. I want to make you fall in love with the new Joe Reilly."

"L-love?" Did he really say that? She searched his eyes for a clue to the truth.

"Don't overthink it. Like I said, just let it happen. Okay?"

The slow smile he gave her curled her toes. Damn! How was she supposed to resist him? Stay sensible?

"Okay."

"Like I said, we won't rush this." His face sobered. "I will never, ever lie to you. That's a promise. All I ask is a chance. Baby steps. Agreed? Can we do that?"

Shay inhaled and blew out the breath very slowly. This was what she wanted, right? And if it all went to hell, she'd survive. But she'd never know if she didn't take the chance. She'd been ready for just really great sex, burying her own emotions. But this? Could she really have it all with him?

You've got the guts. Just go for it.

"Well?" he urged.

Again she searched his face for clues, saw the smile that reached his eyes, the heat blazing in them. Heard the words he spoke. And she nodded.

"Okay. Baby steps, one at a time." She looked hard into his eyes. "And complete honesty."

"Nothing but," he agreed.

Before she realized what was happening he rolled her beneath him and spread her legs with his.

"Do I get my morning reward for truthfulness and good behavior?"

Despite the mental reservations about this whole thing clinging to her brain like barnacles, she was so wet she could smell her own musk. When Joe's eyes widened she was aware he caught the scent, too. Holy crap. It didn't take much for her to be ready for him.

"I don't know about morning quickies."

Joe moved his hips against her, his thick shaft branding itself against her body. His mouth curved in a lazy smile even as the desire in his eyes sent its own message.

"I want you. Right now." He slipped a hand between them, found her cunt, and slid one finger between the lips of her pussy. "And it seems you want me just as much." His breath was a moist breeze against her cheek, his body hard and hot. "Quick and dirty is just as much fun as slow and sultry," he murmured before taking her mouth in a toe-curling kiss. He slid his tongue across the seam of her lips until she opened for him, then thrust it deep inside and licked every available surface.

She couldn't help it. She moaned, and laced her fingers through the silky strands of his thick, inky-black hair, holding his head in place. He broke the kiss and dipped his head to trail his tongue down the length of her neck, stopping to flutter his tongue over the hollow of her throat where she was sure her pulse was beating triple time. Then down to her nipples, first one then the other. The heat of his tongue made her nipples harden like diamonds and her breasts ache with the need for his touch.

More than anything, she wanted him inside her. Just like that. She spread her legs and arched her hips up to him in a silent message.

His laugh rumbled against her.

"I can't wait, either, darlin'."

Joe fished a condom from the nightstand, rolled it on, and in what seemed like seconds was inching himself inside her tight, wet cunt. And oh, sweet heaven, such pleasure raced through her it consumed every part of her body.

"Ride with me, Shay," Joe coaxed, his lips just barely touching hers. "Let me have you. Come on."

While he spoke to her, his hips were moving and his engorged cock moved in and out of her tight clasp. She bent her legs, then wrapped them around his waist, pulling him to her as tightly as she could. It made his movements shorter but more intense, the tip of his shaft dragging each time against her sweet spot. Each time the head of his shaft bumped the mouth of her womb electricity zinged to every part of her body. Could he tell how ready she was? How close to the edge?

"Now." His ragged voice reached into her. "Now, now, now."

"Yes," she begged. "Yes, now."

Two thrusts, three was all it took to take them over the edge together. If she'd thought the release from a quickie would be less intense than one resulting from long foreplay, she was dead wrong. Her orgasm hit the second his did and they shook together so hard she hung onto him to anchor herself in the sensual storm. It was over quickly but she was no less depleted, no less drained. Her heart beat wildly, and she struggled to get enough breath in her lungs.

She felt the hard thump of Joe's heart beating against her breasts, heard the ragged seesawing of his breath until finally he, too, lay limp, still holding her. Neither of them said a word for long moments. Then Joe lifted his head and placed a soft kiss on her mouth.

"Words fail me," he told her in a low voice. "I'm not a big fan of quickies, but Jesus, Shay, you just blow my mind."

"Joe, I—"

He freed one hand and touched a finger to her lips. "Whatever it is, don't say it. Just think of this as a great way to start a Saturday."

She couldn't argue with that, but she had to say this one more time. "This can't just be about sex. I can't be nothing more than—"

"Ssh. It won't. I promise. Trust me. Please. Give me a chance. Give us a chance." Then he grinned and slowly withdrew from her body. "But I have to say, as quickies go it's sure the best I've ever had."

Shay laughed. It was suddenly so easy to laugh with this man, to just enjoy being with him. To cherish every minute.

"You did yourself proud," she teased.

He whisked his mouth over her before rolling out of bed to dispose of the condom. Approaching the bed again, he held out his hand to her. "Time for a shower. Then breakfast." He checked the time on his cell phone, lying on the nightstand. "Better make that brunch."

"Fine by me." Her stomach chose that moment to rumble. Her face heated with embarrassment. Joe just winked.

"Yup, time to eat." His face sobered. "Listen, I have some stuff to do this afternoon that's sort of for my program."

"What kind of things?"

"Just Joe Reilly bullshit, but it goes with the territory. Just a couple of things but they could take up a chunk of time. I can bring you back here after we eat or"—he paused—"you could come with if you want to."

She glanced up at him warily. "You're going to spend the day with me? Even though you have business stuff to do? Are you sure?"

Uncertainty flitted across his face so briefly she wasn't sure she actually saw it, replaced almost at once by a smile. "Absolutely."

She was mulling it over in her brain when his cell phone rang and her automatic reflexes kicked into gear. Of course he'd get a call. She was surprised he hadn't been flooded with them since he'd been in town, women chasing after him as they'd done for as long as she could remember.

He picked up his cell, frowning. "Hello? Yes. No, I was up. No problem. Would it be just as convenient for me to give you a call later? Uh-huh. Yes, of course. Okay, this afternoon. Thanks." He hung up and tossed the phone back on his nightstand.

Shay's stomach muscles tied themselves in a knot, and she had to force herself to relax. "Let me guess. One of your harem is looking for you."

He shook his head. "No, just some business I have to call back on sometime today. God's truth, that's all it is." He cupped her chin and forced her to look at him directly. "If that was just some female, I'd never have taken the call. I made a promise to you and I intend to keep it, no matter how hard it is to get you to believe it. So. Like I said, shower, then brunch, okay?"

"Okay. But we shower separately."

He laughed. "You're no fun."

"Not when I'm hungry." She gathered up her clothes from the night before, holding them against her, and winked. "And I warn you, I've got a big appetite."

"I'll let you get away with it but just this once."

When she reached her own room, she shut the door and leaned against it, closing her eyes. What had she gotten herself into? One minute Joe Reilly was giving her spectacular sex and promising her whatever she wanted and the next he was taking a call he couldn't discuss with her. Maybe it was just business. He was under no obligation to roll out the details of his life to her. She chewed her bottom lip. What if it was another woman, despite what he said?

Okay, enough. She'd made her decision. Time to take a shower, get dressed, and take this one day at a time. One hour at a time if she had to. She'd give herself a chance. Give him the chance he'd asked for.

She'd waited all these years, never expecting this to happen. Now she needed to dredge up some measure of trust to make it true.

* * * *

Joe cursed his luck as he shaved. Timing was always everything in life and sometimes his just sucked. Marge Faraday had some questions for him. As chair of the Reach for Success Foundation, the parent organization of the fundraiser, she wanted all the blanks filled in. Not unreasonable with the event only a week away. He could have just told Shay who it was but he had this crazy-obsessive need to lay the groundwork for everything before giving her the full picture of who he had become. They had been out of touch for so long. He knew with painful clarity how she'd seen him before. It was important for him to find the right moment to tell her about his epiphany and explain the changes in his life and how he lived it now.

Not with another woman, that was for sure. He'd work hard to keep convincing her of that.

It still stunned him to realize with the number of females he'd gone through in his life it was Shay Beckham who pushed every one of his buttons and made him feel something real and special. However he made this whole thing come together, he knew he didn't have unlimited time to accomplish it. The fundraiser was Saturday night and his Coaches Conference meeting the following Monday night. He wanted to take Shay

with him to the fundraiser, which meant getting her totally on board with
this version of Joe Reilly before then.

He would do this right, all the way. Hank could be back any day,
although his two texts in the past few days had been totally uninformative.
Joe wanted to make sure that this thing with Shay was on solid ground by
then. If he screwed up, Hank would dismember him one limb at a time.

He stared at himself in the mirror, noticing the fine lines at the corners
of his eyes, the barest hint of gray threading through his temples. He
certainly wasn't old, but he wasn't a kid anymore. He'd been making all
those changes in his life and now, with Shay, he wanted an anchor. Some
permanence.

He'd probably be getting a lot more calls from Marge Faraday. Maybe
at brunch with Shay he could find a way to work his life changes and the
reason for them into the conversation. He had to do it just right.

But when they walked into Magic Waffle House just before noon, his
plans took an unexpected detour.

"Hey, Rocket Arm!" a voice called to him.

Joe was stunned to hear the nickname. Although a reporter had given it
to him in high school and the name stuck all the way through the NFL, no
one had called him that for a long time. He glanced to the right and saw
two of his former Granite Falls High School teammates sitting in a booth,
each with a woman. He had just seen Rafe the other day at lunch, but the
last time he saw Mike was fourteen years ago. Still, he recognized him
right away. Was his entire past suddenly congregating in San Antonio?

"Is that Mike Lazarus?" Shay asked, peering in the direction of the
voice. "Holy cow, he hasn't changed a bit. What's he doing here?"

"I have no idea."

Mike was motioning for them to come over to the booth.

"Let's go say hello," Shay urged. "Lord, I just ran into Jilly Knight at
the grocery store. Did you know she's married to Jason Mackenzie? Other
than her, it's been ages since I've seen anyone from Granite Falls High
besides you and Hank."

Joe wasn't the least bit interested in making this a social gathering.
Joining a group was not in his plans. He wanted Shay to himself so he
could have a quiet conversation with her and open the door to his life for
her to see the new him. Maybe going out for breakfast wasn't his best and
brightest idea after all.

"Come on, Joe," she urged. "Let's go say hello."

He bit back his objections. "Sure. Let's do it." With his hand at the
small of her back, he guided Shay toward where the others were sitting.

As they approached, Mike rose and held out his hand. "Joe! It's good to see you after such a long time."

"Yeah, same here." The other man in the booth rose and turned to face him.

"Rafe? Damn. I hardly ever see you and now it's twice in one week."

"Yeah. It's great hooking up with you like this. Everything still going good with—"

"Yeah, great," he cut Rafe off.

He glanced at Shay. She looked from him to Rafe and back again. Uh-oh. Immediately she was suspicious. He knew exactly what she was thinking. His lunch with Rafe earlier in the week had been all business, so why hadn't he mentioned it? Rafe was single, good-looking, easy to imagine the two of them having lunch with a couple of sexy women. If he had just casually dropped the fundraiser into the conversation with her the first night, explained it was one of the things he was in town for, he wouldn't feel uncomfortable about introducing it now. If he brought it up now out of the blue, Shay might think he had something to hide. Well, he did, only for reasons he was now thinking might be more and more illogical.

Maybe his stupidity would get him hung. He needed to bring her in on this as soon as possible. Joe gave his brain a mental shove to tune back into the conversation.

"We didn't expect to run into the famous sportscaster when we came here for brunch," Mike was joking.

Joe snorted. "Famous is just a word in the dictionary. I do okay."

Mike pointed to Rafe. "The two of us watch *Inside the Helmet* every season. Damn good job, Rocket." He looked at Shay. "How about introducing us to your gorgeous date?"

Joe draped his arm around Shay's shoulders in a casual yet possessive gesture. "You guys remember Shay Beckham, right?"

Mike's jaw dropped. "Hank's skinny little kid sister? The brat? Are you shitting me?"

Joe gritted his teeth. "Yeah, she's grown up a little, so let's treat her like an adult."

A red flush crept up Mike's face. "Sorry," he muttered. "Nice to see you, Shay."

"You'll have to forgive him," the lovely redhead in the booth said. "He's not at his best when he's sleep deprived."

"Damn." Mike shook his head. "Yeah, excuse my lack of intelligence this morning. I'm just a mess today."

Desiree Holt

She smiled at them. "I never got to see you guys play, but Mike and Rafe talk about it all the time."

"Too true." The brunette sitting in the same booth laughed.

"Since Mike seems to have left his manners at home," Rafe broke in, "let me make the introductions. The redhead is Mike's long-suffering wife, Shana. And this," he nodded to the other woman, "is Shana's sister Annaliese."

"Annie," she interrupted. "The other is a real mouthful."

Shay moved forward a little. "It's very nice to meet you." She looked at Mike and Rafe. "I remember watching the team play. Four state championships in a row. You guys rocked."

"Thanks." Mike smiled at her. "Listen, how about joining us? We just got here."

"No, thanks, I—" Joe began.

"Please," Mike interrupted. "We insist. How often do we get to see each other?"

"Yes, please," Shana urged. "Mike needs as much male bonding as he can get right now."

There was just no graceful way to get out of it. Joe nodded and waited for everyone to shift to a large round table, his hand again resting at the base of Shay's spine, as if to say, I've got your back. She'd been very quiet through the conversations except for her one comment. He couldn't tell if she thought this was a good idea or wanted to bolt for the door. All he knew was his plans for brunch were shot to shit. This was not the intimate little meal Joe had planned, relaxing over coffee while he told her about his afternoon schedule and why he wanted her to go along with him.

"So," Mike began when everyone was seated again and the waitress filled coffee cups. "You and Shay, huh? Wow!"

Beside him, Shay shifted in her chair. "We just, um, that is—"

"Yes, we are," he overrode in a firm voice. Deliberately, he reached for her hand and closed his fingers over it, resting it on the table for everyone to see. If he was going to make a statement, he could just start here. Maybe this would get some kind of message across to her and calm her jitters.

Shana burst out laughing. "I hope the two of you figure it out pretty soon or you're liable to have a problem."

"I've got it figured out," he told them. "Shay just needs to catch up. I'm working on that." He had to steer this conversation in a different direction. "So what's new with you guys?"

A lot, it appeared. The reason Mike and Shana were sleep deprived was their latest addition to the family, Jonathon, one month old.

"We've got two others," Mike said. "They're seven and four. No rest for the weary."

"We caught a little break," Shana told them. "Jon's christening is tomorrow so my folks are in town for a week and they took babysitting duties today. Mike and I get to act like adults for a few hours. The house is a zoo, as I'm sure you can imagine. Mike and I grabbed up Annie and Rafe, the baby's godparents, and escaped the madness for some grownup down time."

Shay looked at the other couple. "Okay, now it's my turn to ask. Are you two—" She waggled a finger between the two.

"Oh." Annie burst out laughing. "Not even on a good day. We've known each other too long."

"Yeah, but look at Joe and Shay," Mike pointed out. "They're—"

"Not a topic for discussion," Joe interrupted. "So what are you guys up to these days?"

"I'm not sure if you're caught up on everyone," Shana said, "but Mike never played after high school. He went on to get his law degree at the University of Texas. That's where we met. He got some good offers when he graduated but the one in San Antonio was the best."

"Never regretted it," Mike added. "Ran into Rafe again when he was training security for one of our corporate clients and, well, here we are."

Rafe looked from Joe to Shay. "Is everyone living in this city now?"

"I'm not but Hank is," Joe told them. "He's an engineer."

"How come he's not here with you guys today?" Annie asked. "Is he antisocial?"

"He's out in Wyoming on a project," Shay explained. "He'll be so jealous when I tell him about this."

"How did the two of you get together?" Rafe asked.

"That's a long story best left for another time." Joe laughed and immediately changed the subject.

Brunch turned out to be a lot more relaxed than he expected. This was the first time Shay had had contact with anyone on the team in years. Everyone seemed to be going out of the way to make her as comfortable as possible. No one referred to her again as Hank's skinny, bratty sister and he sensed her relaxing a little at a time. She participated in the conversation as much as everyone.

For Joe, the meal was both enjoyable and torturous. Shay ordered pancakes she drenched in butter and maple syrup, and he wondered, watching, how she kept herself in such good shape. Every time he slid a glance at her, he tightened his fingers around his fork to remind himself he couldn't simply lean over and lick the tiny beads of syrup from her lips. He hoped to hell no one noticed the pure lust he was sure blazed in his eyes. He was more than grateful the table hid his erection, which seemed to have a mind of his own.

He forced himself to concentrate on the conversation and that helped calm his body down. They talked about those great years at Granite High, some of the games, relived some special memories. The conversation made Joe realize how far he'd drifted from a lot of his high school teammates. Only since he'd begun working with scholarship foundations and fundraisers had he reconnected with some of them. Rafe was already on board. Now he needed to get Mike involved. If he didn't have a chance tomorrow afternoon, he'd get Mike's business card and catch him at his office on Monday.

"Why don't the two of you come to the christening tomorrow?" Mike asked.

"Oh, I'm not sure it would be appropriate," Shay protested. "I mean, none of you actually know me and you haven't connected with Joe in a long time."

"Reason enough to do it now." Annie smiled. "What better way to bond than over a baby? And Shay, you can stand in for both yourself and Hank. One o'clock. Church of the Redeemer."

"We're having a little get together at our house afterward." Mike looked at his wife, who nodded. "It would be great if you'd come." He fished a business card out of his wallet and wrote on the back of it. "My address and cell." He handed the card to Joe.

Beside him, Joe felt Shay's body tighten, but if they were going to be a couple—and he damn sure intended for them to get there—this was a good place to start. He reached for her hand and squeezed. Ride with me, he signaled. "Thanks. That would be great."

"It's very nice of you to include us," Shay told them in a formal voice.

"Y'all should make a point of staying reconnected," Annie told them. "Maybe there are other guys from the team who ended up here, too. San Antonio isn't very far from Granite Falls."

"Some of the guys played for teams in other major cities," Joe pointed out. "But maybe we could make it a point to track them down."

"Oh, honey, that would be great." Shana hugged Mike's arm. "I'd love to meet everyone from that team. You talk about it all the time."

"I run into them now and then," Joe said. "Maybe we could set up a database, or something. Start connecting everyone."

"On Facebook," Annie chimed in. "How great would that be?"

"I'd, um, be happy to set up the database and Facebook page."

Joe looked at Shay, eyebrows raised. "You would?"

"Is that a serious offer, Shay?" Mike wanted to know. "Because we'd seriously accept it."

"What?" She looked from one to the other. "I live on the computer. I'm in the graphic-design business. And Hank would enjoy it, too."

Joe put his arm across the back of her chair and hugged her toward him. "Thanks, darlin'. I know everyone would appreciate it."

Shana smiled at Shay. "I really hope you and Joe will come tomorrow."

"We'll be there," Joe assured them. "Right, Slick?"

"Slick?" Shana raised an eyebrow.

Joe chuckled. "Private joke." He turned to look at Shay. "Right?"

For a moment she hesitated, then gave him a small grin. "Right."

He let out the breath he'd been holding. Okay, then. He'd take small victories where he could get them.

They exchanged contact information and finally Joe managed to get Shay out of her chair and headed toward the door before they tumbled into another long conversation. He was glad he'd reconnected with these guys, but he had other plans for the day.

Monday, though, he planned to get back in touch with them about the fundraiser.

"Are you sure it's okay for me to tag along tomorrow?" was the first thing Shay said when they were back in his car.

He cranked the ignition, then left the gearshift in Park, turning his head to study her face. "Why not? They invited you."

She lifted one shoulder, an almost nonchalant gesture. "Oh, you know, I've got stuff to do. And I'm actually not part of that crowd."

"Shay." He cupped her chin and forced her to look at him. "What's this about? We're together. That makes you part of whatever happens to me."

"Are we, Joe?" Her face was so solemn he wanted to shake her. "And am I with you? You told them we were but what if last night was a mistake? What if—"

"No." He touched his fingers to her lips. "No more. I meant every word I said. If I let you down, which I have no intention of doing, then you can open your mouth and say every nasty thing you want to. You have to let me prove myself to you, though." He leaned across the console, tugging her head toward him. "Give me a chance, Slick. Don't keep sliding away from me. This whole thing—us—is as much of a shock to me as it is to you. Will I make some mistakes? I hope not, but probably. I hope you overlook them. I want to prove myself, okay?"

She looked in his eyes, searching, studying whatever she saw there.

"Okay." She grinned. "We'll give it a shot."

He couldn't help himself. The relief was so great he leaned over and pressed his open mouth to hers, thrusting his tongue inside. God, she tasted delicious and the inside of her mouth was incredibly soft. He fisted her hair in his hand, holding her head close to his. He savored her, licking every inch of the surface he could reach. The scent of jasmine she wore drifted against his nose, whispering through him and caressing his nerves.

He broke the kiss only when he couldn't breathe. Shay gaped at him, a stunned look in her eyes. He was sure his own held a matching one. His heart raced like a speed demon. Last night and again this morning the sex between them had been spectacular. Hot. All encompassing. More than just sexual gymnastics. Something in this kiss was so powerful he felt it in every inch of his body. From her reaction, Shay did, too.

She didn't move, just kept her gaze locked with his. "Wow."

"I couldn't have said it better myself."

If he hadn't already believed there was something special going on here, he certainly knew it now. Maybe now Shay would believe it, too.

* * * *

"So where are we going?" Shay asked as they pulled out of the parking lot.

"Like I said earlier, I, uh, have a couple of business things to take care of this afternoon." He slid a glance at her. "I can still drop you off at the house if you want."

"You said you wanted me to go with you," she reminded him. Was he changing his mind? Regretting the invite? God, this was so ridiculous Of course he wasn't. She had to stop driving herself nuts. She'd take him at his word and trust him until he gave her reason not to. "What kind of business?"

"Just some background work for the show and a stop at a sporting-goods store." He looked over at her again. "You might be bored to death, now that I think about it."

She grinned. "Trying to get rid of me already?"

He reached over and took her hand, squeezing it gently. "Not even a little. You'd mostly just be sitting around, though. I probably didn't think this through."

"But I'll be sitting there with you, right?" She frowned. "Or do I have to wait somewhere while you take care of your stuff?"

"Of course not. If you wouldn't be bored out of your skull, I'd like you right there with me. It's a chance for you to see some of the stuff I do."

His words warmed her. "Then it's fine. I'd enjoy going with you. I mean, if you don't mind."

He lifted her hand and pressed a kiss to her knuckles. "If I minded, I wouldn't have asked. Just remember, I warned you."

"So where are we going first?" She wiggled in her seat in order to see him better.

"The facility for the Mustangs."

"This is about the kid we watched the other night, right?"

Joe nodded. "I need to get a feel for how management and coaching think of him, and maybe some of the other players if they're around."

"This will be fun."

He laughed. "If you say so."

The afternoon proved to be fascinating on many fronts. Shay was impressed with the welcome Joe received from the general manager and the coaches as well as their reaction to him. Despite the fact they worked with NFL stars every day, they treated Joe as a visiting celebrity, even sheepishly asking him to autograph footballs for their offices. Joe was quietly charming and laid-back, answering questions then skillfully easing into the real reason he was there—to get the scoop on their quarterback situation.

The Mustangs had drafted a hot-handed young passer, E.J. Rawlins. He'd led his team to the national college championship and won the MVP award in that game. The question, as always, was whether those skills would translate to the NFL.

"There's a lot of buzz about him," Joe said. "But then, I'm sure you know that."

"Just like there was about you." Dex Franklin, the general manager, grinned. "I hope this kid turns out half as well."

Joe laughed. "I'm sure he'll be a lot better."

After the GM, Joe moved on to the coaches, especially the quarterbacks coach, who reiterated all of E.J.'s strong points. Shay found it interesting listening to the kind of questions Joe asked them about the other quarterbacks, explaining the type of things he was looking for when deciding who to feature on the show.

"E.J.'s got great accuracy," the quarterbacks coach told him. "He has a good three-step drop and he can zero in on his receivers. Most of all, though, he understands the system. Completely."

That was something Shay could relate to. She knew the coaches at Granite Falls High had always raved about Joe's ability to wrap his brain around their playbook. Hank mentioned more than once the coach in college had said the same thing. In the NFL, his quarterbacks coach couldn't talk him up enough to the media. If not for the career-ending injury, who knew where he'd be today. Maybe with a bunch of Super Bowl rings.

But he'd obviously found a new career he loved, one that was made for him. Somehow watching Joe host his program every season, she'd had the idea this was a puff job for him, something to take advantage of his celebrity. She thought other people did most of the work, wrote his scripts for him and he only did a quick read-through before airtime. Today she got to see he actually did his own research, knew what he was looking for in his subject. More importantly, knew what his viewers wanted to see and hear. It seemed there were a lot more facets to Joe Reilly's personality than she'd been willing to give him credit for.

They were at the Mustangs team facility for a long time. In addition to those he wanted to chat with, it seemed several people wanted a few minutes of face time with Joe Reilly. There was a scattering of players working out and several of the management staff, even clerical people, catching up on a late summer Saturday before the first game of the season. Joe was endlessly patient with each of them. Shay was sure they would have been happy if Joe stayed longer but he tactfully brought everything to a close, telling them he had another appointment to get to.

"You're good at this," she told him as they walked to his car.

He laughed. "You say that like you're surprised."

Her cheeks heated, and she ducked her head. "I didn't mean that. I just—"

"It's okay. Most people don't realize how much prep you put into a show like mine. Or any sports show. I enjoy all of it, especially meeting the coaches and learning about the players."

Another layer peeled back, she thought.

"One more stop, right?" she asked as she fastened her seat belt.

"Yeah, at a sporting-goods store. I said I'd sign a few footballs for an event the guy has coming up."

Shay looked at him, curious. "Do you do this a lot?"

Joe shrugged. "I guess. It's only an hour or two out of my time and I'm happy to do it."

Shay sneaked a glance at her watch. They'd spent most of the afternoon with the Mustangs people and still had one more thing to do?

"I need to get going here." He cranked the ignition. "Sure you want to keep tagging along? Again, I can drop you off if you'd rather."

He sat there, watching her, waiting for her answer. Did he really think she didn't want to go with him? She was dying to see today's version of Joe Reilly in action.

"Nope. Not getting rid of me that easy." Not when she was learning something new about him almost every minute. "Let's get the horses going."

She was amazed at his endless patience, at the way he interacted warmly with people. Even more so when they got to the sporting-goods store. Although they were ushered in through the back door to avoid the general shopping mob, the small room where he was set up was crowded with as many people who could jam in there. Again, Joe was calm, smiling, courteous. He sipped from the bottle of water someone brought him, smiled, and wrote his name until he'd gone through the huge box of footballs.

What had she expected? That was an easy answer. A cocky, arrogant, full-of-himself jock who treated people as if they were lucky to be in his presence. As she thought back on their high school years, she realized her image of him was one seen from the point of view of a young teenager. A girl who exaggerated everything to make the man less desirable to her. But would Hank, the brother who she adored—except when he dumped her into a setup—have been friends with someone who was obnoxious? It had been much easier to paint Joe Reilly as an insufferable asshole rather than see the person he really was.

Truth be told, when was the last time she'd actually seen him with half-naked females hanging all over him? Or partying in the off-season at events immortalized on the pages of every tabloid? She hated to admit she might need to do a little research of her own.

It wasn't until they were finished at the store and back in his car in the parking lot she saw him actually relax. Leaning his head back in his seat, he rubbed his face, then raked his fingers through his hair.

She'd snared another bottle of water on the way out. Now she uncapped it and held it out to him. "Here. I'm sure you can use this. I don't know how you do it."

"Thanks a lot." He chugged half the bottle before putting it in the console cup holder. "Just part of the game. A lot of people helped make my career a success. Now it's time for payback. Anyway, Fox Sports encourages this kind of thing."

Even though she wasn't quite ready to admit to him she might have been mistaken about her opinion of him, she acknowledged to herself she was impressed by what she'd seen today. She felt more comfortable with her decision to give Joe the chance to prove himself to her. She still harbored misgivings. After all, old habits died hard. But for the first time since the night she'd embarrassed herself, she thought maybe this just might work.

Maybe.

She was still cynical Shay, after all.

"*The Blind Side* is on tonight," she commented as they walked into the house. It was one of her favorite movies.

"Haven't you had enough football for one day?" Joe teased.

She looked up at him. "It was…nice watching you today."

He quirked an eyebrow. "Nice?"

"Yeah. I mean, I enjoyed it."

He chuckled. "I'm not sure I can stand all this effusive praise."

Shay's face heated. "Okay, so I'm not given to a lot of rah-rah. I did enjoy watching you, though. Seriously. You're really good at your job."

"Thanks." He tipped her face up to his. "Does this earn me some extra points in the 'Joe is a great guy' department?"

"We'll see," she teased.

"If you're dead set on watching the movie," Joe commented, "I'm good with it. I never get tired of it."

"Me, either."

"Why don't you figure out what you'd like for dinner? I'm going to change and grab a beer. Want one?"

"Maybe I need to check my e-mail before I do anything." She'd sent a revised design off to her boss late yesterday and she hoped he finally was satisfied with what she'd created. Sometimes he just drove her nuts with his nitpicking.

Joe lifted an eyebrow. "Work on Saturday?"

She shrugged. "I don't think my boss ever looks at a clock or a calendar. We've got a new design due for an upcoming meeting and we've been going back and forth on it."

"Okay. See you in a few."

In her room, Shay checked her e-mail and sighed in relief when she opened one from her boss and it read, *"Looks great. Send the final."* Her boss wasn't much given to a lot of praise but at least he'd signed off on the project. She pulled off her jeans and light sweater and exchanged them for shorts and a loose tank top, one with little ruffles around the neck and shoulders.

She had unexpectedly enjoyed the afternoon. Tonight they'd be home again. Alone, because her idiot brother was still among the missing. Would they have sex again? At the thought, her nipples tightened and a pulse fluttered low in her pussy. She squeezed her thighs together to still the throbbing, the sudden craving to feel his cock inside her.

Behave yourself.

She didn't want to behave herself. She had obviously lost her mind somewhere in the past forty-eight hours. Besides realizing she had to reevaluate her opinion of him, although she still held onto her skepticism, it seemed she'd developed a sexual craving for Joe Reilly that went far beyond any crush. She certainly couldn't go out there like this. He'd take one look at her face and know what she was thinking. Well, so what? Maybe this wouldn't last, maybe she was dreaming, but at least she'd have the best sex of her life.

Still, she forced herself to wash her hands and face with cold water, take time to brush her hair and pull it into a smooth ponytail and take several deep breaths. She'd loaded up at the grocery store, stocking food for both of them. Maybe she'd fix deli sandwiches and open a bag of chips.

She took a quick moment to text Hank. *"U planning to live in Wyoming?"*

The answer came back right away. *"Ha ha ha."*

"So when u cming home?"

This time the answer took a little longer. *"Soon. Take care of Joe."*

Take care of Joe? Oh, she was doing that, swimming in waters way over her head. She tossed the phone onto her bed and headed toward the kitchen. When she passed the sliding glass doors, she looked out toward the deck and spotted Joe stretched out on one of the loungers. An open bottle of beer sat on the little table beside him along with his cell phone. Had he been making more secret calls? Damn. *Stop doing this,* she told herself. What was she, twelve? He appeared to be asleep so when she opened the door she took a moment to admire his muscular athlete's body. The cutoff T-shirt was hiked up enough to display his flat stomach, and the soft fabric of his shorts nicely outlined... Holy crap! The mother of all erections.

Shay eased herself out onto the deck, moving as silently as she could to allow her to get closer, see better. Shock washed through her as she watched him slide one of his hands into his sweats and wrap his fingers around his dick. Was he masturbating? In his sleep? Shay knew she should just go back inside, wait an appropriate amount of time, and then make a noisy entrance but she couldn't seem to make herself move. The scene in front of her mesmerized her. She flexed her hands to keep from reaching out and wrapping her own fingers around his swollen cock. Finally she shoved them into the pockets of her shorts and just treated herself to the sight in front of her.

"That's it." His voice was raw and harsh with need.

Her cheeks flamed as she realized he was dreaming about her. Doing this to him. Good Lord! As if pulled by a magical thread she moved toward his lounger, careful not to wake him. Her heart pounded and her pulse raced, and deep inside something mysterious unwound and spread through her veins. Silently she knelt beside him, eased her hand inside his shorts, and covered his fingers with her own. Oh, yes. Yes! God, he was blatantly hot and hard. Shivers skated along her spine and over the surface of her skin. Boldly she reached beneath the ragged edge of the shorts to find the sac containing his balls and gently cradled them.

She watched his face, fascinated as she moved her hand up and down with his. Oh, God, he was almost there. She could tell. She could just feel it. She squeezed her fingers hard around his, pumping hard, and—

His eyes flew open, widened when he saw her. He yanked his hand out of his shorts and hers along with it, tumbling her to her ass with the jerky motion.

"Holy shit!"

She didn't know if he uttered the words or she did.

* * * *

Joe had returned Marge's call, answered her questions, and set up a time to meet with her Monday. He checked his messages to see if Lisa had called about Gina but he found nothing. He hoped no news was good news, although a thread of disquiet wiggled its way through his system. Again he wondered how he'd let a good deed turn into a black pit that kept sucking him in. His own stupidity, for sure. He hoped Lisa realized he meant it when he said this was the end. Maybe that was why she hadn't called, although he'd feel much easier if he knew Gina was settled in a job again, better about cutting off the connection.

Putting his phone on the table, he leaned back in his chair. His thought was to wait for Shay out on the deck, catching the nice weather at the end of the day. Share a beer before they started foraging for dinner. A little casual time, then dinner and a movie. A nice evening at home.

Followed by sizzling-hot sex. After last night, he wondered if he'd ever get enough of her. Keeping his cock from standing up and waving a flag all afternoon had taken every bit of self-control he could muster.

All day, even as he'd been talking to people at the Mustangs facility and signing the footballs at the sporting goods store, his eyes had strayed again and again to Shay. She smiled at people, chatted when necessary. Sat back to let him do his thing. Every new thing he discovered about her was another shot of voltage through him. There were so many different facets to her. He thought he could spend his life discovering them and still not know them all. He had it bad, no doubt about it. He just hoped he didn't do anything to fuck it up.

The feel of the sun on his face was soothing, the soft breeze a whisper on his skin. They made his entire body feel weightless and relaxed. He'd closed his eyes for just a moment.

* * * *

"I'm glad we have privacy here in the yard."

Joe looked over and there was Shay, completely naked except for gold hoop earrings.

"Holy shit, Shay! The neighbors."

"They can't see through the screens. It's double thick. Hank likes his privacy."

He shook his head as if trying to clear it. "Are you telling me Hank has sex out here on the deck?"

"Certainly not when I'm around, but I'll bet it's on his agenda." She padded over to him on bare feet, eyes fixed on his erection straining his sweats. "Looks like it might be on your agenda, too."

He couldn't believe how bold she was. Shay was confident, snarky, not shy about anything. But this? He'd never expected this from her.

"What's wrong?" she asked. "You aren't afraid of a naked woman, are you?"

"Hell, no." He grabbed her wrist and pulled her toward him, tumbling her on top of him. "Not afraid at all."

The thin fabric of his sweats might have been nonexistent, providing almost no barrier. He urged her legs apart with his thighs and his shaft pressed itself against her body, seeking her heat. With his hands on her naked hips, he urged her body forward so her pussy embraced him.

Her naked breasts rubbed against his chest, the nipples like diamonds stabbing into his flesh. God, she was a mouthwatering morsel.

Suddenly he knew exactly what he wanted. He yanked off his T-shirt, folded it, and placed it on the deck next to the lounger. Then, balancing her so she wouldn't fall, he lifted her from his lap and lowered her to the shirt, nudging her to her knees. She looked up at him, a question in her eyes. But when he stood, slid off his shorts, and sat again with his legs spread wide she knew exactly what he wanted. She drew her tongue in a slow lick across her lower lip, heat smoldering in her eyes. Damn, but he'd never expected Shay Beckham to set him on fire like this.

Tentatively at first, then more confidently, she wrapped the slim fingers of one hand around his cock and slowly glided them up and down the throbbing shaft. As she eased the other hand between his thighs to cup his balls, that sexy tongue of hers came out to lick the dark surface of the head. She probed the slit with the tip before circling it around and around. Electricity shot through his balls and along his spine and he swore his heart rate tripled.

It was obvious to him that although she'd done this before she was far from experienced. That only made it more erotic, more arousing. Her lips were soft yet firm around his pounding erection, her fingers strong as they worked him up and down, up and down.

He wanted it to last forever.

He closed his eyes, letting the climax swirl in his belly and rise up within his body. She squeezed his cock and he could have sworn another set of fingers closed over hers. He opened his eyes and—

* * * *

He was flat on his back rather than sitting up, Shay kneeling beside him, watching him. His fingers were wrapped around the largest, most painful boner he ever remembered having. He wanted it to be her fingers, just like in his dream, but her hand rested on his thigh, just touching his balls through the soft material of his sweats.

They stared at each other.

Holy, holy, holy hell.

How long had she been watching him working to get himself off?

She drew her tongue across her bottom lip in the little lick that drove him nuts. Then, without saying a word, she grabbed the waist of his sweats and tugged them down just enough to give her access.

"Shay," he began, not even sure what to say. Need and embarrassment fought for control of his brain.

"Ssh." Her voice was a soft caress. "We can't leave you like this."

Well, she was damn right about that. He wanted to be intelligent and respectful and just excuse himself but the moment her slim fingers closed around his erection he was lost. Her lips circled the head and her warm mouth sucked him in. She swirled her sweet tongue around him, licking the skin stretched taut over the muscle and tissue beneath it before moving her head up and down on his shaft. He was sure he'd died and gone to heaven, although he was sure he was supposed to be in hell.

As aroused as he was, it took very little time for her to bring him to climax with her magic fingers and her magic lips, especially when she slipped her other hand between his thighs and squeezed his balls. He dug his fingers into her hair, knowing he was on the edge and trying to pull her away, but she was relentless. Any control he might have had snapped and he exploded in her mouth, coming like a maniac, spurting over and over again.

Shay swallowed every bit of it. When the last convulsion eased, she carefully licked him again before lifting her head and slowly sweeping her tongue across her lip again in a motion so sexy it burned him. Something profound had taken place just now. No denying it.

Last night was all about great sex. Just sex. This? This was something totally different, maybe because last night he'd had the impression she wanted to avoid it so he hadn't pushed her. Now it had the feeling of a special gift. They stared at each other and he could see emotion swirl darkly in her eyes. Though neither of them said a word, it was obvious something between them shifted. Despite any reservations she might still harbor, despite his need to still prove himself to her, they were both very aware that from this moment on there was no going back.

Chapter 7

Shay waited for Joe to make a comment. Say something, anything. She couldn't believe how bold she'd been, but she hadn't been able to stop herself. The act was so intensely erotic, so personal, she hoped he didn't dismiss it with a throwaway line or a "Thanks, that was great." She nearly stopped breathing as she watched him sit, his gaze unreadable as he studied her face. Then he reached for her hands, pulled her closer to him, and gave a soft kiss far more emotional than she expected. He slid his hands through her hair, stroked her cheekbones with his thumbs, and gave her one of his penetrating looks.

He cleared his throat. "That was…unbelievable."

What should she say? Thank you? She didn't remember the last time she'd found herself this tongue-tied. Then the word "tongue" brought the image of her mouth on his cock right to the forefront and heat rushed through her.

"Shay? Look at me."

She lifted her gaze.

"Incredible doesn't begin to describe you." His voice was husky and slightly rough. "You amaze me. Truly amaze me."

The look they exchanged filled her with a whirlpool of emotions. Everything had changed now. Everything.

Finally he pushed himself off the lounger and folded one of her small hands in his larger one. "Okay, Slick. How about seeing what the kitchen has to offer?"

Shay followed along on legs not quite steady. She almost felt as if she'd been the one to have such a tremendous orgasm. She could still taste him on her tongue, still feel the size of him in her mouth. Dinner and a movie seemed almost anticlimactic after what happened on the deck. The air between them was charged now with a different kind of electricity.

As they moved in the kitchen putting sandwiches together, each time they accidentally touched they both stopped whatever they were doing to lock gazes. Heat sizzled in the air around them. Every time their eyes connected, she was consumed by lust. Shay felt as if someone had sandpapered her skin and exposed every nerve.

From the looks he kept giving her, she sensed Joe felt the same way. She'd certainly participated in oral sex before, with only mild enjoyment. With Joe it was different. What she'd done—what *they'd* done—felt beyond pure sex. She couldn't ignore her feelings. Don't say the words, she told herself. There was danger in saying it out loud. Too soon, too soon.

"What time does the movie come on?"

"Seven." She added some pickle chips to the plated sandwiches.

He glanced at the clock. "Almost time. We can catch the rest of *Fox Sports Live*, if you don't mind."

"Sure. No problem. Let's take our stuff in the other room." She took a painted metal tray from the counter. "Here. I've got it. You turn on the television."

She loaded the tray with their sandwiches and two freshly opened bottles of beer, and led the way into the living room. As she helped Joe distribute the food on the coffee table, their hands bumped and again they turned to look at each other. Butterflies did a tap dance in her stomach at what she saw in his eyes and she couldn't help the curl of excitement winding through her body.

"How did you happen to get into broadcasting?" She picked up one of the sandwich plates, settled on the couch, and put the plate in her lap. "I don't think Hank ever said, other than to tell me you were doing it. Did you see yourself in a role like this when you were in college?"

He chewed and swallowed a bite of his sandwich. "Uh-uh. I actually graduated with a business degree. My dad was all about getting an education that prepared you for something." He chased the food with a swallow of beer. "Truth be told, I think he half expected me to come back to the ranch when I was finished with the NFL. Put my degree to use in ranch management."

Shay cocked her head. "And you didn't want to? Go back, I mean."

"I *wanted* to want it," he told her. "But my interests are elsewhere. Being an only child the generational thing was kind of a burden. My dad and I had a long talk about it and he realized I needed to make my own life. I love the ranch but ranching's not for everyone."

"So how did you get to be Joe Reilly, big television star?"

He laughed. "I'm not sure I agree with the big-star thing, but I'm not stupid enough not to acknowledge my success." He took another sip of beer. "When they operated on my knee the last time and I learned my playing days were over, Scott Manchin, my agent, did some hustling. He doesn't make any money unless I have a high visibility factor."

Shay frowned. "But didn't he already make a lot of money from your NFL contracts and your endorsements?"

"He did. But good agents know which of their clients have longevity beyond the playing field and do their best to capitalize on it. Both ESPN and Fox Sports hire a lot of former players and coaches. They bring them on for some of the studio shows, after a little training, to see how they work out. For some reason I just clicked."

"And whose idea was it to create the kind of show you do rather than just adding you to an existing studio show? Or having you do play-by-play or color for the games?"

"Scott and I discussed it and a lot of it concerned my comfort zone. While I understand the game of football, I'm not sure I can communicate it appropriately to the viewing audience. That takes a particular skill. It's a talent you either have or not. Ditto for the color commentary. But a show focused on what I know best? What goes on inside the head of a quarterback? That I got on board with right away."

"You do it very well."

He chuckled. "Surprised?"

Shay thought for a moment, not sure how to answer. "If you'd asked me a couple of years ago, I would have said yes. But now? Especially after today? No, I'm not surprised. I think you're a natural."

He winked at her. "Best compliment I've had today." Then his face sobered. "I enjoy what I'm doing, Shay. I see an entirely new side to the business. It's a real trip learning about other quarterbacks, getting into their heads, hearing what their coaches say about them. Then giving my opinion, which someone actually pays me to do."

She took another bite of sandwich, chewed thoughtfully. It occurred to her this was the first real discussion she and Joe had had about anything. He was right. She had no idea who he was now. "Any idea how long you see yourself doing this for?"

He shrugged. "I haven't thought much about it. I'm enjoying it. I get to spend a lot of time with the players, study the rookies, analyze the different quarterbacks." He grinned. "See a lot of games."

"You're very good at it," she said again.

"Um, thanks." Was that a blush on big bad Joe Reilly's face? "I try hard to make it interesting."

"I think the concept is great. People tend to idolize quarterbacks as the glamour players." She laughed. "I mean, look at Joe Montana."

"Yeah, he's always been *your* idol, right?"

"Yes, and for a lot of other people, too. The quarterback is the symbol of the team and can make or break a game. Knowing what goes on inside his head is important to fans."

"I'm glad you like the show."

Silence dropped between them, thick and heavy.

"Well." Shay uncurled her legs from the sofa and reached for the remote. "Okay. Let's catch the end of the sports show."

They watched the end of *Fox Sports Live* as they finished eating, then clicked over to *The Blind Side.* About an hour into the movie, Shay hit Pause on the remote and stood up.

"I think it's time for dessert. Let me take these dishes into the kitchen and scoop up some ice cream. That work for you?"

"Sure. Let me help you." Joe reached for his plate and empty bottle.

"I've got it." She winked. "You can come help with the dessert."

For whatever reason her hands shook as she filled two bowls with ice cream and got out the chocolate syrup. She was squirting it into the first bowl when Joe came up behind her and touched her shoulder, startling her. She jerked her arm as she turned and ended up squirting chocolate syrup on Joe's T-shirt.

"Oh my God." She took a step away from him. "Damn. I am so sorry. I seem to keep dumping things on you."

He laughed and yanked the shirt over his head. "I should really tell you to squirt it on my chest and then lick it off." When she grinned and pointed the bottle toward him, he wrapped his fingers around her wrists. When he spoke his voice was deep and thick, like warm molasses "But I'm not going to. You know why?"

She shook her head, wondering what was on his mind.

"Because then it would be just sex. And although sex with you is definitely spectacular, I think we've moved into a deeper area."

"Deeper," she repeated.

"What happened on the deck out back was something very special. Something changed for us. Admit it, Shay. You felt it, too. And I think it shocked you as much as it did me."

All she could do was nod, her throat so tight she couldn't force out any words. Did he regret it now?

"That was a special gift," he went on. "And it took us to a whole new level. As much as I want to strip you naked and slide my cock into you, I want just as much to spend the evening just holding your hand, maybe having you cuddle with me. Watching the movie. Getting to know the things that make us up as individuals. We've both carried images of each other that have turned out to be skewed. We need to take the time to correct them. Right?"

"Oh." Her lips formed the single syllable.

"I hope you're feeling the same things I am. The game plan has changed here because our feelings are suddenly much more than either of us anticipated. Everything's out in the open. Raw. Much more intense than I ever expected. Do you agree?"

After the scene on the deck? How could she not? She nodded silently.

He touched her cheek, a brief caress. "I don't want to ruin things."

She looked hard at him and nodded her head. The emotion surrounding them was powerful, the air so thick with it she could barely breathe. Then, before he could move, she pointed the syrup bottle at him and squirted it over his chest. Just like that, the spell was broken and the air lightened.

"Hey!"

He grabbed for her but she was too fast for him. She tossed the bottle on the counter and danced out of his reach, giggling.

"Better get cleaned up, or I'm going to eat all the ice cream."

"You little minx." When he reached for her, she twirled farther away.

"Better hurry or the ice cream will be melted." She raced into her bedroom and closed the door, waited until she thought he'd given up, then cracked the door open a little. She flinched when the hinges squeaked.

"It's okay," Joe called. "You can come out. I put away all the dangerous weapons like the syrup."

She tiptoed into the kitchen where he stood holding the two bowls of now melting ice cream.

"But take heed," he warned, one corner of his mouth crooked up in a grin. "This battle is far from over."

The little byplay took the edge off the intensity vibrating in the air and gave them both some breathing room, which was exactly what she'd intended. They needed to examine this new jump in their relationship so neither of them did anything to screw it up. Especially her. When they settled back in the living room, his posture was more at ease and she relaxed into the couch.

After *The Blind Side*, Shay found another movie she wanted to watch.

"You're kidding." Joe cocked his head. "A chick flick? Don't you know us macho guys don't watch them?"

"My lips are sealed. Come on." She wiggled her eyebrows. "There might be more ice cream in it for you."

"I expect more of a bribe than that," he teased.

"This won't hurt, I promise. And I won't tell a soul." She made an *X* across her chest.

"Okay, but you'll owe me big-time."

She sat on the couch curled against Joe, his arm around her, the warmth of his body seeping into hers. They talked very little. Shay was startled to realize sometimes silence could be as informative as conversation. By the time the second movie ended, Shay felt a quiet peace wrapped around them like a cloak. The ramped-up sexual tension still buzzed beneath the surface only now it had a much deeper quality.

"Wasn't it great the way he set up the seduction scene?' she asked Joe, turning off the television. "Champagne and chocolates by the pool. Expensive champagne, too. And gourmet chocolates. What a guy." She couldn't quite stifle the sigh.

He slid his lips over hers. "I'm amazed some hot guy hasn't pulled out all the stops for you by now."

She only wished, but she wasn't about to tell him that.

"You deserve royal treatment." There was something strange in his voice. Something she couldn't quite identify. An unexpected intensity.

She pushed it out of her mind before she overthought the situation.

"So bedtime?" she asked. "And whose bed?"

The smile he gave her curled her toes. "Let's try yours for a change. Is there something in there you're hiding?"

"Not at all. I didn't know if you wanted to sleep in the middle of a bunch of feminine stuff."

"If it's your feminine stuff, I'm good with it. Come on."

He took her hand and led her to her room, waiting while she folded back the covers, watching her every movement. When she finished, she turned to face him.

"At least you don't have far to go to brush your teeth."

He burst out laughing. "Works for me."

It was at once strange and familiar to be doing these things with him. They stripped out of their clothes and Shay pulled her sleep shirt out of a drawer, sliding it over her head. Joe left his boxer briefs on and followed her into the bathroom. They brushed their teeth side by side at the vanity, and when Shay looked in the mirror and caught his eye, he had the strangest look on his face. Not desire, not discomfort, almost one of longing. Strange.

He slid into bed first and coaxed her body up against his, wrapping his arm around her and tucking her head into the curve of his shoulder.

"You know what I'd like tonight, Shay?"

"What?" What could he have in mind? Something outrageous he thought might turn her off?

"I'd just like to fall asleep like this, with you in my arms, right against my body."

No sex?

"You know this is about more than just sex, right? That it's about being together?"

Had he read her mind?

His lips were close enough she could feel his breath. "I plan to make you totally addicted to me."

She wanted to tell him she was well on the way, but she forced the words back. Too soon, she told herself. Instead she snuggled against him, ignoring his semihard cock bumping against the crease of her ass and the warm hand cradling her breast through the fabric of her shirt. The feeling of closeness and intimacy was like a warm blanket around her.

This was good. Very good.

* * * *

Joe had slept fitfully. His dreams filled with erotic images of Shay on her knees beside him, his cock in her sweet, sweet mouth. Her tongue licking him carefully. Her slender fingers wrapped around his pulsing shaft, stroking him. Her very lack of experience was a huge turn-on—and one of the reasons she'd managed to open his emotional well and send it bubbling to the surface.

Less than forty-eight hours ago, he'd told himself he was in love with Shay Beckham. Hell, he hadn't even known what the word meant until then. It wasn't just the act itself. It was the circumstances. The way she'd thrown herself into such an intimate act with him without question. The way she'd touched him.

The way she'd swallowed every drop. Keeping his hands to himself last night had been sheer agony but he'd needed to let his emotions settle down. When he took Shay to bed again, every stroke, every movement would have special meaning. His mind spun like a top as he thought of the many ways he wanted to enjoy her. To pleasure her. He wanted to build on the new intensity between them, the temperature of their relationship up several notches after the episode on the patio.

At least that was how he saw it. He hoped she did, too. Hoped she wasn't seized with delayed embarrassment. Or worse, sudden regret. She didn't seem to be. So why had she slid out of bed so softly this morning, leaving him to wake up by himself? Did she suddenly have regrets? He gave his head a mental shake. His knowledge of this new mature Shay was so brand new he was examining every signal under a mental microscope.

Meanwhile there was today to get through. Why the hell had he agreed to go to the Lazarus christening? If that wasn't bad enough, he'd committed them to the party afterward. In his addled state, he'd imagined spending the day alone with Shay. Maybe making use of the huge sunken spa tub on the deck.

Damn!

Okay, he'd just have to use the time to plan carefully for tonight.

While he was trying to unscramble his brain, the door opened and Shay walked in carrying two mugs of hot coffee.

"You were so dead to the world I didn't want to wake you." She grinned. "Did I tap into all your energy, big guy?"

He smiled back at her. "Not yet." He took the mug she handed to him and inhaled the aroma of the rich roast. "You are a goddess."

As he took a swallow of the coffee, he let his gaze roam over every inch of her. Her face was free of makeup, her hair messed and tucked back behind her ears, and from what he could see she wore a ratty old T-shirt and little boy sleep shorts. And she looked sexier than hell. Shit, he had it bad.

"So." She sat down on the edge of the bed. "We have to buy a present this morning."

"What? Buy what?" What the hell was she talking about?

She gave an exasperated sigh. "For the christening party. We can't go without a present for the baby."

Oh, yeah. The party. His brain was definitely fried. He scrubbed his hands over his face, set his mug on the nightstand, and swung his legs over the side of the bed. He gave thanks he'd slept in his boxers last night but he kept the edge of the sheet across his thighs in an effort to hide his ever-present erection.

"Okay. Whatever you say." He raked his fingers through his hair. "Give me a few to get my act together."

"How about using Hank's shower this morning, so we can both get ready?"

He reached for her free hand. "How about if we shower together and conserve water?"

She giggled. "Because we'd never get to the christening. Come on. We have to get going."

"We also need food," he reminded her. "We'll grab a bite while we're out getting the present, if you're okay with it. What time do we have to be at the church, anyway?"

"Big help you are. Don't tell me you forgot. And these are your friends." She shook her head. "One o'clock. Be sure to bring Mike's business card. It's got his home address on the back. We can just plug it into the GPS."

"I'll do much better when I've mainlined the coffee," he assured her.

He waited until she was gone before getting out of bed. Thank God she wasn't in the kitchen when he went to fill his mug. He had a boner tenting his shorts enough to let in a small band. First order of business was an ice-cold shower and then giving himself a stern talking-to.

Yeah, like that was going to help.

Outside of the incredibly sexy black dress Shay had worn to dinner, he wasn't used to seeing her in anything except jeans or shorts and T-shirts. When she met him in the foyer his heart nearly stopped beating. How was it just the simplest clothes on her made her so breath-stealing? Navy slacks, a light blue jacket, and a multicolored print top shouldn't have made her look like an erotic goddess. With her golden hair tumbled to her shoulders and tempting gloss on her lips, he wanted to ravish her right then and there.

"You look great," he told her.

"Thanks." She eyed his blazer and slacks. "You're not too bad yourself."

Think Alaska, he told himself. Ice cubes. Igloos. Antarctica. Oh, yeah. He was definitely hooked. Damn straight. And he'd better handle it properly.

"Ready to go?"

She nodded. "And I checked. There's a baby boutique not far from here where we can get a gift. Let's hit it."

He grinned at her and opened the front door. "After you, *madame.*"

* * * *

"Hey!" Mike Lazarus moved away from the small group where he'd been chatting and held out his hand. "Glad you could make it."

"It was nice of you to ask us." Shay handed him the gift. "Just a little something for the baby."

"Totally unnecessary." Shana moved up to stand beside him. "But thank you."

Shay looked around at the people in Mike and Shana's backyard. Even after this long, she recognized some of the Coyotes players from the years Hank and Joe had played. They were older, bigger, some not in such great shape anymore. Most of them were married. Meeting their wives was interesting, learning the kind of women they'd chosen to be with.

Joe introduced her to some of the people, Shana to others. They looked at her strangely at first, as if she'd come from a different planet. Then she realized it was because they still remembered her as a skinny little kid chasing after her big brother and his friends. She hadn't been that person for a long time.

"Let me get you a beer," Mike offered. "Then you can pick your side of the debate."

Joe cocked an eyebrow. "Debate?"

"Yeah. Which championship game was the toughest, the one against Chandler High or the one against West Hills."

Joe laughed. "They were both ball busters, if I remember."

"True," one of the other guys chimed in. "They both had defenders who were after your ass."

"But he always hung in there," Mike pointed out. "Never faltered in the famous three-step drop and hardly ever missed a receiver."

"That's because my golden hands caught the ball." A tall, lanky man with dark brown hair and a familiar face held out his hand to Shay. "Marcus Williams. Running back. I used to hang out at your house sometimes."

"Oh, sure. I remember." Shay shook hands with him. "You were always nice to me."

Some of the women hooted with laughter. "Doesn't say much for the rest of you," Shana pointed out.

"It's okay," someone else added. "They were too busy telling each other what great stars they were and pounding their chests over the females they attracted."

More laughter followed, with a few choice remarks by some of the wives.

"Fortunately they've matured a little," Annie put in.

"Hey." Mike lifted an eyebrow. "We played some tough games and we won them. We deserved a little reward."

"Tough games is right," said a heavyset man, walking up to them. "It seemed like the other teams were always laying for us, ready to pound us into the ground."

Joe nodded his agreement. "But thanks to the offensive line they never could shut us down." He looked at the man who now joined them. "And Rocky here led the toughest defense in our division."

"Okay, enough." Shana held up her hands, palms out. "You guys can hang out and tell each other how great you were. I'm taking Shay to join the ladies. We're much more refined." She winked at her husband.

"I can take a hint." He kissed her on the cheek. "I want to keep on your good side." He winked at her and walked off toward the other side of the yard, the others following with him.

Shana pulled over a lawn chair for her and made sure she was comfortable. It took some time, but eventually Shay began to relax, listening to the conversation and contributing something when she could. She admired the baby, a real cutie. Congratulated Shana. Smiled at the people she was introduced to. Mostly she was interested in watching Joe interact with his former teammates.

She remembered them as high-energy teenagers, ramped up on hormones and testosterone, full of themselves; they were often obnoxious. Those golden years when the Coyotes were champions were burned into her memory. She'd even gone to the championship games with her parents, sat in the stands and cheered and yelled as loudly as anyone when Joe, as the captain of the team, hoisted the trophy for everyone to see.

She'd watched some of them play in college later on, seen their interviews and thought, yeah, well, a little older but not much growing up there. Joe was the only one whose NFL career she'd followed even though some of the others had been drafted as well. Now they all seemed—different. More settled. Even the ones not married.

As usual at functions like this the group separated, men on one side of the yard, women on the other. Snippets of conversation bumped into each other. Until some of the guys, overgrown kids they were, began tossing the football around. She didn't know who started it but soon there were a half a dozen guys lobbing the pigskin back and forth.

"Come on, Joe," someone yelled. "Let's see if you've still got it. Send me out for a pass."

Shay watched from the corner of her eye as Joe uncorked a long one from the other side of the yard. Whoever the man was who'd expected to catch it misjudged direction and the ball sailed right past him. Something clicked in Shay's head as the ball headed toward her. The habits of her long-ago childhood when she'd dogged Hank and Joe in her backyard, the instinctive reaction, kicked in. Leaping up, she plucked the ball out of the air, tucked it into the crook of her arm, and ran to the other end of the yard, just as she'd done all those years ago when she'd tried so hard to make them let her participate.

When she reached the trees, she stopped and looked around, grinning, expecting to see Hank and Joe with fists on hips, glaring at her for somehow stealing the ball again. Just like always when they'd practiced in her family's backyard and she pestered Joe and Hank, shrieking with glee whenever they slipped up and she managed to steal the ball from them.

Only they weren't in her parents' backyard. And Hank wasn't here, only Joe. She was in a strange place with at least three dozen people she didn't know staring at her as if she'd grown two heads.

Holy crap.

Chills froze her skin followed by the hot flush of embarrassment. For a long moment she couldn't breathe, her breath trapped in her lungs. What had she done? And in front of the people filling the backyard? If she prayed hard enough, would the ground open up and swallow her?

Okay. Now what?

Joe pulled her in tight to his body. "Now you know why I call her Slick."

Rafe Ortiz burst out laughing. "Shay, I have to say I'm impressed. I think you learned better than the rest of us. Damn! Maybe we should have been hanging out at your house more often."

Shay had two choices, the way she saw it. She could hide her embarrassment and try to pretend the whole thing never happened, or she could celebrate her skills and laugh about it, hopefully with everyone. Shay clutched the ball to her chest for only a moment before she raised it over her head in victory.

"She scores!" she shouted. "Let's hear some applause." If they thought she was crazy, well, she'd just deal with it.

"Go, Shay," someone shouted.

Applause broke out, peppered with more cheers.

"That's my girl." Joe gently plucked the football from her and placed a soft kiss on her forehead. "Who knew those hours of practice in your backyard would make a wide receiver out of you? Or we'd discover you'd still be so good."

She stood there, wondering what to do next, when she found herself surrounded by a crowd. Women hugged her and men patted her on the back.

"She could have been our secret weapon, Joe," Mike commented. "You know, for when you got hurt."

Shay grinned at the crowd. "Maybe he was afraid I'd grow up and take his place."

"And maybe I should have been practicing with you instead of Hank."

"Oh my God." Annie was still laughing. "You rock, Shay. You have to make Joe bring you over next time we get together. These jocks think they're such hot shit. I'll bet if you helped us we could take them."

"I don't think—" She began.

"Annie's right," someone hollered. "It's time for the women to revolt."

"What did you do to us, Joe?" someone shouted. "We'll lose our jock status."

"She puts every one of us to shame." Mike laughed. "Damn, Joe. You never told us you guys were hatching a standout in Hank's backyard."

"Please." She smiled as she leaned into Joe's body. "I just reacted automatically. I guess I made a spectacle of myself."

"Spectacle?" Shana was there, holding the baby. "Are you kidding? You gave us something to rag on the guys about forever. You go, girl."

"Lucky you," one of the women said. "Getting to hang with Joe. I think all of us had a crush on him at one time or another." She grinned at her husband when she said it.

"Maida!" Shana admonished. "Behave yourself."

"That's no fun." Maida winked.

Before Shay knew what was happening Shana tugged her away from Joe. Someone pressed a glass of wine in her hands. Someone else offered her more food. And everyone was talking to her at once. She glanced over her shoulder at Joe who just looked at her, winked, and gave her a big grin.

Go with it, he mouthed.

In moments she was seated in a lawn chair again in the middle of the group of eager women. Now they were tripping over themselves asking her questions.

"So what was it like being Hank's baby sister?" Annie asked. "Come on, tell all. We're dying to know."

Shay made a face. "Most of the time it was a pain in the ass. *He* was a pain in the ass."

She managed to tell them stories about watching Joe and Hank toss the ball when she was a kid and pestering them to include her. She did not, of course, tell them she'd been in love with Joe Reilly since she was eight years old. Or that unexpectedly they were in a relationship more intense and deeper than anything she ever thought possible.

Time passed in a blur. It was impossible for her to just sneak out, crowded in as she was with the other women. Instead she sipped wine and did her best to make conversation without embarrassing herself. Again. And avoided personal questions about Joe as deftly as she could. Shana opened the baby gifts and Shay oohed and aahed with everyone.

Although they left the topic of Joe alone, she could tell they were curious about her relationship with him. Now and then one of the women would mention the catch again. Shay knew they'd be talking about it long after she left today.

She kept trying to sneak glances at her watch and send signals to Joe. She was answering questions about her job with someone named Lizzie when a warm hand descended on her shoulder.

"Before we move on to any family secrets," Joe broke in with his deep voice, "I think it's time for Shay and me to get going."

She looked up at him and saw the penetrating look in his eyes as if he was sending her a secret message. Thank you, Joe. She was more than ready to leave. She pushed her lawn chair back and stood up.

"Thank you very much for inviting us," she told Shana who was sitting next to her.

"Thanks for livening up the party." Shana smiled at her. "And thank *you* so much for the gift." She took one of Shay's hands between both of hers and gave it a warm squeeze. "I hope the four of us can get together, maybe once I get the little one on a schedule and my houseguests go home."

"Don't make it hard on yourself," Shay told her. "And don't feel obligated to invite us over. I know how busy you are."

"Are you kidding?" Shana laughed. "I want to be best friends with a woman who can catch a ball better than half the men on that team. Poking holes in their ego is a full-time sport."

Shay hesitated a moment. She wasn't comfortable yet putting a name to her situation with Joe. Plus she had no idea how long he planned to stick around. They had carefully skirted that topic. What would happen when he left? Would these people still be interested in her friendship?

"You know Joe doesn't live here, right?"

"Of course. But he's not leaving yet, is he? Let's make time before he's gone for us to at least have dinner together." She put her arm around Shay. "Even after that I'd like for us to get together. We used to see Hank once in a while but he's been gone so much lately we never can seem to connect with him. I had no idea his sister was even living in the city." Her lips twisted in a grimace of distaste. "Oh, wait. That didn't come out right. You're a lot more than Hank's sister. I just—"

"It's okay," Shay assured her. "I know that's how people have always identified me. It's not like I hung out with the team socially or anything. And like you said, Hank's gone a lot. I've hardly seen him myself since I moved back here."

"Forget about Hank." Shana gave her a little hug. "I like you, Shay. I think we could be good friends."

She didn't know what to say. A warm feeling wriggled its way through her. Hadn't she just been telling herself the other day she needed to get out more? Meet more people?

"I'd like it, too," she said at last.

"Good. We'll make it happen. Where's your cell?" She waited while Shay dug it out of her pocket. "I'm going to program my number in here. Please call me. I mean it."

At last they were back in Joe's car and pulling away from the house. Shay leaned back in the seat, trying to relax.

"A penny for them." Joe's voice broke into her thoughts.

She laughed. "I can't decide if I made a real ass of myself this afternoon, or if I want to pump my fist in the air."

"I'd go with the fist pump, darlin'." She could hear the amusement in his voice. "As a matter of fact, if you recall I was clapping louder than anyone."

"Who knew being such a pest when I was a kid would ever pay off?"

Joe laughed, a husky, warm sound. "You were the hit of the party, Shay. I mean, come on. A gorgeous, totally feminine female who can do what you did? I should have taken a shot with my phone."

She punched his arm. "I'm glad you didn't." Then laughter bubbled up from inside her. "I guess I did impress everyone. Some things you don't forget."

Joe closed a hand over her thigh and gripped it gently, tenderly kneading her flesh with his fingers.

"I know what I'm not about to forget." His voice dropped. "The delicious sight of your naked body in my bed."

He slid his hand between her thighs and pressed the edge of his fingers against her panties, rubbing the silk into her cunt. Just that light touch made her internal muscles clench and her blood race. Lordy. Would they ever get enough of each other? She hoped not.

Then Shana's words came back to her, about getting together while Joe was still in town. How much longer would he be around, anyway? He'd told her a couple of weeks or so. Or so? How long a period was that? And then what? Things were moving scary fast between them. What would happen when he finished his business and was gone?

"You're awfully quiet over there, Slick."

"Just mulling things over." She shifted in her seat. "You know."

"I do know. That's why I'm asking. Don't second-guess us, please. We've got something working here now. Okay?"

She swallowed a sigh. By now there was no way she could shove her feelings for him back in the deep freeze. She'd just have to trust this would work out. Too bad trust was a scarce commodity where she was concerned.

* * * *

He was determined to get back to where they'd been after yesterday. Easing his fingers between her thighs, he held his breath, waiting to see if she'd tug it away. When, after what seemed like an endless minute she closed her legs together enough to trap his hand there, he let out a slow breath.

Excellent.

Shay's impulsive catch and run had surprised Joe. She'd laughed about it, raised her hands in victory, but he'd caught a flash of uncertainty on her face. Of vulnerability. Things she kept hidden beneath the snarky attitude she'd always had. Because life kept them apart for a lot of years, except for those few minutes in New York, he'd never really gotten to know her as a person, until now. Currently he was too busy getting her into his bed and proving his feelings to really see who and what she was. *Bad, Joe, Very, very bad.*

Had she always been this person, even as a kid, and he and Hank were just self-involved enough they didn't see it? He remembered her as a brash and confident kid, and then as a teenager. Of course during her high school years he and Hank had been away at college. When they were home, they were too busy enjoying the females who stuck to them like flypaper to pay attention to Hank's baby sister.

The baby sure wasn't a baby any more. Somehow she'd grown up into a woman who was knocking him on his ass minute by minute and he'd been totally unprepared for it. He had eight days left to show her how much she meant to him, to solidify this thing brewing between them that had exploded and deepened, and make some plans for the future. Convince her this was something real, which was made more difficult by the unexpected nature of it all. He'd never expected this at all. Not even a little. But he wanted it and whatever it took, he intended to do just that.

Starting with tonight.

Last night he'd dreamt about the two of them naked, doing all manner of sweaty dirty things. The things *he* liked and hoped she would, too. Friday night had been beyond wonderful but now—now, with this new invisible thread binding them inextricably together, he wanted it all with her. Everything. Tonight he planned to ramp things up. Test the waters, so to speak. Because he just couldn't imagine doing those things with anyone else, ever again.

He needed something special. Something out of the ordinary. Something that showed her he paid attention to more than just her body. Something dramatic was called for, but what?

Then he remembered the chick flick she'd coerced him into watching and the note of envy in her voice at the big seduction scene. He still had a hard time believing some guy hadn't felt compelled to do the same thing for her. After all, she was a desirable woman living all those years in sophisticated New York. It pained him to realize not too many people did special things for Shay Beckham. Treated her in an exceptional way. Made her feel, well, unique.

So now he knew exactly what to do. Everyone else's failures made his idea much better. He intended to make up for her lack starting right now. When he spotted a wine and liquor store in a strip center, he made a quick right into the parking lot and eased into an empty space.

Shay sat up and looked around. "What are we doing here?"

"Getting a surprise. Sit tight. I'll be right out."

"But—"

He leaned back in and grinned at her. "It's all good. I promise. Just relax."

He could feel her staring at him as he entered Zander's Wine and Spirits Shoppe.

"Can I help you?" the man behind the counter asked.

Joe could take champagne or leave it. He liked a good glass of wine now and then although he was more of a bourbon or beer guy. At certain times in his life, however, like when he signed the contract with the Rattlers and when they won the Super Bowl, he'd enjoyed a glass of bubbly courtesy of the team's owner. He hadn't paid much attention to brands at the time. Never cared. But he thought he remembered Wally Jaeger, the owner, saying something about Piper-Heidsieck. If it was good enough for his boss, it was good enough for him.

"Piper-Heidsieck," he told the man. "Two bottles."

The guy raised an eyebrow. "Good stuff. What year?"

"Year?" How the hell did he know? "How many are there?"

The man burst out laughing. "I'd have to say the bubby isn't your drink of choice. Okay, this must be a special occasion, right?"

Joe nodded.

"Then I'd say 2008. The Gilded Cuvée. We don't usually carry it, but I happen to have a couple of bottles by accident."

"I'll take them both," Joe told him, reaching for his billfold.

The man stared at him. "You know they're two hundred fifty a pop, right?"

He wanted to tell the man he dropped larger amounts on dinner sometimes, with people he didn't even like. While he wasn't a person who flashed his money around, sometimes you needed a high-dollar meal.

"No problem. Oh, and can you wrap them so they're completely covered?"

"Sure thing. I can box them." The cash register dinged. "Nice surprise for someone special?"

"Big surprise." Joe grinned. "And very special."

Carrying the champagne, he trotted down to the deli and asked if they could do a cheese-and-crackers platter fast. He'd serve them later. When he asked if the man could also disguise it in a box or carton, the clerk frowned at him.

"You're not planning to poison anyone with this, are you?"

"Nope." Joe shook his head. He didn't care if everyone thought he was weird. He just didn't want Shay to see anything until they got back to the house. "Just putting together a little surprise."

But as he waited for the cheese platter, another idea occurred to him. He pulled out his cell phone, scrolled through an app until he found what he wanted, and made a call.

"Yes, that's exactly what I want. Can you do it? Uh-huh. Okay I'll meet you by the deck in back in, what, thirty minutes? Oh, and can you add…" What? What kind of flowers did Shay like? "A romantic bouquet of some kind? Tell the florist to use his imagination. Oh, and one more thing." He gave one more set of directions. "Thanks."

"You still want the platter?" the deli guy asked.

"Sure. Why not?" They could always snack on it the next day, or tomorrow evening.

When he opened the back door of the car and slid the two boxes in carefully, Shay looked at him with curiosity in her eyes. "Am I allowed to ask what's in those things?"

"No, you're not." His mouth curved in the hint of a grin. "You'll find out soon enough."

"A surprise? For me? People don't usually give me surprises."

He winked. "Maybe they don't know how much you deserve them."

She slouched down in her seat. "Maybe they know how grouchy I get when they do."

"Again maybe they don't pick the right surprises." He slid a glance at her. "Back to your Super Bowl catch this afternoon, you know, every single woman there this afternoon was jealous of you."

"Please. I can just hear Hank laughing his ass off about it when he hears the story."

"Uh-uh. Hank will be jealous. I'll bet he can't make a catch like that now."

"It was fun and exciting, but I've had my fifteen minutes of fame. Can we just not talk about it anymore? Please?"

"Whatever you say, but I promise you you're a hero to those women." He reached over and squeezed her hands.

"Yeah, yeah. Let's move along, okay?"

"Sure." Releasing her hands, he turned on the radio, found a country station, turned up the volume a little. "Do you like Blake Shelton?"

"And if I didn't?" she challenged.

"Then we'd have a problem." He glanced over at her, his smile fading. "If you hate it, I'll change the station."

"No." She chuckled. "Leave it on. I love Blake."

"Good. Let's just relax and let him mellow out the day."

Little by little he was getting to know the Shay no one else saw. He'd finally figured out her snarkiness was a mask for insecurities she hid from the world. Beneath the exterior was a woman with so much to give and he wanted her to give it to him. No one else.

Possessive, much?

He swallowed a laugh.

He pulled into the driveway and turned off the ignition. He wanted tonight to be very special. This wasn't just any woman, this was Shay. She came with her own built-in set of challenges, and tonight he was planning to meet them head-on. He couldn't afford to get it wrong.

Okay. Here we go.

Chapter 8

"Can you get the front door for me?" he asked, climbing out of the car.

"I will if you tell me why you took the long way home."

"Did I? Really? I guess I just wanted to get a better look at the neighborhood where you live."

"Joe." She planted her hands on her hips. "What the hell is going on?"

"If I told you, I'd miss half the fun. Now can you get the door?"

"Do I get a tip for being the doorman?" she asked.

"Depends on what kind of tip you expect." He leaned his forearms on the roof of the car and studied her. "Today was fun. I enjoyed being with those people but more so because I was with you."

Her lips tilted in a crooked grin. "Yeah? And why is that?"

"Maybe tonight I can show you." He winked. "Come on, open up so I can put this stuff away."

She unlocked and opened the door, then stood to the side while he carried the boxes into the kitchen, doing her best to hide her curiosity.

"Do I ever get to find out what the secret goodies are?"

Joe swallowed a smile. She looked like a little kid trying not to shake the presents under the Christmas tree. He kissed the tip of her nose.

"Soon. Very soon. Right about the time I go to work on *your* secret goodies."

A becoming blush crept up her cheeks and she lowered her eyes.

He faced a big test tonight, showing her he wasn't the ego-driven playboy anymore. He thought he'd made a good start so far but tonight he wanted her to see for herself that he was someone who cared for her very deeply. That he was someone she could trust her heart with. Dinner Friday night had been a great beginning. Now he was going to take things forward with a big leap.

She was still in the foyer, frowning, after he stashed his packages.

He tipped up her chin and brushed his lips over hers, then lifted his head a millimeter. "Go to your bedroom, take off your clothes and put on a robe. Don't come out until I tell you to."

"Wow. Aren't you the bossy one all of a sudden."

"I promise it will be worth it."

She lifted an eyebrow. "Is that a directive? Do you order all your women around?"

He smiled against her mouth. "Right now *you're* all my women and ordering you around has great appeal to it. Now scoot. I'll meet you outside in a few."

"Am I allowed to shower first?" She managed a little grin. "I got a little sweaty playing football."

He chuckled, glad she saw the humor in what happened. "Absolutely. As a matter of fact, take a long shower. Now go on." He swatted her ass.

She squealed and made a face at him but headed for her room.

He hustled as much as possible to set things up. First he took the cover off the spa and turned on the jets. Then placed one bottle of champagne where the caterers would be sure to see it and could place it in the cooler they were bringing. Back in the kitchen, he stored the other bottle in the back of the fridge along with the cheese platter. Checking the time, he hurried out to the back deck where the people he'd called were now waiting for him.

"You know what to do?"

The man nodded. "Leave it to us."

"Okay, Just hustle, will you, please? I don't know how long I can stall her." He handed over his credit card, waited while the guy swiped it on his portable reader, then added a big tip.

The man smiled. "Thanks. Appreciate it."

"No, I appreciate this."

He shoved his wallet back in his pocket and pulled the long, thick cushions from the loungers, arranging them by the hot tub for later.

The woman smiled at him. "Your girlfriend is very, very lucky."

"Thanks. I hope she agrees."

He imagined the results and smiled. Who said he didn't know how to set up a romantic scene?

Inside the house, he found the controls for the stereo, punched the button for outside speakers only, and turned the dial until he found the music he wanted. He was on his way to his bedroom when his cell rang.

"What?" he answered impatiently, unbuttoning his shirt.

"Oh, Joe? Sorry. Did I catch you at a bad time?"

Lisa. Damn it. He hoped nothing happened with Gina to derail his plans for the night.

"No, no." He toed off his shoes and socks. "What's up?"

"Just wanted to let you know Gina got one of those jobs she interviewed for. She starts tomorrow. Maybe you could give her a call? Encourage her a little?"

Damn, damn, damn. With an effort he tamped down his irritation.

"Lisa, if I'm going to cut this off, I don't think talking to her would be such a great idea."

"I told her and she understands," Lisa assured him. "I think she'd just appreciate this one last word of support from you."

He swallowed a sigh. With Shay in his life now—at least he hoped she was—he was glad he'd made the decision to break all ties with this situation. Maybe Shay would understand, but he didn't want to take that chance. Not when everything was still so new and fragile.

"How about I call her now?" He took a quick glance at his watch. Crap. "I've only got a few minutes, though."

"If you're busy—"

"I'll just have to make it quick."

"Thanks, Joe. You're the best."

He disconnected the call and pressed speed dial for Gina's cell. He was happy to hear the excitement in her voice, sense the positive attitude, although he wished Lisa had picked a better time for the call. He said all the right words, praised her for the new job.

"Listen, Gina," he began.

"It's okay, Joe." Her voice was soft but steady. "Lisa told me and I understand. You've taken care of me far longer than you needed to. Longer than anyone else in my life except Lisa. I appreciate every single thing you've done for me and now it's time for me to stand on my own two feet. I'll be fine. I'll make you proud of me."

"Just be proud of yourself."

Despite what she said, a tiny feeling of unease still niggled at him. Deliberately he shoved it away and tossed his phone on the bed. He was sure he broke speed records ripping off his clothes and tossing them to a chair. The shower was still running in the bathroom he shared with Shay. That gave him a few more minutes to get his shit together. The towels were in the hall linen closet. He wrapped one around his waist and carried two others out to the deck.

He was just in time to see the two workers getting ready to leave. They'd done a great job. Everything was exactly as he'd ordered.

He hurried back into the house and knocked on Shay's door.

"Can I come out of prison?" she asked.

"Absolutely."

She opened the door. "I'm ready."

"Close your eyes."

She stared at him. "What? Why? What's going on?"

"Shay, just this once will you please not ask questions? Just close your eyes."

"Okay." She frowned. "But just this once."

"And cover them with your hand."

He took her other hand and guided her through the house and out onto the deck. When they were standing in the middle of it, he stopped.

"Okay. Now you can look."

If he wished for anything, it was that he'd remembered to bring out his cell so he could snap a picture of the look on her face.

The place he'd called had outdone themselves. The picnic table had been shoved to the side and in its place was a small round table covered with a lace-trimmed tablecloth. A bouquet of wildflowers sat in a crystal vase in the center of the table and at each place was a china plate with a protective cover over it. Ice water had been poured into the goblets and the champagne was chilling in the cooler they'd brought. Two flutes were waiting on the table. Strewn across the cushions on the floor was an abundance of rose petals. Soft music drifted on the air.

"Ohmigod!" She stared, wide-eyed, at the display he'd set up. "Wow. Are these your carefully concealed packages? No, wait. There's more here than you picked up. Where did all this come from?"

He laughed. "From the romance fairies."

"No, really. How did you do all this?"

"My secret." He took her hand and pulled her toward him. "Good surprise? Like it?"

"Like it?" She blinked, as if she expected it to disappear. "What's not to like?"

"We don't have a pool," he pointed out, "so I hope the hot tub works as well. I thought you deserved a little pampering." He winked at her. "I wanted to spoil you a little. After all, you *are* more than a wide receiver."

Her jaw dropped, and she closed her mouth forcibly, staring. "You paid attention to the movie."

"I did." He tried to read the expression on her face. "Does it work?"

"Work? Are you kidding?" She lifted one of the silver domes from a plate. "Cold entrees. You thought of everything."

Joe couldn't hide his grin. "I didn't want to have to worry about hot dishes. Shrimp remoulade on one and spiced cold chicken on the other. I took a chance so I hope they're okay."

"You couldn't have picked better. And we don't have to worry about warm food getting cold."

"And flowers." She turned in a circle. "And rose petals everywhere. Oh, God, Joe."

Tears gathered in the corner of her eyes. He tucked a finger beneath her chin, lifted her face, and licked her tears away. "Happy tears, I hope."

"Overwhelming tears."

"How about some champagne?"

"I think that would be great." She looked at the label when he lifted it from the cooler. "Holy crap. This stuff you bought costs as much as my car payment."

"I'm lucky the cost doesn't matter, darlin'." He sobered. "I wanted to do something very nice for you. Something exceptional. Something to show you how special you are. Did I get it wrong?"

The soft curve of her lips in a smile eased the tension in his body.

"No. No, you got it absolutely right. Flowers, rose petals. Catered dinner. Music. You didn't miss a trick." She took one of the flutes from him. "When I said last night no one has ever done anything like this for me before, I wasn't hinting. I hope you know that."

"I do. That's part of what made me want to do this. The fact you'd never ask for this. You deserve this and more." He touched his glass to hers. "To us, Shay. And I mean this toast in every sense of the word."

"To us." She whispered the words, almost as if afraid to say them out loud.

Joe swallowed some champagne and studied Shay, his heart kicking over with emotion. Her face was scrubbed free of makeup, and her natural beauty astounded him. She had pulled her hair up into a ponytail and it glinted gold in the fading sunlight. But it was the rest of her that stole his breath. She was wearing a thin shortie robe that left little to the imagination. The fabric fell softly against her breasts, nipples poking hard into it, and the hem barely reached the top of her thighs. As she walked, the material shifted back and forth, teasing him with what lay hidden behind it.

But when he looked into her eyes, the uncertainty had faded, replaced now by an intense mixture of heat and emotion he'd seen there yesterday. The deep connection you either had with someone or you didn't. The invisible but unbreakable thread binding two people together. The kind linking them since she'd given him the incredible and intensely personal orgasm on the deck.

He set his glass down and took hers, putting it next to his, then held out his arms to her.

"Come here to me."

She tilted her head, a question in her eyes. "What's this about?"

He released her hair from the ponytail, combing his fingers through it as it tumbled to her shoulders. "There. Much better." He let the strands sift through his fingers again. "So soft. I like it loose like this."

"I put it up to keep it from getting wet in the tub."

He cupped her chin. "I promise to keep you occupied enough you won't notice if it gets wet. Or care." He nodded his head at the speakers. "Remember how they danced in that movie? I think this one's for us."

He pulled her close to him, making soothing circles on her back with his hand, the tips of her breasts hard against his chest. He knew she sure as hell could feel the boner poking straight out through the towel. Probably the only thing keeping it in place.

Oh, yeah. She could feel it. She pressed herself more tightly against him and shifted her hips slightly in a sliding move.

He chuckled. "Tease."

The stiffness eased from her body, leaving her boneless against him. Her soft little snicker echoed through him.

"You're the one who wanted to dance," she reminded him.

He laughed and did another little twirl. When Faith Hill's *Breathe* kicked in, he asked, "Remember this song?"

"Mm-hmm. Sure do. I love it."

"Me, too. It describes exactly how I feel." He tightened his hold on her for a moment. "Like the song says, I can feel you breathe, Shay. Almost as if you're a part of me. The other night…" He let out a breath and began again. "The other night was very special to me. You have to admit what happened between us was more than just friendship." When she didn't answer, he stopped dancing. "Well?"

"Okay, yes. More than friendship."

He began moving them to the music again. "A lot more. I keep telling you I'm not the person you used to think I was. Okay," he corrected himself. "Maybe that's what I was before, when I was younger and stupid. Life changes, though, and we change with it. When I came to San Antonio this time I never expected to see you. More than that, I never expected to fall in love with you."

She tensed in his arms and stumbled slightly before he smoothly eased her back into the dance. "There's the love word again," she murmured.

"Sure is." He did a fancy swirl and turn, thankful that he'd tied a tight knot in his towel. "Every minute I spend with you, I fall more in love with you. Love. I'm not afraid to say the word. If you'd drop the wall you keep around yourself, the one you keep trying to hide behind, you might admit you feel the same way. At least I hope you do."

"Isn't this a little too fast?"

He dipped and swirled again, then pulled her tight against his body. "Life moves along very fast. You have to grab onto it while you can and hang on with both hands. Good stuff doesn't come along that often."

"I don't—"

He kissed her gently to stop her words. "Tonight is about showing you how special you are to me. Making you feel exceptional. Unique." He dropped his voice. "Treasured." Her breathing quickened, and he could actually see the flutter of her pulse at the hollow of her throat. "About pleasing you sexually. Would you like that? Hmm?"

A long sigh whispered from her throat. "Yes. I-I would." She coasted her tongue over her lower lip, making his dick want to beg and plead. "Is—Is that what you usually do with your women?"

"Not even a little bit." He touched his lips to her forehead. "I keep telling you, you're special. This night is about proving it to you."

She tilted her head back and the corner of her mouth kicked up in a tiny grin. "So far you're doing a good job. I'm totally floored. Who knew a hot jock paid attention to a chick flick?"

"Ex-hot jock," he corrected.

"Well." She looked up at him with an impish grin. "Ex-jock but still hot."

"Yeah? Good to know you think that." They weren't moving now, just sort of shuffling their feet in place, bodies swaying to the beat of the music. There was hardly a whisper of air between them. "Here's a little secret for you. I've never been with a woman who even comes close to making me feel the way I do with you. Wanting the things I want with you."

"Is that right?"

There was still a faint note of skepticism in her voice. He planned to do his damndest to eliminate every trace of it.

"I'm ashamed to admit I probably didn't care enough about any of them," he went on. "Not like this. But that's good, because I've saved it for you." He lifted their joined hands and rubbed his thumb over her damp lower lip. "I want it all with you, Shay Beckham. Everything. But I only want it with you. And you can take that to the bank any day of the week."

When the song ended, he gave her a quick hug before moving away. He took her champagne flute, filled it, and placed it with his on the wide ledge of the tub. Then he hugged her back against him. Tilting her head up to give him better access, he brushed his lips gently over hers, licking the soft flesh with the tip of his tongue before gently probing inside.

She opened for him easily, her mouth a hot well of desire, and he drank from it greedily. Deepening the kiss even more, he spread one hand against a hip and drew her against his body. The thin robe was no barrier. She might as well have been wearing nothing. He could feel every curve and dip and swell as he coasted his hand over the globes of her ass and up the length of her spine until he pressed his fingers against the nape of her neck.

She moaned, a low yet greedy sound and pushed herself against him. Her breasts, soft and round, imprinted themselves on his chest, her nipples stiff and granite-hard. Through the layers of the towel and her robe, he could feel the heat of her pussy burning against his body.

Slow down, he told himself. *You have all night.*

His unexpected problem was just touching her challenged his famous restraint. With great reluctance, he broke the kiss and set her scant inches away from him.

"I think by now the hot tub should be just about right." He pulled one end of the sash on her robe, letting the fabric fall open. At the sight of her nearly nude body, he sucked in a breath, hard. Every time he saw her like this, she took his breath away all over again. "Let's get you into the water, shall we?"

He slid the robe from her shoulders and dropped it to a chair, then held her hand as she climbed down into the tub. He couldn't tear his eyes from the play of muscles in her thighs, the movement of her breasts, the dark blond curls covering her sweet, sweet pussy.

"You, too," she teased. "Looks like someone needs to get rid of his towel."

No doubt. His cock was so rigid it poked the terrycloth nearly straight ahead. His balls were sending him messages of urgent need but again, he was determined not to rush this if he could help it. It didn't help to realize the air of vulnerability he'd sensed wrapped around Shay earlier seemed to have disappeared. Fire flashed in her eyes now, and hunger. Need. Yes, those things he wanted her to feel.

Dropping his towel to the floor, he stepped down into the hot tub, quick to notice Shay's gaze fastened on his very prominent hard-on. She took his hand as she slipped into the tub, submerging herself up to her neck.

He moved a little closer to her. "Do you know you have the most beautiful nipples in the world?"

Her laugh was slightly hysterical. "Is your opinion the result of an extensive survey?"

He shook his head. "Even if I'd never seen anyone else's, I'd know none could come close to yours. Warm and firm and such a nice rosy color." He reached out and gave one a gentle pinch. "I want to suck them until you beg for mercy. Until every touch with my fingers or my mouth sends a message straight to your delicious cunt."

She shivered in reaction.

"Or maybe," he went on, "I'll start by playing with your clit until you beg me to let you come."

A faint blush stained her cheeks and her breathing quickened. Did she like it when he talked dirty to her? Said these things to her? Would she like the other things he had in mind? God, he hadn't been this uncertain since high school.

"Do you know you're an incredibly sexy woman?"

Her eyes widened. "You think so? I always thought you looked at me like a tomboy."

"Sweetheart, that was a lot of years ago when I was a horny teenager and you were a…a…"

She grinned. "Tomboy?"

"I can assure you those days are gone forever." He reached over and snagged their champagne, handing one of the flutes to her, again touching his glass to hers. "To us, Shay. I want to drink to us."

He saw just the barest sign of hesitation before she gave him one of her slow, sexy smiles and nodded.

"To us."

"Just so you know," he said after he swallowed the icy liquid, "I plan to take a lot of time fucking you tonight."

She looked at him, the sexy little smile he'd come to love teasing at her lips again.

"Think you're up to the task?"

"You challenging me, darlin'? Think I can't do it?"

"I think you can give it your best shot," she teased.

Enough. Her words were like a match lighting dry paper. He needed to touch her now, feel her body, watch her response to his touch. As she sipped slowly from the glass Joe eased his leg up until his foot was cradled between her thighs. Using his toes, he stroked the folds of her pussy, easing his big toe into her slit until he felt the hot nub hidden there. Shay sucked in a breath.

"Joe? You're, um—"

"Uh-huh." He nodded. "I am." He wiggled his toes just a tiny bit. "Every part of you I touch with any part of me turns me on, did you know that?"

She shook her head.

"I want to do everything with you, darlin'. Is this what you want, too?"

"Yes." Her breath hitched on the word and she started to move closer. "It is."

"What you did for me the other day, out here? I can't stop thinking about it. It was the most incredible experience."

She blushed again, a deeper rosy hue this time. "I have to tell you, that's never been a favorite activity of mine. Not until the other day. With you, I, um, really wanted to do it." She looked directly at him. "Will you think I'm corny if I say it was almost like a religious experience?"

"Funny you should say that." He gave a strangled laugh. "I felt the same way." *Enough with the talk*, he told himself and pulled his foot back. Now he wanted to give her something special. "Will you try something with me?"

"Try something?" Her brow creased in an adorable frown. "What do you have in mind? Is it something I'll like?"

"I sure hope so." He winked. "I'll bet it's something you've never done before. What do you think?"

She lifted her glass and studied him over the rim. "And if I don't like it, you'll stop?"

"Always. You only have to tell me."

Her lips curved in a slow smile. "Then yes. I'm game."

"Okay. Here's what I want you to do." He watched her carefully. "Lean back against the side of the tub, spread your legs as wide as you can, and sip your champagne. Just that, nothing more. No matter what I do, don't move. Do not try to close your legs. Don't move your hips. Can you do that?"

She nibbled her lower lip. "I-I don't know. I guess so."

"Remember. No matter what I do, keep your legs spread wide."

He moved his foot back into place again, stroking her with his toe.

She sucked in a breath. "W-What are you doing?"

"Touching you. I told you. I love touching you."

"B-But—"

"But why am I using my toe?"

She nodded.

"Because if I put my hands on you right now I won't be able to take this slow the way I want to." He gave her a lopsided grin. "Besides, this way I get to see every reaction. Should I stop?"

"No." She caught her lower lip with her teeth. "No, don't stop. In fact"—she gave him a slow, sultry smile—"if you do I might have to hurt you."

"Are you threatening or promising?"

His eyes never left her face, registering each change of expression, each nuance as he teased and played with her sex. Every time he pressed against her clit, she sucked in a breath. Like a good girl she kept her legs open for him, but he could see her straining to follow his orders. He managed to keep from saying to hell with it and grabbing her right then by sipping his own champagne as he watched her and stimulated her bundle of nerves. Her hazel eyes had turned a stormy gray and color still flared on her cheekbones. The more he fondled her with his toe and his foot, the more uneven her breathing became. The pulse at the base of her throat fluttered hard enough now he could see the beat of it.

When her eyes got that glazed, totally aroused look he eased his foot away, leaving her sitting there with her legs spread wide. He knew her pussy would be spasming with unfulfilled need. What he had in mind he hoped would give her an extra thrill, even though it might not truly satisfy her. He tried to envision her reaction and hoped it would excite her as much as it did him. He didn't want to make any mistakes here.

"Do you know how hot you look sitting there the way you are, spread out in the water, your sweet cunt hungry for release?" He reached beneath the surface and wrapped his fingers around his cock. Blood pulsed through the thick vein that wrapped around it and his balls were sending him urgent messages. He wanted to plunge himself into her now but doing so wasn't part of his plan. No, he wanted her so aroused, so hot for him, that when he finally fucked her it would be an explosion they'd both remember for a very long time.

"Legs still apart," he reminded her, eating her up with his eyes.

He drained the rest of his drink, set the glass down, then took hers and put it to the side, also. Moving slowly in the bubbling water, he moved around until he could maneuver her in front of him. She trembled slightly as he placed her on his lap, draping her legs over his thighs. Sliding his hands up her rib cage, he palmed her breasts, kneading them before capturing her nipples between each thumb and forefinger. He squeezed, hard, just as before.

"You have the most incredible nipples."

"I think you told me that," she reminded him, leaning back against him.

He put his lips close to her ear. "I could spend all night just sucking them. Well, maybe giving them a little bite now and then."

Unbelievably, she blushed again.

Joe laughed. "Does it embarrass you when I talk dirty to you, Slick? Because I love doing it."

She lowered her gaze. "No. It doesn't. I, um, sorta like it."

She said the words so softly he almost didn't hear her.

"Did you say you liked it?" he prompted.

She nodded.

He put his mouth right next to her ear. "Good. Because I'm going to keep doing it while I'm fucking you." He palmed her breasts, kneading them gently. Provocatively. "And playing with these gorgeous breasts. Touching your incredible pussy." He lowered his voice even more. "When my cock is inside you and you're so tight around me I could lose my mind."

She looked up at him now and the spark of mischief in her eyes startled him. "Big talker there."

"Brat." He said the word affectionately. "I'll have to think of some way to get even with you."

"Oh, I think you're already doing that."

He lifted one hand and turned her face, forcing her to look at him directly.

"This thing happening here with us? I want you to know this is no mistake. Not even a little. I wanted tonight to be very special for you, in a lot of ways. I want to make you forget about any other man you've ever been with. Wipe them out of your mind."

"You make me sound like I had a whole collection of men," she baited.

The thought of her with others made his stomach cramp. "You know what? I'm going to pretend none of them existed, whoever they were. There's only this, here and now. You and me." He brushed droplets of water from her cheek. "And I'm going to make you feel real good. I promise."

She gave him the now familiar sly little look again. "You are?"

"I am." He pulled her into him as tightly as he could and still keep her legs spread, the bubbling water sloshing in tiny waves, and put his mouth close to her ear. "That okay with you?"

Her breathing accelerated, and she leaned back against him. "Yes. Very okay."

His heart rate ramped up again and his cock said thank you.

"Good. Because I'm going to make you so hot even the water won't cool you down." He licked the shell of her ear, caressing it with his tongue, and slid his hand down until he found the hot button of her clit. He rolled it in his fingers and tugged on it lightly. She shook against him and he felt the sexual need pulsing through her body. She strained into his touch.

"You'll love this, darlin'," he murmured.

She gasped and tried to push herself into his touch. "Please," she whispered.

"Please what? Please let you come?"

"Yes." Her head fell back against his chest. "Oh, God, Joe."

He knew it was hard for her to move as stretched out as she was but she did her best to push back against him and wriggle her fine ass, pressing against his already painfully rigid shaft.

He swallowed a groan. Now he wanted to touch her everywhere. Get his hands and his mouth on every part of her body.

"Ask me nicely," he teased.

"P-Please," she whispered.

"Please what?" he prompted.

"Please let me come."

"All you had to do was ask."

Every response she gave made his cock throb more painfully, his balls ache more excruciatingly. He reached for a nipple again, feeling it swell beneath his touch. He wanted to fuck her more than he wanted his next breath. Not, however, before he'd gotten at least one orgasm out of her. Focused solely on her.

He concentrated on rubbing her nipple and her clit, squeezing them between his fingers and tugging on them, tormenting them enough to elicit cries of pleasure from her. He could tell she was hanging on the very edge, her body ready for release. Holding her on his lap, he turned them so their bodies pointed at one of the jets. As soon as the stream hit her directly she cried out.

"God. Oh, God."

He knew the instant the pulsing stream of the jet hit her cunt.

"Like how that feels?'

"Yes, yes, yesss." The words hissed from her mouth and she jerked within the circle of his arm. He laughed softly as she tried to close her legs.

"Uh-uh-uh. Keep those legs where they are." He nuzzled her neck. "Feel good, darlin'?"

"Yes, but—"

"But it makes you want to come, right?" He bit down lightly on the soft flesh of her shoulder. "Right, Slick?"

She squirmed against him again, tormenting his poor, hungry cock, not to mention what she was doing to his balls. The other night had been a great start, but he was determined to give her more pleasure than she'd ever known. To show her good sex—*great* sex—was about a lot more than the act itself. To prove *he* was about a lot more than she thought.

Anchoring her firmly to his body he reached for one of the champagne flutes and handed it to her. Then he grabbed his own, still keeping her positioned so the stream of the jet continued to hit directly into her hungry channel. He touched the base of her champagne flute and tilted it toward her lips.

Her giggle had a touch of hysteria. "You expect me to sip champagne while the jet does—while I—"

"Oh, yeah. You can do it." He licked her ear again. "Doesn't the water feel good in your pussy? Like a million tiny fingers, right?"

"Oh my God, you have no idea." Her voice was unsteady.

"Get ready, then," he told her. "Almost there."

* * * *

Shay was giddy. She couldn't believe it because she'd never been giddy in her life. Hysterical, maybe, but not dizzy with excitement like this. The assault on her senses from the very high-priced champagne and the power of the hot-tub jets was making her crazy. Every time she wriggled her ass Joe tensed beneath her, his cock like a steel pole poking at her body.

Crazy with need, she tried yet again to close her legs. Joe Reilly was driving her nuts, just as he said he would. She was still astonished at the incredible surprise he'd arranged, everything from the catered meal, to the flowers, to the scattered rose petals, to…to…everything. Saturday night should have proven to her he wasn't the same Joe Reilly but she'd never expected anything like this.

Joe shifted just enough to tilt her pelvis more toward the jet stream, the pressure now directly on her clit. "Maybe you aren't concentrating enough on what's important here?"

She jerked in his grasp and just like that her brain shut down. "Oh my God!"

"Yeah." His laugh vibrated against her. "That's better."

She wanted desperately to squeeze her thighs together but Joe's hard, muscular ones prevented it. She gripped the forearm pressing against her midriff and dug her fingers into it as the bubbles pounded against her. She wanted to come. She *had* to come. Her entire body trembled with need.

"Please, Joe." She barely recognized her own voice now.

"Please what?" His low voice rumbled in her ear.

"Please let me come. I want to come now. God. Right now."

He closed his teeth over her earlobe. "Hmmm. Maybe." He slid his hand down over her mound to find her sensitive clit. "Keep those legs wide open for me."

Wide open? Could she spread her legs any wider? She wanted to squeeze them together as tightly as she could and give in to the climax hanging just beyond reach.

He stroked her clit with his strong fingers and pinched it, just as he bit down on her ear. She screamed as the walls of her channel pulsed and spasmed, desperate for him to fill it, closing over nothing but the heavy stream of water. His strong arm held her in place, his free hand pinching one nipple hard enough to send flashes of pleasure/pain streaking through her system.

When her body finally relaxed, he moved his legs, allowing her to lower hers into the water and press them together. Even such a slight movement took every bit of her remaining strength. A long sigh whooshed from her and she lay limply in his grasp, at once satisfied yet unfulfilled. She wanted more. She wanted him inside her. She wanted everything. If not for the demanding flexing of his unsatisfied cock against her buttocks, she would have thought him unaffected by it all. She felt his shaft slip into the crevice of her ass and she teasingly clenched her buttocks, trapping him there.

"Minx." He took a gentle nip where the tendon of her neck joined her shoulder, a place she was coming to learn was a very sensitive erogenous zone. "Can you feel what you do to me?"

The devil in her brain prodded her to ask him if he did this with all his women but she was through with that train of thought. Other women didn't matter because this was for her. He'd told her he loved her. She was going to take a leap of faith and believe him. He moved his lips back to her ear, the soft breeze of his breath an erotic tickle. Ohmigod! He already had her motor so revved she'd try just about anything with him. She shifted on his lap, rubbing herself against him.

His laugh was a low rumble vibrating through her body. "That excite you? It does me. Just the thought of turning your sweet ass a nice shade of red, then taking you from behind so I can look at it the whole time? Damn. It would make me harder if I didn't already feel like my dick could pound nails."

His words stroked over her nerves, setting up a throbbing again in the walls of her cunt.

"Joe...." She tried to shift again on his lap.

He raked his teeth over her shoulder. "Okay, I think a little more champagne is in order. Something to cool me down." He moved her very carefully, setting her on the sunken ledge along one side of the tub. Then he refilled the champagne flutes and handed hers to her. "To making tonight memorable for you." He touched her glass with his.

"It already is." She drank some of the champagne, feeling the smooth bite of it as it slid down her throat.

Holding the flute carefully, she leaned back against the wall of the hot tub and closed her eyes. The jets coursed water at her in steady streams, like liquid fingers massaging her muscles. Her body hummed with unfulfilled need even while the champagne and the music smoothed out the edges. She thought she could stay like this forever, partially floating on the water. Almost. If only she could feel him inside her.

She startled, eyes popping open when she felt Joe's fingers on her nipples again, tugging as he pulled her toward him.

"What—" Some of the champagne in her glass sloshed over and she licked the drops of champagne from the back of her hand.

"You looked so tempting just lounging there I couldn't keep my hands off you. My intentions were good, darlin' but you just do it to me." He cupped her mounds, gently manipulating them. "Damn, your breasts make my mouth water. Come here, darlin'."

"But—"

He lifted the flute from her fingers and set it on the rim of the tub. "I'm trying to go slow here, Shay. Do the whole seduction thing just right. But Jesus, I don't think I can wait any longer to be inside you. Come here."

His words electrified her, like a charged wand passing over her nerve endings sending urgent messages to every erotic spot on her body.

Gathering her in his arms, he pushed himself to his feet, water sluicing from his body. His mouth on hers was hot and hungry, his tongue a flame probing the inside of her mouth. Her temperature, already on simmer despite the soothing effects of the hot tub, spiked to the top of the red zone. Reflexively she bit down on Joe's tongue, causing him to groan. Looping her arms around his neck, she pressed herself to him, their bodies slick with the water sliding along their skin.

Earlier Shay hadn't noticed the cushions he'd moved to the deck, as astounded as she was about everything else. Her breath caught as the reason for them hit her. God, he'd thought of everything.

* * * *

Joe tore his mouth from hers as he placed her gently on the cushions, stretching out her body and kneeling beside her. His gaze raked her from head to toe and back again. When he nudged her thighs apart to give him a better view of her mound, she shivered in anticipation of what came next.

He had to turn his head from the sight of Shay spread out naked before him or risk embarrassing himself. He'd wanted to take everything slow, seduce her with the champagne and the music and the games in the hot tub. But the joke was on him. Apparently his control easily eroded where she was concerned. He wondered if he'd ever get enough of her. If anyone told him six months ago—hell, six days ago—he was in love with Shay Beckham he'd have laughed them out of the room. Yet there it was, the truth, staring him in the face. And it was strong enough he'd been willing to lay it all out there for her.

Now he just had to make her feel secure enough to say it back.

God, she was tempting. Did she even know what a completely sexual creature she was? His cock certainly took note of it. Straddling her, his knees on either side of her, he began to kiss his way down her body. As he trailed his lips down her neck and onto her breasts, she arched up to him. He forced himself to move slowly as he licked and sucked her very delicious flesh. The valley between her breasts. Her navel and the curve of her tummy. The crease where hip and thigh were joined.

Sliding his hands beneath the cheeks of her ass, he lifted her and put his mouth directly on her pussy. She tasted delectable as he dragged the tip of his tongue along the closed seam, her juices already flowing and coating his mouth. Soft little moans whispered up from her throat, sounds so arousing he scraped hard for his self-control.

He kissed his way down her legs, past her knees to her ankles, then flipped her over, turning her face down on the cushions and began the same careful treatment on her back. He couldn't resist taking little nips at her buttocks or running his fingers through the cleft between her cheeks. At the slow and easy caress, she tightened her muscles around his touch.

Jesus! He couldn't stop himself from pushing in a little more until one fingertip touched the tight pucker of her anus.

"Ahhhhh." The sound rolled from her, vibrating in the air.

"Feel good?" His voice was so raw with emotion he almost didn't recognize it. "One of these nights I'm going to take you right here. Sink my cock into your tight, hot flesh."

He couldn't seem to stop talking, every erotic phrase and word he'd ever learned spilling out of his mouth even as he sprinkled her ass with soft kisses. Her body quivered beneath his touch as he skated his hand up and down between her closed legs and she made those sexy little sounds. Realizing he was tormenting himself as much as her, he reached beneath the edge of the pillows for one of the condoms he'd stashed there and rolled it on.

He took a deep breath to control himself, then let it out slowly and tugged Shay up to her knees. The sight of her positioned this way, the curve of her buttocks, the glimpse of her luscious cunt between her thighs, nearly caused him to detonate. He dragged his fingertips along her cleft, now rich with her cream and brought his fingers to his mouth to lick them clean. Jesus, he loved her taste. Needing to see every bit of her, he shifted position, spread her legs wide, and knelt between them.

"Joe?" Her voice quivered.

"Right here, honey. Coming right up." He placed his hands on her hips to steady her body and drove into her with one swift thrust.

"Oh, God!" Shay threw her head back and pushed against him.

"Christ, baby. This is just fucking good. So hot, so tight, so damn sweet."

Exhaling slowly again he drove into her over and over, setting up a hard rhythm, whispering his dirty talk to her. Her breasts swayed with the force of each thrust as each movement rocked her. Joe's cock filled every inch of her, dragging against her tight walls as he pushed in and out. His balls slapped with a rhythmic sound against her thighs, underscoring her cries of pleasure.

Sweat dripped from his body as he fought to control himself, to hold off as long as possible. Teasing her only ramped up his own arousal, as hungry for her as he was. His balls felt like steel weights and he was sure his cock swelled to twice its normal size. The moment he was sure he'd reached his limit her walls squeezed around him and her body tightened. *Now*, he wanted to shout. Right now.

They ignited together in an orgasm nothing less than epic. Cataclysmic, even. The spasms shook them both as if they were in the grip of a giant fist. Joe braced himself as much as he could, trying his best not to fall forward and crush her body, but the feel of his cock pulsing inside her nearly destroyed him. He held on until the tremors in the walls of her pussy slowed, easing their tight grip on his shaft. When his arms finally gave out on him he rolled to the side, taking Shay with him, still joined with her. He stroked her arm, her leg, her shoulder, calming her as shivers continued to skate over her body.

At last her breathing slowed, became more even. A tremendous sigh whooshed from her and he felt her relax beneath his hand and tuck her head against his shoulder.

"I love you."

The words were so soft at first he wasn't sure he'd actually heard her say them. Damn! Had she really said that? Should he ask her to repeat it? Maybe his scrambled brain had just imagined it. Totally drained, undone by a climax that shook him to his very soul, he couldn't get his thoughts together. Then the moment passed but he was going to cling to those words as if she'd shouted them.

The other night served merely as an appetizer for this, the main erotic course. Shay wiped the memory of every other woman he'd known from his body and his brain. It seemed forever before his strength returned enough to ease himself from her body, even longer until he could push himself to his feet.

"I'll be right back," he mumbled as he staggered off to dispose of the condom.

Jesus! She just wiped him out.

The water bubbling in the spa sent out a siren call to his aching body. He was sure Shay felt the same way. Somehow he found the strength to guide her up from the cushions and back into the hot tub and to refill their champagne flutes. Shay was like a limp rag doll, letting him push and pull her body every which way.

Neither of them seemed able to do anything for the moment but lean back and let the soothing pulse of the jets ease their sore muscles. Physically sated as he'd never been before, he took a long look at Shay, drinking her in. She leaned her body into a corner of the tub, balanced on the seat below the water, a rosy hue coloring her cheeks, a knowing look in her eyes, her lips curved in a sexy, secretive grin.

"I think it was the dancing that did us in," she blurted out.

Joe threw back his head and laughed. "It was dancing all right, but of a different kind." He rose and reached down a hand to her. "Shall we give that incredible food a taste?"

"I don't know if I have the energy to eat," she teased, but she gave him her hand and let him pull her to her feet. He stopped her when she reached for her robe.

"Naked," he said. "I want you naked when we eat."

She hesitated for a moment, then threw back her head and laughed. "Why not? It's that kind of evening, right?"

"Sure is, darlin'."

He smiled to himself as they sat down at the small table. Now they could begin moving forward again. Because one thing he'd learned this entire weekend. He had no intention of letting Shay get away from him. Ever. What he felt for her was too strong. Too powerful. He could tell she felt it, too.

He just had to make sure he didn't screw up.

Chapter 9

Shay came awake slowly, blinking against the intrusion of sunlight through the slightly open blinds. Before she was even fully alert every memory of the night before washed over her, warming her. Everything was amazing. *Joe* was amazing. A sense of euphoria she'd never felt before wrapped around her. If she'd harbored any lingering doubts about the rightness of being with Joe, last night wiped them away. Everything he'd done, for her, to her… She sighed, a smile curving her lips. Life was good. More than good. It was terrific.

She reached out a hand, wanting to touch Joe's hard male body, only to encounter empty space. Her eyes flew open. He was gone? Had he just left her there and gone about his business?

What time was it, anyway? She looked at the nightstand, hunting her clock radio, only to remember she wasn't in her own room. Or her own bed. She was in Joe's bed except Joe wasn't in it with her. Where had he disappeared to? Had he just gotten up and left the house? After the night they'd spent together? Well, that certainly sucked. So much for his fine words and their fantastic night.

Then she rolled over and spotted a torn piece of paper on the nightstand. Her eyes widened as she read the brief scribbled note.

"Woke early. Coffee will be waiting in the kitchen. I'm on the deck. I love you."

Okay, then.

She picked up the paper and hugged it to her breasts. Love. She looked at the word at least ten times. It was one thing to say it but if he wrote it, then he must mean it, right? She needed to quit second-guessing everything. This was a whole new day with her and Joe Reilly. Last night she'd said the *I love you* phrase. Maybe not right out loud but she was sure he'd heard it. No taking it back now. She needed to tuck away the self-doubting little kid who kept popping up at inconvenient times.

She smiled, unexpectedly energized. Her body ached in a number of places, but it was a pleasant sensation, sparking memories that sent warmth coursing through her. Her embarrassment over the incident at the christening party faded as she remembered the hours that followed at home. Smiling to herself, she climbed out of bed and allowed herself a long, pleasant stretch. Last night was the best. The very best.

She could still feel the way Joe's very talented hands played her body like a musical instrument. She'd never look at the hot tub the same again. Who knew the jets that pushed air into the water could be turned into erotic toys? God! The orgasm he'd wrung from her at the end had raced up from the soles of her feet and consumed her entire body. Thank God for the hot tub that soothed her very exhausted body afterward. Lying there with Joe, sipping the champagne, eating the dinner he'd had catered for them, listening to the music floating out from the speakers...

Magic. That was the only word to describe it.

He'd promised her a special evening and he'd been as good as his word. He'd given her a night to remember, including the unexpected dancing and the ungodly expensive champagne. Who knew he'd paid attention to the movie they'd watched and remembered the things she'd liked about it?

She'd been boneless when he carried her to bed, sure they were done for the night. But Joe had woken her twice more, making love to her thoroughly and completely until he'd wrung one last final orgasm from her. Finally he let her fall asleep for good, his body curled around hers, his big hand cupping her breast. She smiled at the memories, even as the slightest movement reminded her how sore she was. It was a pleasant soreness, however, one she welcomed. Even embraced.

And he loved her! She had it in writing.

Rather than go to her room for something to put on, she searched in Joe's drawers for a T-shirt and pulled it over her head. As she brushed her teeth in the bathroom she and Joe shared, images flashed back to her of how incredible last night had been. Of his attentiveness, his passion, his total focus on her all night. A shimmer of remembered pleasure skated over her.

Shay rinsed her mouth and looked at herself in the mirror over the sink. Her lips were still kiss-swollen, her cheeks still flushed even after a night's sleep. Her eyes shone with erotic satisfaction and secret knowledge. She'd carried her feelings for Joe Reilly in her heart since she was a kid, covering them over with sass and attitude, never dreaming it would ever come to anything.

"I hope I'm not fooling myself," she told the happy face in the mirror. But if she was, so be it. She'd made up her mind beforehand to enjoy this and that was what she was going to do.

Then she deliberately banished the negative thoughts from her mind. It was past time to move forward, accept what was happening and tell Joe how she felt. She was gloriously in love with him and she needed to make sure he knew it. He might be a prize package but so was she and she didn't intend to forget it.

She dragged a brush through her hair and pulled it into a ponytail, then headed into the kitchen. With her coffee fixed just the way she liked it, she carried the mug out to the deck. Joe was stretched out on one of the loungers, his own coffee sitting on the small table beside him, eyes closed against the early morning sunlight, clad in a T-shirt and jogging shorts. Even at this distance, she could see the outline of his erection. Lordy! Was the man primed all the time?

She slid open the glass door and he turned his head, opening his eyes.

"I thought for sure you'd sleep late this morning." He held out a hand to her.

"You, too."

Driven by the same need she'd felt last time she saw him lying out here like this, and bolstered by the words in his note, she bent down and pressed her lips to his. He opened his mouth and let his tongue probe gently for hers, the slide of it a gentle caress. She opened her mouth wider and let her tongue tangle with his, tasting him. He slid his hand up along her arm to her head, winding her ponytail around his fingers and holding her in place. She was nearly out of breath when he finally tugged her head up and broke the kiss.

"Whew." She ran her tongue over her bottom lip. "That was just supposed to be a good-morning kiss."

Joe gave her one of his crooked grins. "Your kiss would make any morning good." He studied her face. "Last night was very special, Shay. I hope you believe me."

Heat skated over her body, sending a shiver from head to toe. "Yes, I know that. I mean, you certainly made it extra special for me."

He reached for her free hand. "It was my pleasure." A corner of his mouth kicked into the beginning of a grin. "Well, I hope not *all* my pleasure."

Shay lowered her eyes, heat creeping up her cheeks as memories of the night flashed again through her brain. The things Joe said, the promises he'd made of things to come… Between her thighs a pulse beat insistently, reminding her of just *how* special last night had been. Swallowing a smile, she sat on the edge of the chair beside him, cradling her mug in her hands.

"You signed this 'love'." She dangled the note in front of him. "I guess if you put it in writing, you mean it."

His face sobered. "Darlin', I told you—"

"Ssh." She touched her fingertips to his mouth. "It's okay." She bent low until her mouth was a breath away from his. "I love you, too. A lot."

His smile would have battled the sun for brightness. "I don't think I'll ever get tired of hearing you say that, darlin'." He wrapped his arms around her, pulling her tight to his chest. "I'll never hurt you. I promise. The old Joe is dead and gone. The only woman I want in my life now and forever is you." He kissed her forehead. "Tell me again."

"Tell you what?" she teased.

He pinched her butt.

"Ow! Okay." She looked hard into his eyes, hoping everything she felt would show. "I love you, Joe Reilly. I think I always have."

"Me, too, Slick. I think we just had to grow into it."

She brushed her mouth over his very lightly, pushed herself to a sitting position, and grabbed her coffee cup from the floor where she'd set it. "What are you doing up this early?"

He shrugged. "Force of habit, I guess. I'm always trying to catch up with my schedule. I slept in a little this week. Now it's time to stop lazing around."

"You have stuff to do today?"

"Unfortunately." He took her free hand and laced his fingers through hers. "Don't you?"

Shay let out a sigh. "Yeah." She looked at him and grinned. "Unfortunately."

He burst out laughing. "We're quite a pair. What's up for you today?"

"I have two designs I have to finish for a presentation to one of our clients." She drank from her mug. "One of them is nearly done but the other is turning out to be a pain in the ass."

"Complicated?" he asked.

"Not so much. It's actually the client who's a pain in the ass. I'll get it done today. I promised my boss he'd have it before he left the office tonight. What's on tap for you?"

"Just stuff. This and that." He released her hand and lifted his mug to drink.

Shay frowned, trying to ignore the little thread of unease beginning to wriggle through her. What was it he couldn't tell her about?

"Stuff like the other day?"

He hiked a shoulder. "Not exactly. These are business meetings."

Why did she have the uncomfortable feeling he was avoiding giving her information?

"Oh? Television business?"

"Um, yeah. Sort of."

She set her mug down carefully. "Is there something you don't want to tell me?"

He turned his million-watt smile on her and coasted one hand casually down her spine. "Not at all, darlin'. I have some business meetings dealing with some of my endorsements. That's all. Some corporate glad-handing, shit like that." He took both of their mugs and lightly bit her lower lip. "I told you these are business meetings, and I told you there's no one else in my life now. Will we ever get to the point where you can believe everything I tell you?"

Shay certainly hoped so. She didn't like this edgy feeling that kept popping up.

Joe tugged on her ponytail. "Well?"

She blew out a breath. "Yes. Of course." As if to seal what she said, she gave him a kiss that scorched both of them.

Joe took her hand and placed it over his very erect cock. "Feel what you do to me? You think I'd get hard like this if there was any other woman in my life?" He stroked a hand down her arm. "Believe me, Shay. Believe *in* me, will you?"

"I already said yes. And I meant it."

She hoped.

* * * *

Joe hated being evasive with Shay. They'd come a long way in their relationship but he knew things were not as solid as he would like them. Although he'd planned to tell her when they went to breakfast, he was glad they'd gotten sidetracked with Rafe and Mike and the others. He felt he had a ways to go to prove to Shay who he was now and what he felt for her. He just wanted to wait until the right moment to tell her about the fundraiser and everything else he was doing. He was just back to the same old twitch, still worried she'd think he only did this kind of thing to make himself look good to the public.

She had no idea how often he argued with Scott to minimize the publicity. He agreed to including his name on the invitations. He twisted all the arms he could reach for contributions, both auction items and cash. He pushed his contacts in San Antonio to buy tickets to events and bring their wallets with them to bid on high-dollar items. And he always made a substantial cash gift himself.

But he just didn't feel comfortable with a lot of media coverage. Listening to Shay, realizing the impression she'd carried of him since she was a teenager, and taking a good long look at himself through her eyes, he was even more convinced he'd made the right decision about media coverage. For the first time he understood he needed to feel good with himself before he could ask others to look at him as a solid citizen. He couldn't begin to count the number of professional athletes with images they needed to polish who manipulated the media to do it but gave lip service to actual good works or changes.

Today he had another meeting with Marge Faraday and some of her committee. They would review the list of items for both the silent and live auctions, check the cash contributions they'd received, and go over the guest list one more time. Then he intended to plant himself at a coffee shop out of earshot of Shay. His idea was to call Mike Lazarus and the others he'd exchanged business cards with yesterday and see if he could hook them into the event, too. He knew if he brought some high rollers, Marge would always find a way to squeeze in extra tables. And maybe they were in some industries in a position to contribute merchandise or gift certificates.

Only six days until Saturday, less than a week to solidify himself with Shay and bring her to the event with him. Despite the amazing mind-blowing sex, despite her willingness to spend time with him and her obvious pleasure, he wasn't one hundred percent convinced that he'd accomplished his goal.

Every time he was near her, his cock stood at attention and his balls ached with need. He wondered if she'd be interested in a quick shower—well, maybe not so quick—before she started working this morning. But as soon as he entered the kitchen he heard music coming from the den. He'd discovered when she worked she stuck her iPod in a docking station and set up one of her playlists to run.

"I think better if I don't have to force myself to think," she'd explained to him.

He didn't quite understand but he liked hearing the music when he was in the house, knowing she was there even if he didn't see her. No couples shower on the horizon. He swallowed his disappointment, refilled his coffee mug, and ambled down the hall to where she was working. He suddenly realized that he'd never actually seen any of her creations. Even the red ball cap she'd worn on the plane only earned a passing glance from him. He knew from things Hank said she was considered one of the best graphic artists in the business. Probably the reason her bosses, rather than losing her, had agreed to the current telecommute situation.

He paused in the doorway, just enjoying the sight of her sitting cross-legged in her padded desk chair, frowning in concentration at the screen. She'd pulled on a pair of sweats, but it pleased him that she still wore his T-shirt she'd dragged on when she got up. He took a moment to drink in the sight of her, wondering how someone could be sexy and adorable at the same time. A few strands of hair escaped the ponytail and drifted onto her face. Her smooth forehead was creased in a frown as she stared at the screen. She was so focused on what she was doing, the music obviously blanking out every other sound, she didn't even see him standing there until he rapped lightly on the doorjamb.

She looked up, startled, then smiled at him. At the sight of her mouth lifting so sexily, his cock sent him an urgent message. He sent one back. *Down, boy. Save it for later.*

"I didn't mean to interrupt you." He stopped and shook his head. "Who am I kidding? Of course I did. I wondered if I could get a peek at what you've got going on here."

"It's just a new design I'm working on, for a midsize college." She pushed pause on the iPod.

"Is it still top secret?" he teased. "Because, I swear, my lips are sealed."

"Um, okay. Sure. I guess for you it's okay." Tentatively she turned the screen, allowing him to see it and sat back in her chair, watching him.

The one the other day had been good but this one was outstanding. The design on the screen was three-dimensional and showed a scowling tiger in a batting stance, ready to take a pitch. He could almost see the animal moving. The colors were so vivid they looked freshly painted.

"That's amazing." He couldn't take his eyes from the screen. "You have incredible talent."

"Thank you." She looked up at him. "I love creating these things from scratch, making them different than the others."

"I can see why your boss wants to keep you happy by letting you telecommute."

"If I can manage it today, I'm going to build the Facebook page for Coyotes football alumni. I can get the Coyotes logo and incorporate it into the banner."

"You know, you don't have to do it. I know how busy you are."

She shrugged. "It's no sweat for me and I want to. I genuinely do."

"Okay, then." Juggling his coffee, he bent down enough to brush his lips over hers. "Gotta get going. I'll probably be out most of the day. How about if I take you someplace casual for dinner? Or would you rather eat in? Maybe I could pick some ribs up from Open Pit Barbecue."

"Um." She rubbed her stomach. "Sounds good." She hesitated. "So, what time do you think you'll be home?"

"Late afternoon. Six at the outside."

"A lot of meetings, huh?"

He knew he should just lay it out there for her, but he was edgy about doing it just right.

"Yes. And I'm meeting a couple of guys from the party the other day."

"Oh, wait. I knew I forgot to tell you something." She picked up her phone and scrolled through it. "Don't forget Jason Mackenzie. Remember I told you I ran into Jilly at the store the other day?"

"Yeah? I wonder if Mike knows Jason's here?"

"I'd say no, since he didn't mention him." She reached for a piece of paper and a pen, then scrolled through her phone. "Here. I'll write his number down for you. He's with some big law firm in town. I'm surprised the two hotshot attorneys haven't run into each other before this."

"So, you plan to get together with Jilly?"

Shay nodded. "She said she'd give me a call. She's going to try and get some of our old friends together, too."

"That should be fun." He took the slip of paper.

"I also called Shana and thanked her again for inviting us to the christening and party." A blush crept up her cheeks. "She mentioned the women want to get up an all-female football team to take on you guys."

Joe laughed. He was happy to see her reaching out to these people. "Maybe you can hire me as a coach."

"Are you kidding? We want to beat your ass."

"That'll be the day. Listen, I gotta run but I'll be home by six." He glanced at the screen again. "You rock it, Slick. I'm very impressed."

And horny. She looked appealing as hell sitting there in his T-shirt and sweats, hair in a messy tail. He wanted to strip her out of her clothes and take her right there on the floor.

Lotta class there, jerk. Save it for later.

Which was exactly what he intended to do.

* * * *

"We've done very well, Joe." Marge Faraday smiled at him. "Actually you're the one who's done it. Without you we'd never hit our numbers. Or have the crowd we're expecting."

Joe thought by this time he should have learned to accept praise graciously. But praise for Joe Reilly, the quarterback was different from Joe Reilly, the private person. What he did here was purely because he wanted to help others, not for any other reason. He took a moment to sip at the excellent espresso Marge had served him.

"I just see it as a way to give back to the community. Football was very good to me. I had a lot of opportunities and I want to make sure others do, too."

"Well, we just want you to know the committee appreciates everything you do for the High School Athletes Scholarship Fund."

"I still say that's a mouthful," he told her. "You ought to find someone to kick in a nice fat check and name it after him. Or her."

She exchanged looks with Lily Volta, her cochair. "We've discussed that very thing in committee," Lily told him. "We're tossing some ideas around. We might even make an announcement Saturday night."

"Yeah?" Joe grinned. "Sounds great." He pulled out his phone and scrolled to his notepad. "I've connected with some other guys on my team. I'm going to hook up with them when I leave here and get them involved, too. If I can convince them to come to the dinner as well as kick in for the auction, can we fit them in?"

Marge laughed. "For people with money we can always find room." She leaned forward and touched his arm. "I wish your folks were in town. I know they enjoyed being involved in the other events."

"Yes, they did. They really wanted to be here and hated having to send their regrets. In fact"—he reached into his pants pocket for his wallet and plucked out a check—"they also asked me to give this to you."

Lily looked over Marge's shoulder, her jaw dropping. "That's a very large amount. Are they sure about this?"

He nodded. "Absolutely." He chuckled. "Mom said to tell you since I managed to be gainfully employed they can do something with the money they planned to use to support me."

Marge gave a hearty laugh. "I don't think your folks spent one moment worrying about you. Like Hank Beckham, you were always an overachiever."

"You know we expect you to say a few words at the event," Lily reminded him.

Joe shifted uncomfortably in his chair. "I thought we already discussed that. This isn't my night. It's yours. The whole committee. You're the ones who do ninety-nine percent of the work."

"And you and your friends are the ones who make it possible," Marge pointed out.

Joe set his cup down and stood up. "Can we please not ruin a very nice meeting with an argument? I get plenty of recognition in my job. The important people here are the donors and the kids who benefit from the scholarships. Let's leave it at that, okay?"

Marge rose, also, sighing. "I hear you. Please know how grateful we are for every bit of this."

"I'll call you later this afternoon. I hope to have more big-ticket items to add and some high rollers to attend."

"We look forward to hearing from you."

When the women both looked as if they wanted to kiss him on the cheek, he quickly maneuvered to shake hands with them. He made a cordial getaway and escaped to his car.

He did feel good about the things he'd accomplished with his philanthropic efforts. Hooking up with Mike and Rafe the other day had given him an idea. Maybe they could use the Facebook page when Shay had it set up to contact others from that old Coyotes team. At some point he'd like to get the entire team together, if it was possible. Maybe together they could make more things happen.

As he pulled into the parking lot—if you could call a tiny stretch of pavement a lot—for Java Junction, his cell rang. He lifted it from the console where he stashed it when he was driving and looked at the identification. Scott.

"Let me guess," he said. "Marge called you."

Scott's laugh echoed in his ear. "You haven't lost your skills. Yes, I just got off the phone with her."

"The answer's no," Joe told him.

"Joe." Scott's sigh was so heavy it vibrated across the connection. "We have to have a talk about this. Wait. We *have* talked about this. You're a valuable commodity to them. Let them use you."

"I'm just as valuable without making speeches." He shifted and leaned back in his seat. "I'm not sure you know what a wakeup call it was when I had to retire from the NFL and you made me take a good look at the way I'd been living my life."

"Not in a way to interfere with the game," Scott reminded him. "You never did that."

"No, but I sat down one night and Googled myself and found a shitload of photos and stories from the Saturday night parties I thought were such hot stuff. Not to mention what went on during the months between the end of the season and spring practice. I didn't like what I saw. I made the change as much for my own self-esteem as I did for this job. I won't do anything to make people think I'm just putting on a show."

"But you're not," Scott argued. "You're doing some great stuff. Hey, I know exactly how much money you help raise for these scholarships. That's not puff stuff. The public at least needs to acknowledge you."

Joe opened the car door and stepped out. "I'll think about it. How's that?"

"Think hard." Then he was gone, as usual without a good-bye.

Joe rubbed his jaw. Sooner or later Scott was going to push hard enough he'd have to cave, at least a little. He needed to start thinking about how he was going to do that. But first he needed to tell Shay. No more dancing around this. Besides, he had to let her know about Saturday night.

Things were going really well between them now. His body heated when he remembered exactly how well. Images of the two of them naked did an erotic dance in his brain. But this was about more than sex. A lot more. It was about how much fun they had together, the interests they shared, the way they finally felt comfortable with each other. If they were indeed going to have a future together, he wanted her to understand who Joe Reilly was these days. That all this wasn't just for show. And he was going to do it soon.

* * * *

Shay climbed out of the shower and reached for a towel when her cell phone rang. Damn! She quickly wrapped a big bath towel around her and shoved her dripping hair out of her face before picking the phone up from the vanity counter. The screen readout showed Jilly Mackenzie's name. Why did people always call at the most inconvenient times? But she pasted a smile on her face, even though Jilly couldn't see her, and hit the Accept button.

"Hey."

"Hey. Shay. Bad time?"

Not if Shay didn't mind dripping all over the place. She sat down on the vanity bench and pulled her towel tighter.

"No, not at all. What's up?"

"I called a couple of the girls we hung out with in high school. One of them lives here and two of them are still in Granite Falls. Anyway, they're very excited to know you're back in the area. Are you by any chance free for brunch on Saturday?"

"Wow!" Shay felt a touch of excitement. "I'd love to, but I need to be home by midafternoon."

"No problem. How about eleven-thirty?"

The thought of reconnecting with women she hadn't seen for a long time was exciting. She'd have plenty of time to get home, primped, and dressed in case Joe wanted to take her someplace Saturday night. On the other hand, maybe she could prepare a special night for him the way he had for her.

Really, Shay? You're already planning?

It was just hard not to, the way things were going.

"That would be just great." Jilly named a restaurant known for its excellent brunch as well as being a great gathering spot. "You okay with the time?"

"I am. I'll see you there."

After she hung up Shay stared at herself in the mirror, blotting drops of moisture from her skin with the corner of the towel. All she could think about was last night and Joe and how incredible he'd been. She still couldn't wrap her head around how special he'd made the night for her.

She closed her eyes as the memory of his touch slid over her skin. Talk about an attentive lover. Every touch, every caress had been designed to give her maximum pleasure. She could still feel his hands and his mouth on her, coaxing and teasing, pushing her from one orgasm to another. And the thing with the jet stream in the hot tub? Even now she shivered with pleasure as she remembered it.

It was more than just sex, though, no matter how spectacular that was. Her emotions were all tied up in it. She was truly in love with Joe Reilly.

That scared the hell out of her.

Shay had never thought of herself as an insecure person. She was smart, savvy, a respected graphic designer, had good friends and now was renewing old friendships, and hadn't lacked for dates either in college or New York. She'd even had three long-term relationships. They might not have imploded if she hadn't unconsciously compared each of them to Joe.

For so long she'd seen him as unattainable, convincing herself she wasn't interested in the horny playboy she believed him to be. Believing she wasn't even on his horizon, what with the abundance of over-the-top females who threw themselves at him, everyone from the cheerleaders to homecoming queens to sophisticated models. Now the game had changed and she allowed herself to trust the idea this was something real.

It is, Shay. Very real. He is real. The real Joe Reilly. He loves you and you love him.

She did. She'd made up her mind, finally, to take Joe at his word and now the thought of where this might go filled her with excited anticipation.

She had no idea what would happen when Joe had to leave. He hadn't mentioned anything beyond this time in San Antonio and Shay wasn't pushing him. It would work out. She was determined to believe it.

Again memories of the previous night danced through her brain, so sharp and clear a throbbing set up in her pussy and her nipples tightened and ached. She cupped them through the towel and squeezed her breasts, pretending the hands were Joe's. Electricity sizzled through her and she squeezed her legs together against the thudding pulse between her thighs. Was that slick feeling on her inner thighs from the shower or from her juices sliding from her overheated cunt?

Damn, Shay! Get your act together. You have work to do.

She thought of the photo of Joe Montana on her desk, hoping it would center her. It had been her most-prized possession since she was in high school. When Joe Reilly had paid little attention to her she could always count on Joe Montana to be there. At least his autographed picture. Some nights she'd hugged it to her body and told herself both Joes were equally unattainable.

But now it seemed fate had handed her the opportunity to have her dream man. She wondered idly if she could get Joe Reilly to sign a picture for her. And if he would sign it *Love, Joe.*

Chapter 10

"Shay?"

Joe's voice carried back to her office where she'd been huddled by her computer all day.

"Back here," she yelled.

He leaned against the doorjamb, arms crossed as he took in the sight of her. "Have you even been out of here since this morning?"

She blinked. "Out of here? You mean the house?"

"No, Slick, I mean the office. Have you even eaten?"

She blinked again and took in his mouthwatering image. He'd been dressed in full business attire when he left that morning for his "meetings and stuff" but somewhere on his way to her office he'd ditched the jacket and tie. His dress shirt was open at the throat and he'd rolled up the sleeves to bare his muscular arms covered with a fine dusting of hair. She barely restrained herself from jumping up and licking each arm from wrist to elbow.

Holy shit. She needed to get hold of herself.

"So did you?" he prompted. "Eat? Today?" He frowned. "Slick, are you okay?"

She gave herself a mental shake. "Sorry. Um, yeah. I ate. Sort of. I've just been fixated on getting these two designs done." And doing him.

She slammed that door in her brain tight shut.

"Okay. Enough." He walked over. Lifted one hand and put it on her mouse. "Save this, shut it down, and come with me."

"To do what?"

"I know you grocery shopped, but I couldn't remember what was in the fridge or freezer. And I had a feeling you'd be stuck to your computer since I left. I didn't know if you'd want to get dressed to go out so I brought home ribs with corn bread and coleslaw."

She sat up straighter. "From Open Pit like you said?"

"Uh-huh. But before I let you sit down at a table with me it's off to the shower with you." He lifted her bodily from her chair.

"Hey!" She wriggled in his grasp. "I already showered today."

He buried his face against her neck and inhaled. "And you smell damn good, too." His grin was one of pure lust. "But it's always more fun to shower with a friend."

"Wait! I have to save the document first and shut down the computer."

"Well, get it done."

He tilted her enough to reach the keyboard and her mouse. As soon as the screen went dark, he strode toward the bathroom.

She wound her arms around his neck. "Are you going to bathe me or something?"

His laugh vibrated through her body. "I'm going to bathe both of us, Slick. And then some." He winked at her as he stripped. "There's nothing like shower sex."

"Shower sex?" Why was she just repeating his words?

"You'll love it. Trust me."

He stood her on her feet and peeled off her clothes, taking a moment to place a kiss on each nipple and at the hollow of her throat. By the time he reached in to turn on the shower she was already hot and wanting, just from that brief contact and the thought of what was to come.

He cupped her face, pressed his mouth to hers, and gave her a heated kiss, his tongue tracing the seam of her lips. "I love you, Slick. Have I told you yet today?"

"I don't think so," she whispered. "Maybe you'd better tell me again."

"I love you. I mean that more than you can know."

"Love you, too," she murmured.

A shiver raced over Shay's body, and it had nothing to do with being naked. Well, okay, maybe being naked with Joe. Anticipating what was to come.

When Joe was satisfied the water temperature was where he wanted it, he stepped into the large shower stall, took her hand, and brought her into it with him. When he slid the door closed, steam enveloped them, and Shay wasn't sure it was entirely due to the water. She drank in the sight of him, her gaze moving slowly from head to toe. Joe's magnificent body glistened with drops from the spray, the curls of dark hair on his chest gleaming. Rivulets ran down his well-muscled thighs to his calves. The muscles of his arms and his abdomen stood out in stark relief.

They weren't the only thing standing out. His cock, looking twice as big as the last time she'd seen it, pointed its darkly purple head directly at her. She couldn't help it, she licked her lips.

"I'd rather have you use that tongue on me." Joe's voice was rough with need and hunger.

Shay blinked and looked up at him. The heat in his eyes nearly scorched her body. She rested her palms on his chest, leaned forward, and ran her tongue over first one nipple, then the other. She heard the hiss of his breath and felt his muscles tighten beneath his palms. Teasingly, she closed her teeth over one flat male bud, biting just enough to light a fire in his body. When she moved her mouth to the other one, he placed his palms on either side of her face and eased it away.

"Jesus, Shay. I had a hard-on all day just thinking about you. You touch me like that and I'm ready to go off like a bottle rocket."

Her lips turned up in a satisfied smile. "Just as long as you've got more than one in you," she teased.

"Oh, I've got a lot more where you're concerned, Slick." He took one of her hands and wrapped the fingers around his shaft. "It's waiting for you right there. But I have other things in mind first."

He poured some of her shower gel into his palm, worked it into a lather, and began spreading the soapy bubbles over her skin. His hands were light and gentle as they coasted over her shoulders, her arms, along her neck, and down to her breasts. His slippery fingers kneaded her breasts, his fingers pinching her nipples. Her breathing accelerated as his fingers moved lightly over her, igniting her nerves and sending jolts of electricity through her system.

His palm was warm as he massaged the frothy gel into her tummy, pausing to trace the swirl of flesh in her navel before continuing down, farther down, to her cunt. When she widened her stance in anticipation of his fingers, he simply slid over the soft skin and knelt on the tiles. More gel, more lather, and he massaged it into her legs with infinite care. His touch was as light as a feather as it skimmed from ankle to thigh and back again. She hitched her hips forward, silently urging him to touch her there, but he just gave a low rumble of a laugh.

"All in good time, Slick. All in good time."

Nudging her, he urged her to turn and face away from him, placing her hands on the shower wall, leaning slightly.

"Stand just like that." He placed his mouth next to her ear. "Just. Like. That."

He gave the same intimate attention to her back he had to her front, sliding his large hands down her spine and over the curve of her ass, down her thighs to her ankles again and back up. This time, instead of withdrawing, he slid his soapy fingers into the crevice of her buttocks, lightly rubbing the sensitive skin. When one finger pressed against her puckered opening, she sucked in her breath.

One of these days he was going to take her here. He pressed the tip of one finger to her opening, pushing just enough to breach the tight ring of muscle. Dark need consumed her, a lust unlike anything she'd ever felt before. Fire shot through her, her pussy throbbed, and she clamped down on the intrusive finger.

"Joe!" His name was almost a scream.

When he slid his finger out she wanted to cry out in protest. But then he turned her around, cleaned his hands and soaped them up again. Kneeling before her, he turned his attention to her very needy cunt. The feel of his slippery, soapy finger running the length of her slit made her knees weak and sent heavy vibrations pulsing through her. He paused to touch her clit, just brushing back and forth across the tip, but he might as well have been using a live wire to touch her. She closed her eyes, letting every sensation wash over her, moaning low in her throat at Joe's erotic touch.

When he thrust two fingers into her, she lurched forward, catching herself with her hands on his shoulders, digging her fingernails into his slick flesh.

"Hold on here. I'm going to make you come. Hard."

"Yessss." She rocked back and forth on his hand, erotic heat blazing through her body like a fiery torch.

One of his large hands cupped a cheek of her ass, steadying her as he worked his fingers in and out of her, adding a third as her internal muscles tightened around him. He shifted the angle of his hand slightly so with every slide of his fingers his thumb also brushed across her clit.

Ohgodohgodohgod!

She could hardly stand. If not for her grip on his shoulders she would have fallen to the slippery tile. Steam from the rain mist showerheads billowed around them, carrying the peachy fragrance of her shower gel.

The orgasm started low inside her, unraveling like a tightly wound coil of steel as it surged into every nerve in her cunt. Her legs shook, her breath caught, and she lost all sense of self, of time and place, as Joe coaxed an even higher and hotter response from her. She sucked in her breath when she teetered on the edge of release, but he eased her down despite her moaning protest. Again he took her up and again he backed off. Three times he brought her to the brink until she was sobbing, begging him to let her come.

"Ready?" he asked, his voice rasping in her ear.

"Yes. Oh, yes. Please."

"Okay." He pinched her clit hard, triggering the tidal wave of sensation.

"Joe!" The cry escaped her in a sound so guttural she didn't even recognize it as coming from her.

"That's it. Let it come. Let go. Let it come now."

Did he think she could stop it? Her entire body shuddered as if a giant fist shook her and the muscles in her pussy spasmed again and again. Joe kept up the motion of his fingers and thumb, riding her through the storm. Tremors shook her, the intense orgasm robbing her of breath. If he didn't have his arm wrapped around her to steady her, she would have collapsed to the wet floor.

At last, boneless, gasping for breath, heart thudding against her breastbone, she melted into Joe's embrace. He smoothed her wet hair back from her face, peppered wet kisses over her cheeks.

"We're not done yet, you know." His breath blew against her skin.

Shay lifted her gaze to his face. "What? How—"

"My turn," he whispered, lifting her up.

He placed her on the seat built against one of the short walls of the shower, pulled a condom she hadn't even known was there from the shelf holding shower products, and before she could blink had himself fully sheathed. Then he picked her up as if she weighed nothing.

"Spread your legs, Slick," he whispered.

When she did he positioned her and slowly lowered her onto his rock-hard cock, one incredible inch at a time. When he was fully seated inside her he let out a long, steadying breath.

Shay wound her arms around his neck, anchoring herself, clamping down on the thick rod inside her. God, he felt good. She'd have sworn she didn't have another orgasm in her, that she needed more time to recover. But the moment the head of Joe's cock bumped the mouth of her womb, her nerve endings in every erogenous zone stood up and did a happy dance.

"So good." His voice was a low growl. "So hot. So sexy. I could fuck you forever, darlin'."

Cupping her ass with his hands, he let out a slow breath and began a steady rhythm, driving in and out of her, the sound hot and wet. Shay closed her eyes and hung on tight, letting the sensation build in her again.

They didn't need words. They let their bodies speak for them and the unspoken words were loud and clear.

Over and over he thrust inside her, the thickness of his shaft rubbing the sensitive walls of her channel. Every time he slammed into her the nest of curls on his groin abraded her sensitized clit. God, she was close to the edge again. It shocked her to discover he could coax another response like this from her this quickly.

"Joe?" She pressed down on him as hard as she could, arms tight around his wet neck.

"Yeah, me, too. Jesus." Suddenly his body tensed and his fingers dug into the soft flesh of her ass. "Go with it, Shay. Go with it now."

The explosion matched the force of a fireworks display, powerful and bright and gripping, invading every bit of her body. Joe shuddered from head to toe, every muscle spasming. She couldn't do anything but hang on for dear life until the violence of the storm passed. Finally Joe lifted her from his body and moved enough to place her on the seat again. Almost in slow motion he turned off the shower, opened the door, and pulled her out onto the bath mat with him.

She was surprised he had the strength to dry them both off. Wrapping a towel around her, he lifted her, despite his depleted condition, and carried her to the bed. When she lay stretched out on the sheets, he crawled in next to her.

"My hair," she murmured. "It's soaking wet."

"You can fix it later. Besides," he managed to joke, "I like the wet, bedraggled look." He pulled her against his body and tucked her damp head beneath his chin.

Shay snuggled her body against his, pressing her backside into his—what the hell?—once more hardening cock. Lord, did that thing never rest? A low rumble in her stomach reminded her they hadn't eaten.

"Food," she mumbled. "Ribs."

Joe's low laugh vibrated against her. "I think the ribs will have to wait. I don't think I have the strength to chew right now."

She let out a soft sigh. "Me, either, I guess."

"Nap first." He cupped her breast with one large warm hand, fingers lightly grasping the nipple. Just when she was sure he'd fallen asleep he kissed the lobe of her ear. "Love you, Slick."

A feeling of incredible warmth surged through her. "Love you, too, Joe."

She smiled, closed her eyes, and drifted off to sleep.

Chapter 11

Joe stripped off his jacket and tie as soon as he entered the house and dropped them in his bedroom along with his briefcase. He'd spent the day in more business meetings about both the fundraiser and the Coaches Conference meeting coming up on Monday. He was more than ready for some downtime with Shay.

Shay.

Falling in love was bigger than he'd ever imagined it would be. And with Shay? It was like getting the pot of gold at the end of the rainbow. At first he'd astonished himself at how fast this thing with her happened, until he realized he'd probably been half in love with her for a long time, even though they hadn't seen each other since they were kids except the one time. Now he was convinced fate—or maybe Hank Beckham—had a hand in this. Whatever, he was going to grab onto it with both hands and not let go. Because what he felt for Shay was lasting and real and solid.

Today as he'd gone about his meetings he was smacked by the thought in less than a week he'd be finished here in San Antonio. The fall season would be starting soon and he had obligations to fulfill, beginning with his program. His career. He had to sit down and talk to Shay about what came next. Moving to San Antonio wouldn't be practical for him, but would she uproot herself to come to Houston with him? Would she believe they'd reached that stage in their relationship yet? He'd told her he loved her. Now he realized he wanted to marry her, but had he proven himself to her enough that she'd accept his proposal?

Shit. Why did things have to be so complicated?

Well, whatever. There was very little time left to figure it out so he'd better get his brain busy.

As usual, Shay was in the den at her computer, concentrating hard.

"Shay?" He said her name softly, trying not to startle her.

"What?" She jerked her head up. "What time is it?" She looked at the clock on her computer. "Holy crap. It's after six o'clock." She leaned back in the chair and blew out a breath.

Okay, this was getting to be a habit.

"I think you need a keeper, Slick. This is the second time I've come home and found you all wrapped up in your work. I get it that you have to concentrate. I know the feeling." He tugged on her ponytail and when she tilted her head back pressed a brief kiss to her lips. "And again, I'll bet you didn't eat today. Right?"

"Um, I'm sure I did." She wrinkled her forehead. "I just can't remember what."

"You definitely need a caretaker." Joe laughed. "Time to shut down for the night. I thought about taking you out to grab a bite but I've had a long day and the evidence tells me you did, too. I opted to pick up fresh sandwiches from your favorite deli and a six-pack of Lone Star. Let me get out of these clothes and I'll meet you in the kitchen." He took a slow breath. "There's some stuff I want to run by you, too."

She quirked an eyebrow. "Run by me? Sounds pretty ominous."

Way to go, slug. Very romantic.

"Not at all. In fact, probably just the opposite. I mean—" How did he suddenly get so tongue-tied? "It's good. Very good." He hoped.

"If you say so. But I want to show you something first. Come here." She crooked a finger at him.

He walked over to stand behind her, eyes widening at what he saw. "You created the Facebook page. Wow! It looks terrific."

She'd designed a banner that incorporated a version of the Coyotes logo as well as a graphic of the championship trophy. Somehow she'd worked in an animation of two guys throwing a football back and forth.

"How the hell did you do that?"

She flexed her fingers and gave him an impish grin. "Talent, of course. Lots of talent."

He bent down and planted a kiss on her lips. "Of course," he repeated. "I knew it all the time. Great job, darlin'." He tugged her ponytail. "Let's eat and we can go over it again later. You can tell me what you still need and we can begin to create a list of the players."

"I'll bet a lot of them are already on Facebook. Everyone is on Facebook these days."

"That will make it easy. We can do it together. After—"

"After we eat. I know. Let me just grab a quick shower." She grinned at him. "By myself. Much as I love your version of showering together, I

Desiree Holt

think tonight I'd like to eat before the late news." She saved the file and unfolded herself from the chair. "Ten minutes, fifteen tops. Okay?"

"I'll change and get everything set out."

But he stood in the doorway a moment watching her walk away, admiring the sway of her hips and the sexy movement of her ass.

Face it, Reilly, you're a goner.

He was. Tonight after dinner they would have a serious conversation. If she felt about him the way he felt about her—and he was pretty sure she did—they could make plans for the future. First, he'd give her the skinny on the fundraiser and the Coaches Conference and the other things he spent his time on. And tell her he wanted her with him Saturday night.

He decided they should eat first before he got into anything heavy. The food and beer would mellow them out and he could just coast into the conversation. Coast. Yeah. Very smooth. But what he planned to say was more important than almost anything else he'd done in his life and he didn't want to screw it up. He damn sure didn't want to be living in a different city than the woman he loved.

The more he thought about it, the more determined he was to make this work. She'd told him she loved him. He'd keep hanging onto that.

He made small talk during dinner, telling her about a couple of the interviews coming up for his show. Asked her if she'd finished her designs and what her boss thought. And what she had on tap next. They were sitting in the living room with fresh drinks when he brought up the subject of Hank. He wasn't sure exactly how his friend would react to this situation, or if it had been his doing to begin with.

"Have you heard from Hank lately?"

"No." She shook her head. "Not even a text for a couple of days. What about you?"

"Me, either. I tried him today but didn't get an answer."

Shay laughed. "Wherever he is in Wyoming they must be surrounded by the Grand Tetons with almost no reception. Usually I can at least get a text through but I haven't been able to since the beginning of the week."

"Me, either."

At that moment, however, both of their cell phones went off. Shay pulled hers out of her pocket and laughed. "Speak of the devil."

Joe looked at his and every muscle in his body tensed. Lisa. What now?

"This is business," he told Shay. "I'll take it outside. I don't want to bore you with this stuff."

"Hey. Your business doesn't bore me."

He faked a smile. "But I might have to do some yelling, and I don't think I want you to hear me."

Without making more of a big deal than it was, he headed out to the deck, sliding the glass door shut behind him. Sucking in a deep breath, he answered the call.

"Yeah, Lisa, what's up?"

"Joe." Panic laced her voice. "Joe, I need your help right now. You have to come."

He struggled to keep his voice calm. "Is this about Gina?"

"Of course it's Gina. Why else would I call you? Please, Joe, you have to come."

"First you have to tell me what happened." He looked at his watch. "It's eight-thirty at night. Are you home? Did something go wrong at work for her?"

He could almost see Lisa dialing it back before she spoke. "Yes, something happened. She got fired. Canned. Booted out the door this afternoon."

Joe frowned. "Why? I thought this was a good thing for her. Jesus, Lisa, she just got hired."

Silence hummed across the connection.

"Lisa?" he prompted.

"Apparently she went to lunch with a couple of the other girls and drank one cocktail too many. She was sloppy drunk when she got back to work and they terminated her right then and there."

"Jesus Fucking Christ." Joe wanted to throw something. Would the woman never learn? How many stints in rehab would it take? "Where are you? At the apartment?"

"No. See, that's the problem."

"*What's* the problem? Damn it, spit it out. What's going on?" Silence. "Lisa? Tell me."

"We're at a bar near Westshore. I guess she came here after she got fired. Joe, she's so blitzed she can hardly stand up. The bartender got my number from her somehow and called me. But I can't handle her myself, and she's about to cause a scene."

Fuck, fuck, fuck.

He did not need this right now. He'd get Gina out of the damn bar and get her home and then he'd remind both of them he was well and truly done. He'd discharged every sense of obligation he'd ever felt. If she couldn't make the smallest effort on her own, he was done with it.

"All right. I'm on my way. Get her into the ladies' room if you can. I'll call you when I'm out front."

"Thank you." There was no mistaking the relief in her voice "You know I wouldn't have called you unless—"

"Yes. I get it. But Lisa? I'm done after this. Period."

Shay was standing in the kitchen when he opened the door from the deck, studying him with narrowed eyes.

"So what was such a big deal you went outside to have your conversation?"

Here was the tricky part.

"I hate to do this to you, but I have to go out for a little bit. I won't be long." He hoped. "I promise."

"Can I come with? I'll keep you company."

"I'd love it, but I can take care of it faster myself." He pulled her in tight to his body and kissed her hard, his tongue sweeping into her mouth. He was breathless when he lifted his head. "Think that will hold you until I get back?"

"Um, sure." She looked slightly dazed.

"And then we'll have the conversation I mentioned."

Suspicion flashed in her eyes. "Care to give me a hint what you want to talk about?"

He brushed his mouth over hers one more time. "No, but I promise you'll like it. Word of honor." At least he hoped she would.

In less than five minutes he'd changed into jeans and T-shirt, shoved his bare feet into deck shoes, and was out the door and in his car. Driving as fast as traffic allowed to the bar where Lisa had told him they were, he alternated between swearing under his breath at how he'd let his involvement with Gina drag on this long and praying he hadn't fucked up his relationship with Shay because of it.

The Hot Spot sat right on Kennedy Boulevard and luckily there was a parking spot right in front. He cursed the fact there was no alley where he could slip in and out easily, or no parking lot in back but it was what it was. He pulled out his cell and dialed Lisa.

"I'm out front. Can you manage to get her out by yourself?"

"I don't know." She sounded panicky again. "Can you meet us inside? I can at least get her out of the ladies' room."

Fuck. Double fuck.

"Yeah, okay. Get moving."

He eased into the bar and hovered near the front door until he saw Lisa emerge from the restroom, holding Gina up as best she could. In two strides, Joe was next to them.

"Thank you." She blew out a breath. "I don't know what I would have done—"

"Yeah, yeah, yeah. Save it. Let's get her ass out of here."

"Joe? Thass you?" Gina looked up at him bleary-eyed. "Good ol' Joe. Always bails me out. Gimme a big fat kiss."

Joe bit back his immediate retort. "Come on, Gina."

"Hey, evr'one." She waved her hand at the room. "Look who's here. The fam's Joe Reilly. Gimme a kiss," she repeated, pursing her lips.

"Yeah, Joe," someone hollered from the crowd. "Let's see you give her one of those famous Reilly kisses."

Shit. Shit. Shit.

"Hey, Joe." A tall, beefy guy in a T-shirt and jeans swaggered up to them. "If you don't want her, hand her off to me. Or maybe we could make it a threesome. I heard rumors you used to like threeways." He looked at the crowd and grinned when people began clapping.

Joe gritted his teeth and forced a calm to his voice. He didn't need to antagonize this guy. "Look, man, I'm just trying to help a friend. Get her out of here."

"Yeah, I know all about your 'friends.'" He winked and turned back to the crowd. "Right, everyone? We know all about Joe Reilly and his women."

"We sure do," someone yelled. "Go, Joe."

Joe was about to lose it. "Do us both a favor," he told the man, "and go back and sit down. Don't make a bad situation worse."

Instead the man took a step forward. "You gonna make me?"

Great. Just what he needed. A confrontation. "No, I'm just asking you man-to-man, to please give me a little space here to help my friend."

"Hey." Gina looked up at him, hair falling over her face. "Did someone say threeway? Always wanna'd ta have one with you, Big Joe." She pursed her lips. "Gimme a kiss," she begged again.

"Please, Gina." It took tremendous effort to keep his anger in check. "Let's just get out of here. Come on."

"No." She stopped, nearly falling backward. He barely caught her before she landed in someone's lap.

"Guess you're having trouble with your women," another guy joked.

Joe used every ounce of control to rein in his temper when what he really wanted was to smash the guy's face in. The last thing he needed, though, was to get into a bar fight. He glanced at the patrons and realized by now the little scene was the focus of everyone's attention. Conversation in the bar was reduced to a muted hum as people turned in their seats at the tables and at the bar to watch what was going on with avid interest. A woman in a barely there dress hopped in front of them with her cell phone and snapped a series of pictures.

Fuck again.

"Please, everyone, I'm asking nicely. Just get out of our way," he ground out through clenched teeth. He made another attempt to clamp Gina to his side and steer her to the door, but she dragged her feet.

"Not leaving." She grabbed his shirt to steady herself. "Came to have fun."

"Come with me." He gritted his teeth and grabbed her arm. "Right now. Come on, Gina."

Lisa reached for her friend's other arm, but Gina jerked it away.

"Leave me alone," she shouted. "Hey, everyone!" She waved her hand wildly. "Lookit me with Joe Reilly. But holy damn shit! He won't gimme a kiss." She puckered up her lips again and made loud kissing sounds.

"You tell him, lady," someone shouted. "Give us a lip-lock for a good picture."

"Jesus Christ." Joe swore under his breath and reached out to yank Gina against his body again. "Lisa, get on her other side."

He had to get out of here before he punched someone in the face.

Gina was as determined not to be contained as Joe was to keep her in check. She pushed Lisa away and gave Joe an unexpectedly hard shove, pushing him sideways into an empty chair. He threw up an arm to balance himself and clipped Gina right on the jaw.

"Ow!" she hollered. "You hit me! He hit me, everyone."

Holy Jesus Fucking Christ.

He reached for her and caught her blouse instead, the fabric tearing in his hands as Gina tried to pull away from him. Somehow she lost balance and tumbled to the floor. She continued shouting at the top of her voice, swearing drunkenly, slurring her words.

"Hey!" she yelled from her crumpled position. "Lookit, everyone. He hit me and now he tore my clothes. Big Joe Reilly beats up women."

"Get away from her," a man yelled. "You into physical abuse with women?"

Someone else grabbed his arm and when Joe tried to jerk it away the guy swung at him and connected with his nose. There was no mistaking the blood trickling down his face.

Shit!

The guy still had hold of his arm. He shoved the man as hard as he could, pushing him into the people crowded behind him. More voices shouted at him and, crap, now everyone was getting into the act. By the time Joe could reach down to pick Gina up bodily from the floor, lights were blinking around him. Goddamn it! Half the patrons had their cell phones out videoing the whole fucking mess. They crowded close like hungry spectators at a rock concert or a crime scene. Joe Reilly in a bar fight manhandling his drunken girl friend.

Double fuck.

When he tried to lift Gina she gripped his shirt and pulled hard enough that it tore. Shit. What else could happen? No, not tempting fate with that.

The crowd was pressing in on him.

Thank God the bartender moved into the scene and moved to restore as much order as he could. Lisa was damn little help.

"Get to the door," he snapped at her.

It didn't help matters that he caught the toe of his shoe on something and staggered through the open door, nearly dropping Gina. Or that a crowd had gathered outside, watching with avid curiosity. He knew exactly what this looked like, Gina drunk as a skunk with her torn clothing and a bruise blossoming on her cheek, and him with a rip in his shirt and blood dripping from his nose.

Fucking great.

Of course half the damn bar followed them outside.

Cursing under his breath, Joe yanked open the passenger door of his car. He got Gina into the car and buckled in, and motioned Lisa into the back. Doing his best to ignore the mob with cell phones still in video mode, he jogged around to the other side of the car, using his shirttail to swipe at his face. He threw himself into the driver's seat, cranked the ignition, and laid rubber as he peeled away from the curb.

Shit, shit, shit.

* * * *

Shay clicked through the channels yet another time without finding anything to watch. Nothing seemed to catch her interest. Oh, who the hell was she kidding? The only thing her interest was focused on at the moment was Joe Reilly and his mysterious phone call. If it was just business, why couldn't he take it in the house? Why did he have to go outside as if he was hiding some mysterious secret?

All her carefully hoarded opinions of Joe "The Playboy" Reilly came thundering back at her. Maybe he'd just been playing a part this past week or so. Maybe he just wanted to get in her pants.

No.

Wait.

There were many panties Joe Reilly could get into without having to scam someone. She was being ridiculous.

Wasn't she?

Cycling through the channels again, she came to one of the Fox Sports channels showing a repeat of the Joe Montana program and stopped on it. Maybe she should have stuck to this Joe and not gotten in way deep with the other one. But he'd been so damn good to her, warm and caring. Not to mention the hot sex. She'd finally believed him when he said he loved her. She'd certainly lost her heart to him, although truth to tell, she'd given it to him a long time ago.

Where the hell was Hank when she needed him? Her big brother could talk her through this, point out how foolish she was. Convince her this really was the new Joe, not the old one.

So where had Joe disappeared to? What about that call was so secret he couldn't share it with her? If someone had an emergency, maybe she could even help.

Unsatisfied with her previous text exchange with Hank, she hit the Message icon on her phone and selected his number.

"Where r u? When r u coming home?"

There was a long pause and she wondered if he was out in a no-contact zone again. Then her phone chimed.

"Still working on project. U and Joe doing ok?"

Yeah, just great. She'd gone and fallen all the way in love with him and now she was afraid she'd let herself be tricked.

"Sure but be nice if u could b here."

The answer came back almost at once.

"Glad things r good. Wrapping up here. Hope to be home soon."

"Good."

She wanted to say sooner rather than later would be good but she also didn't want him asking probing questions from hundreds of miles away.

She tried to concentrate on the Montana special but her mind kept wandering. When she glanced at her watch she realized Joe had been gone three hours. What could possibly take him away at night for so long? What wasn't he telling her? She was about to send him a text when the ring tone on her phone sounded. She was surprised to see Jilly Mackenzie's ID. What on earth could she want this late?

"Hey, Jilly. What's up? Everything okay?"

"Depends on your definition of okay, I guess." Her voice sounded strained.

Shay's stomach knotted. This didn't sound good. "What do you mean?"

"Jason just got a disturbing phone call." She said the words slowly.

"From?" Shay prompted.

"One of the guys at his firm who knows he was a Coyote. About Joe Reilly."

Nausea threatened to rise to full bloom. "What about him?"

"Is he still there? Are you and he still, you know…"

Yes, we're still "you know."

"He's out right now. What's going on, Jilly?"

"I don't know how deep your situation with him has gotten, but there's something you should know about."

"Like what?" She bit back her frustration. "Tell me why you called. I promise you the new Joe Reilly is nothing like the old one." She hoped. "Just spit it out."

"Okay." She heard Jilly blow out a breath. "This guy told Jason his kid saw something on YouTube he should check out. At first Jason thought it was some kind of joke." She paused. "I'll warn you ahead of time it's not pretty."

"Oh my God." Panic surged. "Was he hurt? In an accident?"

"Mm, not exactly. Go ahead and pull up the site and type in his name. I don't have any details about it but you can call me back after you see it. I'm here for you."

"Okay, thanks."

What the hell?

Shay hung up, pulled up YouTube on her phone, and typed in Joe's name, her hands shaking. What she saw made her literally ill. She swallowed back the nausea bubbling up in her throat, blinked her eyes, and forced herself to focus again. The video was poor quality, obviously from someone's cell phone camera, and it was rather dark and fuzzy but there was no mistaking what she saw. Joe Reilly with a woman she'd never seen before, in a bar. It was obvious the woman was drunk and causing a scene, but Joe didn't look too great himself, especially when he nearly fell into a nearby chair. It was also very apparent she was no stranger to Joe. There was a familiarity about their interactions that made Shay want to throw up.

Another woman was with them, also unknown. Was Joe out with the two of them? She couldn't make herself tear her eyes away from the hideous video as it unrolled. By the time all of them exited the bar, Joe stumbling at the door with his shirt torn and the woman in his arms, Shay had passed being upset and was high-voltage mad. She watched as Joe buckled the drunken woman into the car, hurried around to the driver's side, and drove away from the curb, tires screeching. That was where the video ended.

Shay sat for a long moment, wondering if she was going to faint. Joe, with two drunk women in a bar. Joe, nose bleeding. Hitting a woman. His shirt torn. And on the verge of a full-out bar brawl. Joe, stumbling out of the bar to his car. Who the hell had let him drive off, anyway? The way he looked he might kill someone.

Finally she forced herself off the couch and into the kitchen. She drank a glass of cold water standing at the sink, trying to calm her shattered nerves and pull her thoughts together. She was still holding the phone when her ringtone sounded again.

Jilly.

Pulling a calming breath, she answered the call.

"Are you okay?" were Jilly's first words. "You didn't call back."

Was she okay? A hysterical laugh threatened to escape. No, she was far from that but she wasn't about to let Jilly know.

"I think it's either a mistake or someone was playing a trick." Shay was proud of how together she sounded. "I'm going to call Joe right now. If he's seen it, I'll bet he's having a fit."

"Shay?" Jilly sounded concerned. "Honey, I hate to tell you this but that video's already gone viral. It's got over a million hits in just a short time. And the kid who posted it is already tweeting he saw it firsthand."

Anger began to replace the nausea, chills raced over her body, and her hands shook. How could he do this? To himself? To them? To his career, for God's sake? He'd done the big romantic night and captured her heart and now this?

"Shay? You still there?"

She swallowed twice before she could speak again. "I'm here. I'm sure there's a rational explanation for this. Joe isn't like that anymore. He certainly wouldn't hit a woman. That's so far from who he is."

Or was it? Maybe she had just been stupid enough to let herself be fooled.

"Well, if he was caught up in a bad situation, he'd better jump on it right away."

"I'm sure he will."

"Let me know if we can do anything, okay?"

"Uh, yeah. Thanks, Jilly."

Thanks for ruining her night. Oh wait, Joe had done that.

She disconnected the call and dropped into one of the chairs at the kitchen table. Before she rushed too badly to judgment she'd call Joe. Talking to him was the first order of business. Find out exactly what this was about. But the call went directly to voice mail. She waited a few minutes then tried again. Same result.

She glanced at the clock and realized it was now close to midnight. Her anger spun through her, resentment at whatever Joe had done to put him—and them—in this position. Several more attempts to contact him gave her the same results. There was no way she was going to sleep tonight, not with the miserable video out there and a mountain of questions swirling around in her brain. She fixed herself a cup of coffee and carried it into the living room, where the television was still a low hum in the background. She sat down on the couch to keep trying Joe's phone. And to wait.

Chapter 12

Lisa shoved her hair back from her face and looked up at Joe.

"I gave her ibuprofen and some ice in a baggie for her face."

"Yeah, sorry about that." He shoved his hands in his pockets. "Not a fun night."

"It was her fault." A sad expression crept over her face. "She really has no one to blame but herself."

By the time they'd gotten Gina back to the apartment and up the stairs to the second floor, she'd gone from drunk and shouting to drunk and sobbing and finally to drunk and sick. She'd vomited until Joe was sure not even the lining in her stomach was left. Then he stood her in the shower, fully dressed, turning it gradually from warm to cold until she was aware enough to stand on her own. He left her sputtering and swearing while Lisa helped her into boy short pajamas and into bed.

He took a moment in the bathroom to wash the blood from his face and examine his war wounds. Gina had scratched him in a few places, but his nose didn't look as bad as he expected. He wiggled it a little and gave thanks it wasn't broken.

Now he was faced with the wreckage the night caused.

"I don't know how to thank you," Lisa said. "I never could have managed without you."

He bit back his wrath. "I understand, but this is the end. I mean really the end. If she gets in trouble again, it's all in your hands."

"But—"

"I mean it. I told you the other day. I've been bailing her out and helping her for years. Nothing ever seems to take for her and I can't put myself through this anymore. I have a life of my own to live."

Which may be in ruins, he thought, *if anyone posted that video on YouTube.* Which they probably had. The thought of Shay seeing it made him physically ill.

Lisa twisted her hands. "But she has no one. You know what a mess her family is."

"I can't make it my problem anymore." He blew out a breath. "Here's what I'll do. Tomorrow I'll find a good residential rehab facility and she signs herself in for as long as it takes to get her straight. I mean with counseling and everything."

"And then what? She'll just go right back to the same old thing."

"If she stays until they say she's good to go, joins AA, and gets her shit together, I will send you a check once a month until she gets on her feet. But only for six months. After that she's on her own. I mean it." He gave Lisa a tired smile. "You're a very good friend to her. I hope she appreciates it. I don't know why you haven't washed your hands of her before this."

"She's like the sister I never had. And when she's sober, we take care of each other."

"Well, I wish you good luck." He reached into his pocket, pulled out his money clip, and handed most of what it held to Lisa. "This should help with whatever you need for the next few days. I'll make the arrangements I told you about and text you the information. But pay attention. I meant what I said. You can't call me anymore. At all." He rubbed his scruffy jaw. "I have things going on in my life now, and I can't let this spill over into them."

"I understand. I absolutely do." She sighed. "I'll have a long talk with Gina in the morning and I'll watch for your text." She studied his face. "Listen, do you want some ice for your nose?"

"No, thanks. I think that's the least of my worries. I'd better get going."

Back in his car he pulled out his cell, which he'd placed on mute earlier, and swore. Messages and missed calls from Shay. A lot, mostly in the past hour. Why? Same from Scott. At this time of night? What in hell? Texts and missed calls from his producer? From Marge Faraday? What the fuck was going on? Who had a stick up their ass and about what on a Thursday night? He wanted to call Shay, but if Scott was hot after him this time of night, something was wrong. Swallowing an oath, he punched his agent's number.

"You asshole," were the first words out of Scott's mouth.

"What? Hey, what the fuck? What did I do?"

"You swore to me you'd changed. That you'd cleaned up your playboy act." Scott's voice was tight with anger. "That you were the original solid citizen."

"I am. For five years now."

"Yeah? Really? Or were you just hiding it well?"

Hiding it? Was he kidding? "I don't know what the hell you're talking about."

"I'm talking about your drunken disaster at a bar tonight," Scott snapped, "with an equally drunk woman. No, make that a full-out brawl, both of you with your clothes ripped, you with a bloody nose and some woman with a bruise on her cheek, your hand gripping her torn blouse. The only thing missing were the nude dancers."

Shit. Damn fucking shit.

"Um, Scott?" He shifted uncomfortably in his seat.

"Don't 'um Scott' me, asshole. I'm sending you a link to a video with more than a million hits already. Watch it and call me back. Immediately."

"But I—"

But the man was gone. In a moment he got the sound of an incoming text and opened it. Hit the web link embedded in it. Watched the video. And nearly passed out. He had no idea which of the many people with cell phones had uploaded this but they'd caught every miserable moment of it, including his near fall going out the door. And if he knew human nature, this wouldn't be the only one. Of course it looked like they were both drunk as skunks and could barely navigate.

Joe gritted his teeth and restrained himself from tossing the phone out the car window. More than almost anything he wanted to find whoever posted the video on YouTube and wring their neck but there were more important things for him to do. Like massive damage control. Reaching for some measure of sanity, he called Scott back.

"I can explain," he began.

"You damn well fucking better," the agent snapped. "Hitting a woman? Ripping her clothes? Getting a bloody nose? After everything we've done to clean up your act, after all the time I've spent—"

"Will you just take a breath and listen to me?" Joe interrupted. "I know what it looks like but it was…something else."

"Then explain it to me."

Joe did, in great and awful detail, going all the way back to Granite Falls High School. When he finished there was nothing but silence humming across the connection.

"So," Scott said at last. "Let me get this straight. This girl took your virginity when you were in high school so you have a soft spot for her. She shows up a few years ago and you bang her for one night. Then she shows up a couple more times and you discover she's got a problem with alcohol. Am I right so far?"

"Yes." Joe rubbed his forehead, trying to ease the pounding pain. Even to his own ears it sounded incredibly stupid. What the fuck had he been thinking about, not just tonight but all this time?

"So you help her because you say she's got no one else. But fucking shit, man, for seven years? That doesn't make you a saint, it makes you a fucking idiot. You have no other relationship with her, you've moved on to other things in your life, she needs to be someone else's responsibility."

"Listen to me. She's had a really tough life. Her family—"

"I don't give a flying fuck about her family. You're the one who concerns me. So, tonight when her friend called, you jumped in your car and risked everything you've worked for, not to mention your new relationship with Shay, for a female who can't stay sober? Did I get that right?"

Joe squirmed in his seat. The man was right. Dragging it out for as long as he had was completely irrational.

"She's had a tough life," he repeated.

"Yeah? *I've* got a tough life with the mess you made of it now. You gonna take care of me?"

"I'm sorry, I—"

"Sorry doesn't cut it, asshole. I've had Marge Faraday screaming in my ear all evening. Fox Sports wants to break your contract. Your Coaches Conference is on hold as well as your endorsements. I've got your sponsors screaming for your blood. I guess the whole world plays on YouTube."

Shit, shit, shit.

Joe pounded his fist on the steering wheel. What a gigantic clusterfuck. All his own fault. He should have cut Gina loose long ago. Was he just pandering to his own ego, playing the patron saint? Any personal connection that existed long ago had disappeared.

"What do you want me to do?"

"I want you to put me to sleep and when I wake up none of this will have happened. Since that's not possible, I have no choice but to fly out to San Antonio and see how we can clean up this mess. Go home and stay there. Don't talk to anyone. Don't answer your phone for anyone but me. Can you manage that, hotshot?"

"Yes." Did he even have a choice? "Well, I hope so."

"What the hell does that mean?"

Joe shifted uncomfortably in his seat. "I, uh, I mean—" Jesus! Why was he stammering like this? "I need to get home and talk to Shay."

"Damn straight you do." Scott's voice was so loud Joe was sure he could hear it without the phone. "Wait until Hank finds out."

Joe cared more about Shay's reaction than Hank's, but he wasn't looking forward to either conversation.

Scott pitched his voice lower. "You'd better not screw her over, or there'll be even more trouble."

"Damn it, Scott." Joe raked his fingers through his hair. "I've been behaving myself since our come-to-Jesus meeting five years ago. And Shay is the very last person I would screw over."

"Then you'd better hope when you get home she doesn't throw your ass out in the cold. Or roast your balls. Or both."

Then he was gone.

Joe stared at his phone. Yeah, he'd better hope that. And pray.

* * * *

Shay hadn't bothered to turn on the light in the living room. After crying for nearly an hour her eyes were too light sensitive so she'd curled up on the couch in the dark. As the minutes passed so did her pain, replaced by overwhelming anger. So Joe got into a bar fight? And punched a woman? What the hell? When she saw him he'd be lucky if she didn't punch him herself.

She was still sitting there in the dark when headlights swept through the window, illuminating the room, and she heard the sound of Joe's car engine in the driveway followed by the slam of the car door. Next came the scrape of his key in the front lock, the door opened and there he was. He stood there for a moment, silhouetted by the light from the street, obviously unaware of her presence. After a moment he closed the door, wandered into the living room, and dropped into the big easy chair. He looked so defeated, for a very brief moment she almost felt sorry for him.

Almost.

Hitching herself up, she snapped on the lamp on the end table and blinked at the sudden intrusion of light. Joe lifted his head and stared at her, the expression on his face a mixture of dread and embarrassment and a few things she couldn't name. Not to mention the disaster that was his nose and the tear in his shirt. After seeing the video she wasn't surprised by his appearance.

"Before you say a word," she told him, "I want you to move out. Tonight. Now."

He leaned forward, elbows on his thighs. "Can I just ask you to listen to me for a minute? There's been a big misunderstanding here."

"Yes," she agreed, "there has. And apparently I'm the one who misunderstood." She rose from the couch, proud of the fact that she had pulled herself together. She would not let him see what this had done to her. "I texted Hank to tell him about this. Of course I had to put emergency in the subject line to get him to respond but he did call. He agrees you going to a hotel would be best."

He pushed himself out of the chair and she tried to ignore the look of abject misery on his face.

"I have to talk to you. There's so much you don't understand. Give me ten minutes. Five minutes." There was no mistaking the desperation in his voice. "Anything. Just let me explain to you."

"I got all the explaining I needed on YouTube." She swallowed the bile rising in her throat. "Nice video, by the way. From the number of hits it has already you're a big star again. Congratulations."

He reached for her arm, but she backed away from him.

"Hit me." His voice sounded like rusty nails on gravel. "Kick me. Do whatever. It's nothing I haven't been doing to myself. But just give me a chance to tell you what really happened."

"What really happened?" She shook her head in disbelief. "I saw it all in living color. If there was something wrong, you could have told me before you raced out of here like the world was ending. I thought we had something good here. Something real. That we could tell each other anything. Apparently I was the only one on that side of the equation."

She turned and headed out of the living room. She had to get away from him.

"Wait. Please. I'm begging you."

She stopped. "I waited for hours. I'm done waiting. I believed you, Joe. I gave you my heart and you just trashed it. But I won't let you trash my pride. We have nothing else to say to each other."

She was proud she made it to her room without faltering. But once inside, with the door closed, she collapsed on the bed, fresh tears running down her cheeks, only this time they were tears of anger. How dare he do this just when things were going so right for them? Damn him anyway.

Burying her face in a pillow, she did her best to ignore the knock on the door.

"Shay? Open the door and let me talk to you."

"Go away," she shouted. "And don't come back."

"Not until I have a chance to explain to you."

"I don't want to hear it. It's just more lies, anyway." She thought about pulling the pillow over her head to shut out the sound of his voice but she didn't have the energy.

"No, it's not," he called through the door. "I should have told you about this situation before. I know I screwed up and I'm sorry. I was just waiting for the right time."

She couldn't help herself. She jumped off the bed, shoved her hair back from her face, and yanked the door open. The rage she'd been keeping a lid on bubbled up to the surface. No more tears for asshole Joe Reilly. She was done.

"The right time? The right time? Wouldn't that have been when we first—When we got—When you said—" God, she sounded like an idiot.

He looked at her, pain evident in his eyes. "When I told you I loved you?"

"Yeah, then."

"You're right. But you were finally getting to believe in me and I didn't want to screw things up. I never expected it to blow up in my face like this."

She glared at him, hands on hips. "You mean the fact you already had a girlfriend you got drunk with tonight? Or is she just part of the harem you say you don't have anymore? You certainly ran out of here like your ass was on fire when she called."

"Shay, listen." He reached for her.

She took a step back. "I told you. I'm done listening. Pack your stuff and get out of here. And don't knock on my door again."

She slammed the door shut and dropped onto her bed. Maybe if she wished very hard it would all disappear, as if the whole thing with Joe had never happened.

* * * *

Joe stood in his hotel room, looking out the window at the early morning light and wondering how the fuck he was going to fix this incredible mess. He'd taken time before leaving the house to clean up his face and change his clothes so he could make it past the registration desk. But that was the only thing he'd been able to fix. When his cell rang, for a brief hopeful moment he thought it might be Shay, but when he looked, Scott's face popped up.

"You here?" Scott asked. "The front desk is pissy about giving me your room number."

"Eleven twenty-seven. Come on up."

When the knock sounded on the door, he took a last slug of his coffee, set the mug down, and went to let his agent in.

"Man, you look like shit," were the first words out of Scott's mouth.

"Not surprised because I feel like shit, too."

Scott bulled his way into the room and put his valet bag and his briefcase on the bed. "I think you've finally outdone yourself. Hit the low point. Driven the final stake in your career." He looked at Joe, hands on his hips. "What the hell possessed you, anyway? Things have been going incredibly well for you. Or were the past five years just a scam on your part?"

"Absolutely not." Joe shoved his hands in his pockets and paced back and forth from the window to the bed.

Scott sat in one of the big chairs. "Okay. We need to do some heavy damage control here. For one thing, Marge Faraday is breathing fire waiting for me to contact her."

The fresh coffee he'd ordered arrived at that moment. Joe poured a new cup for himself and one for Scott.

"All right, big shot. Tell me again, everything, and in complete detail."

Drinking and pacing, he laid the whole story out again for his agent. The man listened attentively until Joe had spilled every miserable detail. Hearing himself talk about it, Joe realized he'd lived in some kind of fantasy world. Scott was right. Gina had made herself an albatross around his neck because she knew she could. Good guy that he was, he'd let her. What he'd told Lisa last night? He should have done it years ago. Where had his brain been?

Sucker. That's what he was. A sucker for a sob story.

He refilled his cup and waited for Scott to speak.

"For once I'm actually stunned." Scott shook his head. "To begin with, I don't know how you've managed to keep this quiet for so long. Especially when you were on the Top Ten gossip list. Didn't you ever think it was time to stop playing Santa Claus to this woman?"

Joe let out a huge sigh. "Yeah, a bunch of times. First it was just once she needed help. I found out almost by accident when a friend of hers got in touch with me."

"In touch with you? Listen to me. You have to stop giving out your cell number to everyone. That's an order."

"It really wasn't that bad." He rubbed the back of his neck. "Until recently."

"Yeah, recently." Scott snorted. "She's been riding the gravy train for a long time now, buddy boy."

"She had a tough life, and she was always special to me."

"Because she took your virginity?" Scott shook his head. "Please. If every guy felt that way, a lot of us would be paying through the nose."

Joe wanted to argue but for the first time he saw the situation for what it was. Had Gina taken advantage of him? Had he just let her? Yes, he should have cut it off a long time ago but he was too softhearted. Or softheaded.

"It just never seemed the right time to end it. This time I thought she finally had her shit together. I was getting ready to cut her off. I told her and I told her friend. I wanted to come clean on this with Shay, but I had to end it first. I mean, I couldn't move forward with Shay unless she knew. No secrets between us. I promised. Then this happened."

"Your timing sucks." Scott refilled his own cup.

"Tell me about it." Joe dropped onto the bed. "So now what? Is it possible to clean up this mess?"

"Maybe with a garbage truck."

"Thanks for the support."

"Support?" Scott swallowed some coffee. "Jesus, Joe. Be realistic here, okay? I have to see what I can do to save the fundraiser, for one thing. I guess it's good you didn't let them use your name in the publicity, but we still want you involved. Then I have to contact the coaches you were meeting with next week and see what we can do there. And last but not least, make sure Fox Sports doesn't follow through on their threat to cancel your contact. None of this will be a lot of fun, sport."

"I know, I know. Sorry I snapped at you, I just—"

"Yeah. Okay. But first I want the name and phone number for that broad you've been so protective of."

"You want to talk to Gina?"

Scott nodded. "Or at least her roommate. If they don't know already they need to understand the mess they dragged you into."

"I was planning to make arrangements to get her into rehab today," Joe told him.

Scott jabbed a finger at him. "You stay away from her. From both of them. Tell me what you want done and I'll take care of it, but you have no further contact or communication with either of them ever again. You hear me?"

Joe rubbed his forehead. The headache had bloomed to full power. "I do."

"Fine. Give me the numbers. You stay in the room until I get back here. Whenever that is. Order from room service. And don't talk to anyone but me."

"What if Shay calls?"

Scott barked a laugh. "You think that's gonna happen? If you do, then you're deluding yourself. No talking on the phone to anyone but me." He drained the last of his coffee. "Okay, I'm off with my big roll of duct tape."

"Scott."

"Yeah?"

"Thanks. I mean it."

"Don't thank me yet. We've got a long way to go."

The door closed behind him and Joe lay back on the bed. How could what he thought was giving help to a friend turn his entire life to shit? By tomorrow every bit of it could be gone—his reputation, the fundraising, the Coaches Conference. His fucking job, for God's sake.

And Shay.

You've really done it this time, buddy boy.

He closed his eyes and wished himself any place but here.

* * * *

After tossing and turning most of the night, Shay finally dragged herself out of bed at seven in the morning. Her eyes burned and her throat ached from all the crying she'd done. She hadn't thought it possible to have such a flood of tears. But what hurt the most was her heart. She'd finally given it willingly to Joe, and he'd stomped all over it. What a fool she was. An idiot. Stupid. There weren't enough adjectives to describe her.

But her self-pity had been replaced by anger. She was madder than she ever remembered being, enraged that she'd allowed Joe Reilly to treat her so badly. She didn't deserve it. She was worth a lot more than that and people—Joe—were going to realize that. She would not give him the satisfaction of any more weeping and wailing. She'd mend her broken heart and take better care of it in the future.

The hell with Joe Reilly. She was through pining for him. Reality had smacked her in the face, and it was time to get over him, once and for all.

Deciding her first order of business was a shower, she headed toward the bathroom, the one she'd shared with Joe. Damn. Could she even walk in there now, looking for his personal items and not seeing them? Sniffing the fresh scent of his aftershave only to find nothing but air?

When she heard the front door open and close she stopped in her tracks. Oh, no. Surely he didn't have the nerve to come back here. Not after what he'd done. She yanked open the door to her room.

"Don't you dare set foot in this house," she called, stomping toward the foyer.

"But I live here," an unexpected voice answered. "Where else would I go?"

She stopped short at the wonderfully familiar sight of her brother standing there with his suitcase, looking like he'd walked from Wyoming instead of flying.

"Hank?" She whispered his name.

"Who else would I be?"

He held out his arms and she ran into them, pressing herself into his warmth, feeling those arms close around her. Shockingly, fresh tears welled and in a moment she was sobbing all over his shirt.

"Let it out, kiddo. Let it out, every bit of it."

They stood there like that for endless minutes until Shay finally managed to pull herself together. She scrubbed her wet cheeks with her palms and looked up at her brother.

"I'm done crying. This time for sure. He isn't worth it." She looked up at him. "How did you get here? When did you get here? And why are you here?"

"Plane, a little more than an hour ago, and because you need me."

"I thought you were still tied up on the big project out there."

He hugged her more tightly. "Never too tied up when you're in the middle of a shitstorm." He looked down at her, sympathy evident in his eyes. "I stayed away longer than I needed to because I'd hoped—Never mind. It was a stupid idea."

"Hoped what?" she prodded.

"Never mind. Later. Nothing could have kept me there after I found out about this, okay?"

"Okay." She sniffed. His words almost made the tears start all over again but she took a deep breath and swallowed. Anger, not self-pity. She needed to hold onto that. She was better than that. "How did you find out, anyway?"

"To give him a tiny amount of credit, Reilly called me himself. Said he thought you might want me at home."

"I appreciate it and I always want my big brother." She took in a deep breath and let it out slowly. "But I'm okay. Really. By now I'm more pissed off than anything, more at myself than him. And regardless of what you say, I know this is all a big hassle for you. But… Thank you, Hank. I feel better with you here."

"That's what big brothers do."

"And you are just the best big brother ever."

"If you think so, maybe you could scare me up some coffee. I haven't had a whole lot of sleep."

"Coffee. Yes." She dug up a smile of sorts and headed toward the kitchen. "I could use some, too."

When they were both holding full mugs and sitting across from each other at the kitchen table, Hank studied her ravaged face.

"Okay, let's have it. The whole story. And don't leave anything out."

"Did you see the video?"

He nodded. "Yeah, Joe sent me the link. I have to tell you, Shay. There's something not quite right about it."

"I don't understand."

"I know Joe Reilly probably better than any other human being, including his family. Even in his hottest playboy days this just was not his style, especially getting drunk. He just was never into booze and beer the way some others were."

"Like you?" She tried on a weak grin.

"Never. You know me better than that. It wasn't my style and it never was Joe's. And he certainly never hit a woman. Ever. That's not who he is and I don't care what that damn video shows. I'm telling you the truth here. Hand to God, I swear."

"Maybe he was just so hot for this babe he broke his own rules." She inhaled the steam from the coffee, hoping it would soothe her nerves. "Did you think about that?"

"Not even for a second. I know Joe better than I know myself. Has he screwed up? Damn straight. But before we go roasting his balls permanently, I think we need to find out the details."

"Let me ask you something first." She sipped at the hot liquid in her mug. "You knew I'd be here in the house alone. Why did you tell Joe he could stay here? Were you playing some kind of game?"

Hank's mouth curved in a rueful smile. "Busted."

"What do you mean?"

"I knew how you felt about Joe. You can't hide things like that from your big brother." He rubbed his jaw. "And I knew how he felt about you, even if he didn't."

"What's that supposed to mean?" she demanded again.

"I don't know exactly when it started, but I do know ever since he saw you in New York, Joe has shown a lot more than passing interest in you. As a woman. I think he was afraid to say something in case I kicked his ass for it. But I love Joe and I respect him. Even more, I trust him—"

"Stupid of you," Shay interrupted.

Hank went right on as if she hadn't said a word. "And I thought the two of you could use a little nudge."

"That sure worked out well." She snorted.

"I'm sorry about this, kiddo. This is the very last thing I expected from him."

She shook her head. "This is all on me. I was a fool to believe anything he said. I don't know if I'm madder at him or at me."

"Don't bury him just yet. The first thing I'm going to do is get hold of him and find out the skinny on this. I've seen too many videos on YouTube turn out to be not what they seemed. I want to check into this one before I rush to judgment. Then we'll see where we go. If he did this? If he led you on and then did this to you? There won't be a place for him to hide. But I want to hear it from him."

"One thing." She put her hand on his arm. "If there's any ass kicking, I'm going to do it. You can back me up, but I can fight my own battles, big brother."

"Fair enough." He pulled his cell from his pocket and dialed Joe's number. He listened for a moment, then frowned.

"What?" Shay asked.

"It went to voice mail. Let me try again." He punched the numbers once more. "Damn."

"What?" she repeated.

"Now I get the message his voice mail is full. What the hell?" His mouth set in a determined line, he punched something into his cell. "I'm texting him, and he damn well better answer me."

As if on cue, his cell rang.

"What's this with not answering your phone, you jerk. What? Uh-huh. Uh-huh." He was silent for a long moment, listening. "Tough fucking shit. I don't care what Scott Manchin said, this is my sister we're talking about, so I want some answers."

"Hank," Shay protested, reaching out to take the phone away from him. She didn't need him to fight her battles for her, no matter what he thought.

He pulled back from her, still listening. "Uh-huh. Uh-huh. Well, here's something for you to pay attention to. Tell me exactly where you are because I'm going to head there now. Manchin can do his thing, but I'm doing mine. And don't give me any crap about it." He hung up and put the phone back in his pocket. "Can you fill a travel mug with coffee for me? I think I'll need the caffeine."

"Hank, don't do this. Please. I'm a big girl. Besides, I'll bet you got hardly any sleep last night what with traveling and all. You can wait to see Joe."

He shook his head. "Uh-uh. Not gonna happen. This needs to be taken care of now. And say what you will, I was the one who created this mess to begin with, so it's up to me to see if it's all ruined." He stood up and put his mug on the counter. "Have that coffee ready in five minutes, okay?"

When Shay rose from her chair, Hank pulled her into a hug again. "I'll leave enough of his ass for you to kick, squirt. Rest assured."

"Stop calling me that," she snapped, but it was just a knee-jerk reaction. The old nickname gave her a certain measure of comfort and security right now.

"This is a fucked-up mess for sure," he told her, "but don't write Joe off until I get to the bottom of it. Okay?"

"We'll see, Hank. If it wasn't his fault he's got a lot of bowing and scraping to do. And a lot of begging for forgiveness."

"I'll be sure to pass along the message. It's what big brothers do."

* * * *

Joe watched his friend pace back and forth in the hotel room.

"I can't understand why you let this go on for as long as you did," Hank repeated yet again. "Once or twice I can understand, but you've been helping her now and then for fifteen years. What kind of idiot does that for a woman he's not even in love with?"

Joe rubbed his jaw, now sporting a thick scruff. "At first it was just the one time. I didn't mind doing it and she seemed so sincere."

"Sincere." Hank snorted. "I'll bet."

"I'm not kidding. I didn't hear from her again for a couple of years. Then it happened again. When I refused to take her next call, she had Lisa contact me. Told me Gina just needed a little help again and pleaded with me. It just kind of dribbled on from there."

Hank stopped his pacing, placed his hands on his hips, and looked at him. "If you weren't such a nice guy, I'd have to tell you what a jerk you've been. Jesus, man."

Joe threw himself back on the bed and closed his eyes. The headache was now the tempo and density of a full marching band.

"So what now?"

Desiree Holt

"Well, buddy, I'd say a lot depends on you. Scott's taking care of business, right?"

"Yes. He's meeting with everyone in San Antonio this morning, and then he's got another conference call scheduled with Fox Sports. After that it's on to my endorsement contracts."

"It's a good thing he's such a magic man. He's got the touch to fix this. Any other agent might not."

"I know. I'm lucky to have him." He sat up, rubbing his temples. "But none of this means shit if I can't fix it up with Shay."

"Answer this for me. Do you love her? I mean, are you thinking forever?"

"You bet." He answered without hesitation. "No question of it."

"Then the first thing we have to do is hook up with Scott. I'll bet he's already got a game plan in play. We need to be part of it."

"I'll call him right now." Joe grabbed his cell from the bedside table. "Hank, I swear, I'll do whatever it takes to be with Shay."

"I'm taking you at your word. But if you screw up again, there won't be a place anywhere you can hide."

"So noted."

He speed dialed Scott's number.

Chapter 13

Shay didn't remember the last time she'd spent a more miserable day. Dumping the pity party hadn't left her with much else to do. She was so angry she couldn't concentrate on anything. She tried working at her computer, but her brain was on vacation. She pulled on shorts and a T-shirt and went for a jog, but jogging made her think of Joe and his habit. That made her remember the feel of his hands on her body, the touch of his lips to hers, the way he told her he loved her. And she'd broken her own rule and said it back to him. What an idiot she'd been.

"You're pathetic," she said to her reflection in the mirror. "Stupid and pathetic."

Jilly Mackenzie called about noon to check on her. Despite the fact Shay said she was okay, she showed up thirty minutes later with three flavors of ice cream.

"Getting mad is a good thing but nothing cures a disaster like ice cream." She held out the containers. "Either it makes the pain go away or you get so full you don't care. Come on. Let's dig in."

Shay was grateful for Jilly's presence. She was amazed this woman she hadn't seen in years, not until they recently reconnected, was there for her without reservation.

"Once a Coyote, always a Coyote," Jilly joked when Shay said something. "Come on, have more ice cream."

But nothing seemed to take the edge off, not even cursing Joe and calling herself a fool.

"I thought I was smarter than that," she said at least a dozen times. "Ha-ha on me."

Jilly just murmured soothing words and kept plying her with ice cream.

Hank called several times to check on her, but when she questioned him about Joe he said, "Later."

"No, not later. Tell me now. Right now, Hank. I deserve to know."

She heard his sigh all the way through the connection. "I would if I could. If it was up to me, that is. But stuff's going on and I promised to wait."

"Promised who?" she snapped. "I should be your first priority."

"You are," he assured you, "but I have to wait for...stuff."

"Stuff?" She was so angry she saw purple dots in front of her eyes. "What the hell does that mean?" she finally asked.

"It means I'm sitting on Joe to give Scott time to take a big broom to this mess. Please, please, please don't ask me more right now. And Shay?"

"What?"

"Don't write him off yet, okay?"

She gripped her cell so tightly it made ridges in her palm. "How can you even ask that of me? I hate him for doing this to me."

"No, you don't. Listen to me. Have I ever steered you wrong? I mean, when it counted?"

"No, but this is different." Why couldn't he see that? He wasn't that dense.

"We'll see. I'll check in again in a little bit."

He called back late in the afternoon and told her he was on his way home and bringing Joe with him.

"No. I don't want him here. Don't do this to me, Hank."

"I promise you I know what I'm doing, kiddo. Don't give me a hard time here."

"Give *you* a hard time? Are you kidding me?"

It didn't matter how much she raged at him, though, and called him a traitor. He refused to change his mind.

"I'm asking you to do me a favor here." His voice was so calm she wanted to reach through the phone and smack him. "You're my sister and I love you. I know how badly you're hurting but trust your big brother just this once, okay?"

"Damn it, Hank." She wanted to stamp her foot. She was the injured party here. Why did she have to make concessions? "I guess I have no choice. But someone better have answers for me and damn soon."

Jilly lifted an eyebrow. "Hank giving you a hard time?"

"Yes, damn him." She chewed her bottom lip. "He knows how upset I am. Why is he doing this to me?"

"If you trust your big brother, then you have to believe he knows what he's doing and has your best interests at heart."

Shay snorted. "Do you have to be such a voice of reason? I thought you were on my side."

"I am." Jilly smiled. "That's why I'm telling you to trust Hank to take care of you."

When they finally heard Hank's car in the driveway, Jilly rose from the couch and picked up her purse.

"Getting out of the war zone?" Shay asked.

Jilly grinned and she gave her a hug. She opened the door and nodded at the two men standing there on her way out.

Shay glared at her brother and Joe, not sure who she was angrier with at the moment.

"I told you I don't want him here. Get him out of my sight."

"Go pull yourself together," Hank whispered to her. "Take a shower and get out of that jogging outfit. You're sweaty."

"Thanks for the compliment, but I'm good enough for Reilly."

Joe stood in the little open foyer, looking as if he expected to be shot any minute. Too bad she didn't have the equipment to do it, although she could think of far more painful things she'd like to do to him. She noticed he'd cleaned himself up and changed his clothes. His nose looked a lot better than it had the last time she'd seen him but she didn't know if that made her happy or not. She wanted him to be in as much pain as she was.

She was so angry with him she had to restrain herself from leaping at him and pounding her fists on his chest. She wanted to smack him and ask him if he had any idea how he'd made her feel and the wreckage left in the wake of his actions.

Hank took her arm and pulled her toward the hallway.

"Scott Manchin's on his way over. Dress for him. Besides"—he grinned—"don't you want to give Joe a last look at what he's missing?"

For the first time all day, she actually smiled. "Of course."

When she walked back into the living room, ready to do battle, Hank handed her a cup of her favorite herbal tea.

"No caffeine for you today," he teased.

"Things must be pretty bad if you're tending to me like this."

He just grinned, even though she didn't see anything the least bit humorous about the situation.

Joe had moved away from the front door and now stood looking out the living room window, hands in his pockets, tension visible in every line of his body. He tried twice to talk to her, but she ignored him.

"Hank, what are we doing?" She had a full head of steam by now. "How long before Scott gets here and what's he got? Some kind of magic pill? If there's an explanation for all this, I want to hear it."

"I told you. Soon." Hank winked at her. "Trust your big brother."

She sneered at him. "I did and look how that turned out. You left me alone in the house with an asshole."

"I'll tell you again. Scott has answers for us. At least that's what he assured me."

"Somebody better have them."

Shay sat gingerly on one end of the sofa in the living room, Hank on the other end. Scott arrived shortly but he ducked her questions and spent ten minutes pacing and talking on his cell phone. The atmosphere was so thick with tension Shay was sure even a knife might not cut through it. Joe was like a statue in front of the window, staring into space except when he threw pleading glances her way.

She turned to Hank. "So? When is this supposed to happen, whatever it is we're waiting for? I'm running out of what little patience I have."

"We're almost there," he promised. "Scott will let us know as soon as he gets off the phone."

Manchin finally finished his call and stood in the middle of the room, looking from one to the other, his gaze finally resting on Joe.

"Reilly, I have to say, you've been more of a pain in the ass than all the rest of my clients rolled into one. It's a good thing you make a lot of money for me, or I never would have done this. And just so you know." He looked at each of them in turn. "I called in a damn lot of favors to pull this off. You, Joseph Andrew Reilly, will owe me for the rest of your life."

"Okay." Shay couldn't keep silent any longer. "I want to know right this minute what we're waiting for. Because if it's not some damn miracle I want Reilly out of my house now. And out of my life."

"Shay," he began.

"Don't 'Shay' me," she spat.

"Stuff it," Hank told her. "And I mean it."

She glared at him and opened her mouth to say something else, but Scott jumped in.

"Calm down, kids." He looked at his watch. "It's just about time. Hank, where's the remote?"

"We're going to watch television?" Shay squeaked. "Are you for real?"

Scott ignored her, took the remote from Hank, and turned on the set, flipping through the guide. Finally he stopped on the local Fox channel where the five-o'clock news was on.

"We're watching the news?" Joe glared at him. "This is your big surprise?"

Scott gave a huge sigh. "Considering the big fucking mess you created, you ought to do anything I tell you to. Now sit down and shut up."

When the segment of the news that was on ended, a teaser came up for sports.

"And tonight," the reporter was saying, "we have an interesting piece for you, brought to you live from our studios here in San Antonio. Stay tuned."

They waited impatiently as a series of commercials rolled out. Then the reporter was back.

"We have something a little different for you tonight. Every one of you know Joe Reilly, star of the Granite Falls championship football team. College All-Star. NFL standout. And now Fox sportscaster. But none of you know the side he keeps hidden, a side leaving him open to vicious attacks by a number of people. A video circulating on YouTube created a false impression of Joe. Now Fox 29 is happy to bring you this exclusive interview we expect will clue you in to the real truth. And we hope those people who were willing and anxious to push the video out there and smear a great guy are watching."

The camera shifted, and Joe jumped to his feet.

"What the fuck?"

"Sit down." Scott literally shoved him back onto the couch.

Shay stared at the woman on the screen. She was beautiful, although at the moment her beauty looked a little worn, despite the studio makeup. It was obvious she was nervous.

"Pay careful attention," Hank whispered to Shay and took her hand.

"My name is Gina Rivera, and I've known Joe Reilly since we were both students at Granite Falls High School. We were friends. Good friends for a while, but then we drifted apart."

"If this woman's going to tell the world she and Joe have found each other again, I'm going to shoot both of you." Shay ground out the words between clenched teeth.

"Quiet," Scott ordered, "or you'll miss the best part."

Gina went on to describe her battle with alcoholism. How she'd reached out to Joe a few years ago because she had no one else to ask for help. How since then he'd helped her despite the numerous times she'd fallen off the wagon.

"I don't know why he kept helping me," she went on, "but I'm extremely grateful he did. I was the one who abused the privilege. The ridiculous video that's been flooding the Internet? It was taken last night. My friend Lisa called Joe because I'd had a little setback, fallen way off the wagon, and she needed help to get me home. She called him and he came right away. The scene that you saw? All my fault. Every bit of it."

She paused, seemed to gather herself before she continued.

"Everything you saw was accidental. People in the bar got involved and the situation went from bad to worse, through no fault of Joe's. All he was trying to do was help me. It was my drunken actions that precipitated the bar brawl that caused all the damage. I take full responsibility. Joe Reilly took a lot of abuse trying to get me out of there. He just wanted to get me home safe and sound, and I was so far gone I nearly made it impossible for him."

She paused and let out a slow breath. "I can't believe so many people would think badly of a man who has done nothing wrong. Who supports scholarship charities. Who holds conferences for coaches, where he conducts workshops on developing a positive coaching culture. Who has made himself an example for other athletes to follow."

She paused again, then looked directly into the camera.

"I understand he's fallen in love with a wonderful woman. I'm sorry the video made her question everything she feels for him. If you're watching this, please understand what a distortion it was and what a real and honest guy Joe Reilly is. How much he loves you. He's definitely one of the good guys. He would never cheat on you or betray you in any way. I hope one day, when I get my act together, I'm fortunate enough to have a man like him love me the way he loves you.

"To everyone else out there watching? Give Joe your support. He's one of the world's truly good guys. You're lucky to have him in your lives."

She paused again, swallowed, obviously pulling herself together.

"After this broadcast I'm leaving for a residential rehab facility. This time I'm determined to get completely clean. Without leaning on Joe or anyone else. Thank you, Joe Reilly, for everything you've done. I'm truly sorry for the problems I've caused you."

The studio cut back to the reporter, but Scott muted the sound. No one spoke for a long moment. Shay was shaking so badly she had to clench her hands together to steady herself. Everything she'd ever thought about Joe Reilly was jumbled in her head, but one thing stood out. He wasn't involved with another woman. He hadn't gotten drunk. He'd been doing something nice and been crucified for it because some idiot thought he was being funny and cute and hip. This woman she didn't even know had more guts than she did, going on television to bare herself to the world to help Joe.

She'd been just as bad as everyone else, jumping to conclusions and not giving him the chance to explain. Blinded by anger and nursing her pain, she'd let the past override the present, something she'd have to fix.

She wanted to still be angry with him, to find someplace to put all the rage that had built up over the past hours since she first saw the video. But she looked at Joe and there was no way he could fake the misery on his face and in his posture. Truthfully, if she cut him out of her life she'd be punishing herself as well.

But trust? He'd have to earn that back, not for what he'd done but for what he hadn't done—trusting *her.* She'd make sure he knew that.

"This went live on Fox Sports at the same time," Scott told them. "Also I arranged for the other sports channels to pick it up. By tonight it will outplay the other video on YouTube by numbers higher than you can count."

"Jesus, Scott." Joe sounded awed. "How the hell did you pull that off?"

"I told you, I'm the magic man."

"Wait a minute." Joe frowned. "How did you convince Gina to do what she did? And what's it going to do to her life? I mean, exposing her like that?"

"Her life's going to be just fine, jackass. She's going into that rehab facility and when she's clean she'll come out with a sponsor, a place to live, and a job if she stays clean."

"You did that," Hank guessed.

"Better me than Joe." One corner of his mouth kicked up in a grin. "Although it is Joe's money paying for it."

"What about the fundraiser?" Joe asked. "And the Coaches Conference? And my job?"

"I told you I'm magic. You spend a few minutes with your lady here. Then I'm taking both of you to meet with Marge Faraday. I did a lot of fast-talking there and I think Shay will help smooth out the rest of the wrinkles."

"And my job?"

Scott barked a laugh. "Still intact, but no more secrets."

Joe nodded his agreement. "No more secrets."

Hank leaned over to whisper in Shay's ear. "I think you should take Joe out to the deck for a private conversation. The guy looks more miserable than I've ever seen him."

Shay pulled herself together and nodded. When she stood up, she held out her hand to Joe and forced a smile. "I think you got some 'splainin' to do, Lucy."

"I'll tell you anything you want to know. But not until I do this." Before she realized what was happening he took her hand and pulled her tight against him. His mouth came down on hers in a kiss that scorched through to the soles of her feet. His tongue swept in, teased and danced, licked her soft flesh. It stole her breath and ratcheted up her heartbeat. She knew Hank and Scott were watching and she just didn't care.

Only Hank's wolf whistle interrupted them.

Joe cupped her face and smiled. "Now we can talk."

* * * *

"So that's all of it." Joe rubbed his jaw. "Everything. I was just trying to help someone."

They were out on the deck, Shay sitting on one of the chairs and Joe pacing as he talked.

"You could have told me about it before you ran out of here like your pants were on fire," she reminded him. "Or given me a call and told me a friend had an emergency."

He nodded. "I could have done a lot of things but I didn't. I made some bad decisions, errors in judgment, and you'll never know how sorry I am. I was stupid."

He'd fucked up royally, and now he realized how badly.

"Tell me something." She tilted her head to look up at him. "I'm curious. Why, when I was ragging on you those first couple of days, didn't you tell me about the fundraiser coming up? Or the other activities you're involved in? Why not tell me about the Coaches Conference? I mean, those things are huge. The old Joe Reilly would never commit his efforts to stuff like that."

He rubbed his forehead, a rueful look on his face. "You know, I'd like to think he would have. I mean, I did get involved in a lot of philanthropic activities when I was with the NFL."

"But those were league activities or team projects. This is stuff you do on your own."

He shrugged. "I guess I wanted you to believe in me first. I didn't want you to think I was doing stuff just to create an image for myself."

"I'm ashamed to say I might have." She smiled at him and the tightness in his chest eased slightly. "But not anymore. Now I do see the real Joe Reilly and he's someone I'm very proud of."

He stopped in front of her. "Proud enough so there's a chance you can forgive me? A chance we can start over?"

When she shook her head, a sharp pain pierced his body. Damn. They weren't leaving this deck until he convinced her they could start over. He loved her and he had no intention of losing her.

"No?" He stared at her. "Are you saying no, we can't start over?"

"That's what I'm saying."

He crouched down in front of her and took her hands in his. "But I love you, Shay. And you said you loved me. I didn't imagine it. What we had—have—is real. We can't just throw that away."

"And we're not going to." She touched his cheek, sliding her palm over the scruff on his skin. "But we're not going to start over. We're going to pick up where we left off and go forward. Doesn't that sound like a better idea?"

Relief surged through him. "It sounds like a damn good idea. Damn good. Starting right now."

The kiss he gave her made the earlier one seem like little more than a tiny spark. He explored her mouth with his tongue, dueling with her own tongue, tasting every inner surface. God, he'd never get enough of tasting her. With his mouth still fused to hers he lifted her, turned, and sat in the chair with her in his lap. His cock immediately thickened and tried to stand at attention, his body so hungry for her he wanted to rip her clothes off.

When she unbuttoned his shirt and slid one hand inside to the hard wall of his chest, his breath caught. But that was nothing compared to the light scrape of her fingernails over his nipples. A deep groan tumbled up from deep inside him. He had just tugged up her T-shirt when someone cleared their throat close by. Shay jerked in his grasp and he turned enough to see her brother standing by the sliding door, watching them, a shit-eating grin on his face.

"You guys might want to take things someplace a little more private," he pointed out.

His face heated. Damn, was he blushing? Yeah, probably. Poor taste to let Hank see him pawing his baby sister, even if he did intend to marry her. He pulled his hand back from her T-shirt as if he'd caught it on fire and began rebuttoning his buttons.

"Uh, yeah, good idea."

Shay planted a small kiss on his cheek.

"Maybe you need to spend some time with Scott before we do anything else. I'm sure he has a lot of things to go over with you."

"We can talk on the way over to Marge's. She's waiting for us." He looked at Shay. "You good to go with us?"

Shay looked up at Joe and smiled. "I am. You just have to fill me in on everything."

"Not a problem." Joe grabbed her hand and squeezed it. "Whatever Scott says, that's what we'll do. I know he spent most of the day in meetings straightening out my life and I'm sure he's got a laundry list of to-do items for me. After I get down on my knees and kiss his feet."

"Although that's an appealing image, I think we can make better use of your time."

He looked past Hank and saw Scott walk out onto the deck.

"Ready, guys? I called Marge and gave her a heads-up. After that I think a little celebration is in order, so how about I take everyone out to dinner? Joe and I will probably need to discuss some business while we eat, if you all don't mind. And Joe? Since you aren't keeping secrets from your lady anymore we ought to let her in on everything."

What he really wanted was to drag Shay off to his hotel room.

"That's very nice of you," she answered for both of them. "Thank you. We accept your invitation. Don't we, Joe?"

The other two men laughed at the look of pain he knew was on his face.

"Yeah, thanks," he managed. "Sure."

Shay put her lips close to his ear. "Later on I'll let you take me back to your expensive hotel room and we'll put the bed to good use."

"I'll hold you to that," he told her.

She grinned. "Yes, you will."

* * * *

Shay sat at the table in the ballroom and watched people milling around. Joe was busy, as he had been throughout the evening, talking to people, working the crowd, doing what the committee people expected of him. Even Scott, who'd accompanied them, was involved in his fair share of glad-handing. She was happy Hank stuck by her side, her anchor as the evening swirled around them and Joe continued to bring people over to introduce to her.

The past few days ran together in a blur. Following Gina's television appearance the video of her with Joe virtually disappeared from the Internet. As soon as the link for that sound bite was posted on the station's Web site it immediately hit YouTube and had already surpassed two million hits. For his part, Scott worked miracles with Joe's endorsement sponsors and with Fox Sports, who then put out reams of favorable publicity about what a good guy Joe Reilly was. People called and texted him with messages of support, and Scott made sure he got the details of the arrangements for Gina's rehab.

"I know I'm going to be on probation for a long time," he told Shay. "Scott was very clear about that. Perception is everything. From now on whatever I do is going to be under a microscope, including my reasons for my philanthropic work."

She knew that bothered him more than anything. He'd deliberately avoided the publicity circus about it so people wouldn't think he did it just to create a better image and now all that was down the drain. He was exactly where he didn't want to be.

But Shay would help him with that. The two of them had spent hours talking—about everything—and working out their problems. There would certainly be more to come, but now they'd face them together until people believed in him again. If she could do it, so could they.

He'd turned down Hank's insistent invitation he move back into the house. He was still at the hotel but for a different reason now.

"What I plan to do with your sister isn't going to take place under your roof," he'd joked.

Shay had blushed but emphatically agreed with him. Having sex with Joe knowing her brother was two rooms away could put a real damper on things. After a twenty-four-hour marathon when it seemed they'd never get enough of each other, they'd finally emerged for air. Joe had business to take care of, and she had work to do. She'd spent her days at the house and Joe, usually with Scott, did whatever was on his schedule. But the nights belonged to them at the hotel.

They did, however, at Joe's insistence, make time to visit a jewelry store.

"We're getting married," he told her the moment they could take a breath. "Period."

"That's some romantic proposal," she teased.

"Okay, okay. I guess you deserve the real deal." He took both of her hands in his and looked hard into her eyes, putting everything he felt into his. "Shay Beckham, will you do me the very great honor of becoming my wife?" He grinned. "Better?"

She laughed and threw her arms around his neck. "Much better. Most definitely."

He sobered. "You know how much I love you, Slick. Right? I mean, the real deal?"

"Yes, I do." She only had to look into his eyes to see the truth. "And I love you the same."

Hank teased her when she took down the picture of Joe Montana on her desk and put it in a drawer.

"All done with Big Joe?"

She winked at him. "I've got the real Big Joe now. And he's a lot better."

And he was, in more ways than she could count.

Besides the fundraiser, the Coaches Conference meeting and a few more cleanup details from the disastrous video, they had a to-do list that could choke a horse. Joe had to be back in Houston in a few days and he was determined they be married before then. Her mother nearly had a stroke when Shay called to tell her there would be a wedding that quickly.

"You're not pregnant, are you?" her mom had asked. "I thought I taught you better about birth control."

Shay giggled. "No, Mom, not pregnant. Just anxious."

Then the Beckhams had jumped on a plane to San Antonio and her wonderful mother began putting a plan of action together.

Shay had agreed they would live in Houston. She was good with that. She could work from anywhere under her new contract terms and as she told Joe, it wasn't as if she had a house to sell or anything. Her mother had been handling the wedding details, which freed her up to pack her stuff at Hank's and get it ready to ship.

Now here they were at Joe's big event. The ballroom was jammed, people milling around talking, drinking, checking out the silent auction items one more time. Joe was off in a corner now with Marge Faraday, who'd greeted Shay with a warm smile.

"Huge crowd tonight," Shay commented. "Is it always this big when Joe does one of these?"

"Mostly," Hank told her. "They'll probably draw even more after this now that Joe's going to let them publicize his involvement. He was always so adamant he not look like he was trying to cover himself with glory. But he personally raises a lot of money, not including what he contributes himself, and it's time for people to know what a good heart he has."

"Now he's got more of the Coyotes involved, too. Joe said the ones he contacted came through with cash as well as auction items. He's been busy."

Hank lifted her left hand. "Not too busy to do a little jewelry shopping, I see. That's some rock, kiddo."

Shay laughed. "I tried to talk him into something smaller, but he said he wanted everyone to be able to spot from a mile away that I was taken."

"I always knew you guys would end up together. You both just had to do some growing up first."

She punched his arm lightly. "I don't know whether to thank you or be insulted."

"I'd say thanks would be the proper response." He laughed. Then his face sobered. "Seriously. I had the feeling with the right circumstances you guys would figure out you belong together. We suffered a few glitches, but in the end it worked out."

"Glitches? Is that what you call them? I'd like to know what you think a real catastrophe would be."

"Let's hope we never find out." He sat up straighter in his chair. "I think something's about to happen." He pointed to the front of the room where Marge Faraday stood with Joe on a raised platform in front of a microphone.

"Good evening," she greeted them. "If I could ask everyone to take their seats, please?" She waited until people found their tables and everyone was settled down. "Welcome to the Annual High School Athletes Scholarship Fundraiser for high school athletes. This is our third year and it continues to grow."

She waited as the crowd applauded.

"A major reason for our success is due to Joe Reilly," she continued and looked at Joe. "Former NFL star, Fox Sports sportscaster, and star of the Granite Falls Coyotes championship team. Despite dealing with a little unpleasantness this week"—she paused to clear her throat—"Joe came through for us again in grand style."

"A little unpleasantness?" Shay whispered. "Talk about the understatement of the year."

"Hush. She's still talking."

"The committee and I met this afternoon. Because of the efforts Joe has put into this, because we agree as a unit we would never raise what we do without him, we would like to announce from now on this will be known as the Joe Reilly Athletic Scholarship Fund."

"Wow." Hank let out a low whistle. "That ought to go a long way to helping restore his reputation.

"I hope so," Shay told him. "He needs to know people will still believe in him. And you know he'll work his ass off to prove he deserves this."

"He learned a valuable lesson these past days, and he learned it the hard way. I don't have to tell you Joe's one of the really good guys now."

Shay grinned and flashed her ring at him. "Would I be wearing this if I didn't think so?"

Hank dipped his head toward the stage. "Your guy looks shell-shocked. I'm sure he didn't expect this after what happened."

Joe did indeed look stunned, blindsided by the announcement as everyone in the room rose to give him a standing ovation.

"Joe?" Marge turned to him. "I think a few words from you before we begin the live auction would be appropriate."

"Thank goodness he's pulling himself together," Shay told Hank in a low voice.

"Comes from all those years being in the public eye."

They watched Joe step up to the microphone and look around the room.

"I have to say I'm stunned. And completely honored by this. Thank you, Marge, and everyone on the committee. I assure you, this is an honor I won't take lightly."

More loud applause filled the room.

"I want to thank the football players," he continued, "from the Granite Falls Coyotes to those in the NFL, people who helped make this successful. I owe you big-time for this." He looked across the room. "There's someone else who needs to share this with me, too. Shay Beckham needs to be here with me for another important announcement."

Shay tried to back away as Hank pulled her up from her chair.

"What is he doing?" she demanded. "What's going on?"

"Go up there with him, kiddo. This is his big night, and he wants to share it with you."

Smiling even as she cursed under her breath, Shay made her way to the microphone where Joe pulled her into his side.

"I don't want to do this anymore without you," he told her in a quiet voice. Then he looked at the audience. "I want you to meet this very special woman in my life. This week she agreed to marry me, even with my many flaws, and I'm never giving her a chance to change her mind."

Despite the formality of the occasion, the crowd clapped and whistled and hooted.

"I'll kill you," she told him in a low voice. "I hate being the center of attention."

"Get used to it, Slick." He grinned at her. "Wherever I go for the rest of my life you'll be right there with me. Always, right?"

How could she not smile at him when he said things like that?

"Always, Joe. It's your game plan now, quarterback, and I'm ready for whatever you can throw at me. I love you."

"I love you, too, Slick. Now and forever."

"Forever," she agreed.

As the crowd whistled and cheered even more loudly, he wrapped her in his arms and gave her a kiss that sizzled all the way to her toes. Forever was definitely good for her.

Meet the Author

Referred to by USA Today as the Nora Roberts of erotic romance, Desiree Holt is the world's oldest living published erotic romance author. A graduate of the University of Michigan with double majors in English and HIstory, her earlier careers include agent and manager in the music industry, public television, associate vice president of university advancement, public relations, and economic development.

She is three times a finalist for an EPIC E-Book Award (and a winner in 2014), a nominee for a Romantic Times Reviewers Choice Award, winner of the first 5 Heart Sweetheart of the Year Award at The Romance Studio as well as twice a CAPA Award winner for best BDSM book of the year, and winner of the Holt Medallion for Excellence in Romance Literature.

She has been featured on CBS Sunday Morning and in The Village Voice, The Daily Beast, USA Today, The (London) Daily Mail, The New Delhi Times, The Huffington Post and numerous other national and international publications. She is also the Authors After Dark 2014 Author of the Year.

Turn the page for a special excerpt of Desiree Holt

Finding Julia

Can a moment of passion outlast years of secrets and misery?

For Julia Patterson, meeting Luke Buchanan awakens within her a
passion she's never dared dream possible. He claims her body and
and helps her remember what it means to be a woman. But Fate has
a twisted sense of humor. Just when Julia is ready to step over the
threshold into a wonderful new life, her almost-ex-husband is diagnosed
with a heart condition that puts her divorce on hold. Turning her back on
Luke is the most difficult thing she's ever done. But Julia has a secret,
one that Charles discovers and uses against her.

Years later, when Luke walks back into Julia's life, the passion between
them is just as explosive. But Charles is still controlling her from the
grave, and the secret Julia has hidden for fourteen years could destroy
their dreams forever.

On sale now!

Chapter 1

Julia Patterson put her suitcases in a precise alignment in the front hall and, through the narrow window, eyed the trickles of rain dripping down the pane of glass. San Antonio, Texas might suffer droughts but when it rained it most definitely poured.

Damn.

She hated flying to begin with. Now she worried the flight would be delayed taking off, or worse, they'd run into bad weather en route. Well, nothing to be done for it. She had to make the trip. The anticipated contract was too lucrative to pass up, and her partner in Bright Ideas was tied up on another project.

For the tenth time, she looked at herself in the powder room mirror. Navy slacks sharply creased. Check. Tweed jacket hitting the hips at the perfect spot. Check. White silk turtleneck draped just so. Check. Even the gold hoops at her ears hung in symmetry. If there was one thing she'd learned from Charles, it was to be precise and exact. "Details, Julia," he repeated ad nauseam. "In our circles it's the details that count." Sometimes she felt as if her entire life was a series of checklists.

Charles. His name sent a tiny shiver the length of her spine. One more stroke of a pen and she'd be rid of him altogether. These weeks of torturous haggling and draining telephone calls were coming to an end and his methodical, dictatorial presence in her life would finally be finished. She and the twins, seven-year-old Andy and Beth, could finally move ahead. Luckily, though sadly, Charles had never made himself an integral part of their lives.

There was just today to get through and Thanksgiving, three days from now. The reminder made her stomach cramp. That damn dinner. She was irritated to have it hanging over her. In a moment of total insanity, she'd agreed Thanksgiving would be here at the house. Her house, now. Or almost. The dinner from hell with Howard and Elise Patterson, Charles's parents who made ice cubes look hot, and his sister Evelyn, her husband Mark and their ten-year-old daughter. If Charles was bad, the rest of the Pattersons were worse.

"We have to be civilized about this, Julia." Charles had delivered the pronouncement in his usual clipped voice, still focused on the holiday. "Until you come to your senses."

"I have come to my senses," she'd insisted, forcing herself to be calm. She couldn't let him bait her the way he always did. "Dinner. Fine. Nothing more."

"It's the least you can do," Charles had argued. "You're the one who insisted on this ridiculous divorce. Don't you think you owe something to me? To my family?"

How about a hit man?

His voice gave her the same feeling of discomfort as a hangnail. Too bad she couldn't just clip him away.

Shaking off the anger always lurking beneath the surface, she turned into the kitchen. Miranda Black, her indispensable housekeeper, stood at the counter, making notes on a pad of paper. The woman had arrived a week after the twins were born, agency reference in one hand, suitcase in the other, and she'd been there ever since.

At first Julia had been so grateful, pleased that Charles was thoughtful enough to get her help. Still stunned that a man like Charles from such a rarified privileged environment wanted her. But then the charming prince who'd swept her off her feet turned into a frog. No, a dragon. It was unfortunate she'd gotten pregnant in only the second year of their marriage but he had no intention of letting children upset his life. It was time now for her to involve herself in appropriate community and social activities. Perform in a way demanded by his position in the community.

All Julia had wanted was a stable home and family environment. Her own certainly hadn't fit that bill. Secretly she'd been happy to be living far away from her dysfunctional parents and hadn't argued when little by little Charles cut them out of her life. With Charles she'd been so sure she had her dream, the chance to create a secure family environment. Instead, the courtship, wedding, and honeymoon now seemed as if they'd belonged to someone else. She was left with the villain of the piece.

Without Miranda, she wasn't sure how she'd have survived. She was more family than employee, an anchor in the turbulence of her life.

"I'd like to check the lists again." Julia reached for the pad of paper.

Miranda grinned. "Julia, you've checked them five times today already. I have everything on there for tomorrow's grocery shopping and everything to prepare on Wednesday. This won't be the first holiday dinner I've helped you put together. Let your mind rest, okay?"

But they both knew Julia's mind seldom rested.

She inhaled slowly to center herself. By tonight, she'd be in Boston. Tomorrow she'd be making a key marketing presentation to Hot Ticket, a major sports apparel company, on the proposed plan for their new line. This was the largest bid yet by Bright Ideas. She and Claire worked hard for opportunities like this. As important as this meeting was, she didn't want to leave anything behind because she'd been careless.

What a rage Charles had been in when she'd opened the agency with Claire. But she was no longer the vulnerable young college student swept off her feet by the handsome and privileged prince. It still shocked her to realize he'd married her for that very vulnerability, assuming he could mold her into the wife he expected her to be. She'd certainly tried, despite the fact she began to hate every minute of it. But somewhere along the line, trying to be someone she wasn't, she'd lost herself completely.

Until her friend Claire Westbrook had quite literally dragged her into the partnership.

Somewhere she'd found the strength to deal with Charles and defy him. She was sick and tired, at last, of being little more than his puppet. And angry with herself for allowing it to happen. Even his threats to use his influence to damage the agency, destroy its reputation, hadn't stopped her. Its growing success only angered him more.

And now she was moving on with the rest of her life. Each day was still a struggle but she was getting there, slowly but steadily. If he would just sign the damn papers. She wanted to avoid a three-ring circus in court, if possible. Meanwhile she had to focus on her trip. This account would be a launching pad for Bright Ideas, solidify them, so she had to nail it down.

Yesterday, going over everything one more time in the office, Claire had been full of encouragement. "You'll nail it. I have every confidence in you."

"You have to say that. You're my friend." And one she gave thanks for every single day.

"Have you seen my briefcase and computer?" Julia asked Miranda now, mentally running down her last minute checklist.

"Right by the back door with your luggage. I wanted to make sure you had your things together."

"Oh, thank God." She exhaled in relief. "The car service will be here any minute. It's starting to rain and you know what San Antonio traffic is like in bad weather. This whole area is subject to flash floods. Besides, I want to get to the airport before the weather closes in."

"Not to worry." Miranda smiled at her. "You're all set."

Julia gave her an impulsive hug. "Whatever would I do without you?" She stepped back, grinning. "And don't let me find out. The twins are in the family room?" Miranda nodded. "I'll just say goodbye one more time."

Andy and Beth were planted in front of the television, staring with rapt attention at a cartoon.

"Hey, kiddos." Julia crouched down to their level. "You guys be good for Miranda, okay?"

"Will you be home tomorrow?" Beth asked, sliding her gaze away from the set.

"Not tomorrow, but the day after, and then we'll have fun making Thanksgiving dinner. Okay?"

"Me, too?" Andy wasn't going to be left out, but his eyes remained glued to his program.

"You, too, sweetie. Now both of you give me a big hug and a kiss."

The tap of a horn outside drew her to the door.

"Damn," she muttered. The familiar knot of tension settled into place in her stomach. Of course he'd show up, try to throw her off her game, aware she didn't want to deal with him today. "How the hell did this happen?"

Rather than the dark sedan the car service used, Charles's grey Lincoln sat impatiently in the driveway. In a moment, he got out of the car, slammed the door, and stomped up to the front porch.

Julia pulled the door open. "What are you doing here? I'm leaving in a few minutes. The car service is due any time."

"I canceled them. It's raining. I came to talk you out of this ridiculous trip with bad weather closing in, and discuss ending this sham of a divorce."

Not today. Please not today. She would not let him get to her. Cause her to fall apart.

"I can't believe you took this on yourself to do," she told him. "It's too late to call them back. I'll have to make other arrangements. Damn."

"I forbid you to go."

Flat, cold words, as if what he said was law. For a moment the uncertainty she fought every day flared inside her but she tamped it down.

"Charles." She curled her hands into fists. "I'm going. You no longer have the right to tell me what I can and can't do. And there is nothing to discuss about the divorce except when you're finally going to sign those papers." She turned to go into the kitchen. "Never mind. I'll see if Claire can take me."

"Julia." He used a tone of controlled patience, one she'd grown to hate so desperately. "You are the most irritating woman. Fine. If you insist on going despite everything, I'll take you. But I think it's ridiculous to take chances when we have dinner coming up on Thursday."

Yes, of course. Dinner was the most important thing.

At that moment, the twins rushed into the foyer from the family room. At the sight of their father, however, they stopped so suddenly they bumped into each other. Smiles faded from their faces, replaced by looks of uncertainty.

"Julia." Charles stood in his perfectly tailored black suit and midnight blue topcoat, not a crease in sight, not a wrinkle, not a smudge. Everything was as perfect as the day it came from the tailor. His mouth was set in a thin line as he observed the children, staring at him. "Must they run around the house like common animals?"

"They're just being children, Charles." She ground her teeth. "I should think you'd be glad to see them."

Charles's cold attitude where the twins were concerned bothered the hell out of her, but now was not the time to begin an argument, one she had no chance of winning. She'd discovered the hard way in the Patterson family, expressions of emotion were strictly forbidden. No wonder he'd grown up to be the way he was.

Miranda, eyeing the situation, gathered the twins and ushered them into the kitchen, soothing and distracting them.

"Are you ready?" A muscle jumped in Charles's cheek. "I'd like to get going. It's raining and the traffic will be a mess."

"Yes, I am." Julia picked up her purse, briefcase, computer, and warm duffel coat. The weather report for Boston was snow, snow, and more snow. "If you'll get the suitcase, we can leave."

She hurried to the car and buckled herself into the passenger seat. A dull ache began to build behind her eyes, the result of the tension always in the air between them. Leaning her head back, she prayed for a moment of quiet peace. Raindrops spattered against the windshield, a waterfall parted by the regular motion of the windshield wipers. A good representation of her life, a curtain falling, parting momentarily, then dropping back in place like a shroud.

She felt the anger vibrating from Charles as he navigated the wet streets and traffic. In the nearly ten years of their marriage, he'd become steadily more dictatorial, more autocratic, more controlling. Vulnerable and insecure, she'd allowed it for far too long, losing herself until she no longer had an identity of her own. She'd finally found the courage to break away, but things turned as nasty as she'd expected.

Telling Charles she was divorcing him had been her most difficult task yet. Worse, because he'd fought her at every turn, assuming as an attorney he'd hold the upper hand and emerge the victor. Lucky for her, Claire had found her a shark who could draw blood.

"Once more, Julia, you have made an irresponsible decision." Charles's words interrupted her thoughts now, tiny pin pricks bringing her back to the present. "I don't know why you have to go away during this particular week. You know my parents have very definite ideas about Thanksgiving dinner."

Yes, she certainly did. More than she wanted to. She should have just told him they could have it at their house but it was one more argument she hadn't wanted at the time.

"Charles, I'll be back Wednesday afternoon." She forced herself to bite back her automatic retort. "Miranda is doing the grocery shopping, she'll have the table set by Wednesday night and everything ready for me to finish cooking Thursday morning. I'm only doing this for the children anyway, so don't push me or there won't be any dinner at all."

"May I remind you of the generous monthly stipend your attorney screwed me out of? There are certain conditions for you to continue receiving it."

"As if I could stop you," she snapped.

"My parents like to eat Thanksgiving dinner at three," he reminded her. "It's a tradition. Nothing should disrupt that."

"God forbid we should ever break with tradition," Julia muttered under her breath.

"What did you say?" Charles cast a sideways glance at her.

"I said don't worry, I'd never break with tradition. Dinner will be on the table exactly at three."

Charles made no comment, his attention at the moment riveted on steering through the traffic with precise moves. "I don't know why Claire couldn't have gone instead." A note of petulance tinged his words.

"Claire is doing the Thanksgiving Festival starting Friday, as you well know." Julia was irritated. This wasn't the first argument they'd had about this. "They have no children. This way I can spend the long weekend with the twins."

"I'd rather you didn't work at all and stayed home where you belong."

"I will not have this discussion with you again at this particular moment." She fisted her hands to hold her temper in check. "Your choices are no longer a factor in my life. I'm sick of the whole thing."

"No more than I am. Julia, I'm tired of waiting for you to come to your senses and call off this ridiculous divorce activity."

Slap, slap, slap. The windshield wipers were a metronome keeping time to the throbbing in her head.

"It's not ridiculous, and it's almost final."

"Almost being the key word."

"Charles..." Oh, God, why wouldn't he shut up?

"Never mind." Charles's hands tightened on the steering wheel. "You were right. This is neither the time nor place to discuss this. But trust me, we *will* be talking about this when you get back."

"I can hardly wait," she muttered and moved as close to the door as her seat belt would allow.

They sat in silence the rest of the way to the airport. Charles let her out at the Departures entrance, and confirmed her return time and flight with her.

"I'll pick you up." It was as much an order as an announcement. Would she never have space to breathe with this man?

"Why do you do this?" she asked. "It's over, Charles. Over. I don't want you hovering and caging me in. I'll take the airport limo home. Or arrange for the car service."

A muscle jumped wildly in his cheek. "Any moment now you will come to your senses and stop this ridiculous charade. I may not be able to sleep in my own bed for the moment, but it is my responsibility to make sure you arrive home safely. We have dinner planned for Thursday."

Ah, yes. The dinner again. It would be a damned shame if she killed herself before the obligatory holiday meal.

Tired of the argument, she simply nodded and slammed the door.

Charles pulled quickly away from the curb, water spraying out in a rooster tail from beneath the wheels. The only thing more drenched than the pavement was her heart.